THE
NAUGHTY
CORNER

Jasmine Haynes

HEAT
New York

THE BERKLEY PUBLISHING GROUP
Published by the Penguin Group
Penguin Group (USA) LLC
375 Hudson Street, New York, New York 10014, USA

USA I Canada I UK I Ireland I Australia I New Zealand I India I South Africa I China

Penguin Books Ltd., Registered Offices: 80 Strand, London WC2R 0RL, England
For more information about the Penguin Group, visit penguin.com.

This book is an original publication of The Berkley Publishing Group.

Library of Congress Cataloging-in-Publication Data

Haynes, Jasmine.
The naughty corner / Jasmine Haynes.—Heat Trade paperback edition.
pages cm.
ISBN 978-0-425-26623-6
I. Title.
PS3608.A936N38 2013
813'.6—dc23
2013002894

PUBLISHING HISTORY
Heat trade paperback edition / October 2013

PRINTED IN THE UNITED STATES OF AMERICA

10 9 8 7 6 5 4 3 2 1

Cover photograph: Tied Hands © Boyan1971 / Shutterstock.
Cover design by Diana Kolsky.

To my husband, Ole,
for standing behind me 100 percent in everything I do

ACKNOWLEDGMENTS

Thanks to my special network of friends who support me, brainstorm with me, and encourage me: Bella Andre, Shelley Bates, Jenny Andersen, Jackie Yau, Ellen Higuchi, Kathy Coatney, Pamela Fryer, Rosemary Gunn, and Laurel Jacobson. Thanks also to my editor, Wendy McCurdy, and my agent, Lucienne Diver.

1

"NOW *THAT* IS ONE HOT MALE ANIMAL." FROM HER PERCH IN THE bleachers, Lola Cook pointed with a small flick of her finger at the football field below as the coach strutted in front of his line of players, counting out their jumping jacks.

Coach Gray Barnett was a hell of a fine specimen.

"He's old." Charlotte Moore, Lola's best friend since they'd attended this very same high school, made a face. "He must be close to forty-five."

Lola laughed. "That's only seven years older than we are." Which made him an excellent match for Lola. She preferred seasoned men who wanted good sex without entanglements. Just the way she liked it. At least she did when she found time to date, which certainly hadn't been much in the last few months.

Charlotte, on the other hand, with her curly red hair, emerald green eyes, and petite buxom frame, took her pick of buff, outdoorsy younger men, *her* favorite kind. "I mean, he's goodlooking and all . . ." She trailed off, leaving the *but* unsaid.

Lola studied him. At this distance, his dark hair almost seemed to gleam in the morning sun. He was tall and broad-shouldered, had the calf muscles of a runner, and his butt in those shorts was definitely squeezable. "So he's some big CEO?" Not a full-time coach.

"Yeah. A global manufacturing company headquartered in Mountain View." Close to Google and a bunch of the other Silicon Valley giants. "This is his way of giving back to the community. It's his fourth year coaching the football camp."

In addition to being a psychologist with a list of private patients, Charlotte was also a guidance counselor at the high school, and she'd given Lola a heads-up to enroll her two nephews. Without the camp, Lola hadn't a clue what she would have done with the boys for the summer.

The *boys* were now prone on the ground, obviously incapable of the push-ups Coach Barnett wanted out of them. He stood over them, coaxing. It was Tuesday, the first day of camp, and at a little before nine, the July sun was already warm on her head; the high school football field would be roasting by midday. Andrea would kill her if the twins got heatstroke, but barrels of iced sports drinks lined the benches, and a huge thermos, presumably filled with water, sat on a table along with baskets of fruit and power bars.

"So what did Andrea say when she heard what you did?"

Lola snorted. "She had a hissy fit. But I told her it was either football camp or I was shipping Heckle and Jeckle to her over in Europe."

"Heckle and Jeckle." Charlotte snorted a laugh in return.

"Oops." Lola covered her mouth with her hand. That was her nickname for the twins, after the naughty magpies from the ancient cartoon. And that's how she thought of her nephews, as naughty brats. "I mean Harry and William," she said with a dramatic elongation.

On her best days, Lola wasn't a *kid* person, but where the twins were concerned . . . she shuddered.

"They're fifteen and a half years old," Charlotte groused. "I don't understand why Andrea has to have a nanny, for God's sake."

"Because my sister is a freak." Which Charlotte knew well. Andrea was five years younger than Lola and so overprotective, it was pathetic. Though in a way, Lola couldn't blame her. Andrea had suffered through four miscarriages before she conceived the twins. She thought she'd never have her own child. But honestly, the experience had warped her. She'd been terrified of coughs and colds, scrapes and bruises. She hadn't even let the boys have bikes in case they were hit by a wayward car. What kid didn't know how to ride a bike? Overprotective to the extreme, their mother had turned the twins into brats. Naming them Harry and William after the English princes said it all.

This summer Andrea had planned to take the boys on a whirlwind tour of Europe while her rich executive husband visited each branch of his company in every foreign country. What fun for them all. Until the nanny fell ill. Horrors. What was Andrea to do with the boys while she attended all the company functions and parties? After all, as the president's wife, her presence was a requirement. Her big idea to solve the nanny debacle had been for Lola to go with them and squire the twins around Europe because, after all, Lola's job was of no importance when compared to Andrea's need. An all-expenses-paid trip through the best of Europe's hotels did have a certain appeal. And they'd make a visit to the south of France where her parents had retired to three years ago. It all sounded great. Except that Lola would have to spend every waking hour with Heckle and Jeckle, oops, Harry and William. She'd rather clean toilets. Even more important, she had the Fletcher Cellular job to finish. It was the first major tech-writing project she'd had sole control of since she started her own business. No way was she screwing it up for her sister's convenience. She was *not* going to Europe, and she wouldn't have taken the boys at all if Andrea hadn't started crying. And begging. And making Lola feel guilty. Not to mention Mom's call from the south of France.

So thank goodness for Gray Barnett's altruism and his football camp for high school boys, which was six weeks long, Tuesday through Saturday, eight in the morning until one. Lola had also enrolled the twins in a driving school, lessons on Mondays, Wednesdays, and Fridays. Problem solved. She'd barely have to see the little magpies at all.

"Your sister needs therapy," Charlotte said, ever the loyal best friend.

"She's already *in* therapy." Andrea wasn't born rich, but after she'd married Ivy League Ethan Penfrey-Jones and given him the little princelings, she'd become the stereotypical rich society matron. "I used to like her once upon a time," Lola mused. "She was a good kid." Money had spoiled her the same way she'd spoiled the twins.

"She sure has your number. The twins for the whole summer." Charlotte rolled her eyes.

The coach now had the boys running the track. Lola counted sixteen charges, none of whom appeared particularly athletic. Then again, the football camp wasn't about training next year's great players. She'd been diligent enough to read the mission statement on the website; the camp was about giving kids some self-esteem. Lola admired the coach for that.

And she certainly admired several other things about him. By the benches, he downed some water and snacked on a banana. Lola had a vision of the old commercial where the half-naked construction worker drank his diet soda. Watching Gray Barnett gave her the same heated sensation.

Charlotte might have been remembering the commercial when she said, "Well, I can't sit here all day watching men get sweaty."

Lola could, if the sweaty man was Gray Barnett. "Yeah, I gotta go, too." She had a meeting with one of the engineers from Fletcher Cellular. She'd watched long enough to be able to assure Andrea that the boys were in capable hands.

She certainly wouldn't mind spending six weeks in Coach Gray Barnett's capable hands. But she had work to do.

SHE WAS A LONG-LEGGED BEAUTY IN A DENIM SKIRT, WITH A SLEN-der, almost boyish figure. The gentle breeze up on the bleachers ruffled her black hair. Gray liked long hair he could wrap around his hands.

Was she the mother of a boy on his team? She neither waved nor tried to catch the eye of any of the kids as she and her friend glided down the bleacher steps together and headed to the exit gate.

The rear view, a very shapely bottom, was equally impressive. And all that hair swishing across her back.

The two women had been the only adults in attendance. Most parents had simply dropped their kids at the curb.

The boys finished another lap. He started camp early to miss the heat of the day. Marshaling them to him with a wave of his arm, he kept one eye on the lady's rear assets. Very nice.

"Line up," he called out. She turned, watched him a moment, then preceded her friend through the gate. "All right, we're going to do some lunges."

"Come on, Dad, we just did laps—" Rafe started.

"Coach Barnett," he corrected.

Rafe muttered and fell into line with everyone else. Gray

couldn't give his son special treatment. It wouldn't be fair to the other kids. He was glad Rafe had signed up again, but he couldn't fathom his reasons since he'd always seemed resentful of every moment spent on the field with his dad. Though Gray had started the football camp four years ago as a community service, he'd also done it with the idea of spending quality time with Rafe, but it hadn't brought them any closer. Gray was hoping this year would be different. Rafe had just turned seventeen; he was almost a man. Maybe he could start to understand. If his mom gave him half a chance. Gray didn't want to blame his ex-wife for the state of his relationship with Rafe—he'd caused the problem himself with too many hours at the office or traveling and not enough time with his son—but Bettina hadn't lightened up in the five years since the divorce.

"Here's what I want you to do." He demonstrated a lunge. The boys, ranging in age from thirteen to seventeen, were not athletes by any stretch of the imagination. Most were out of shape, spending too much time with their iPods and computer games or in front of a TV. The whole point of the camp was to get them some exercise, teach them to be team players, and bolster their self-confidence and esteem. With only sixteen players, he didn't have a full contingent to make two complete teams, but they could still accomplish a lot during the six weeks. If the boys finished the course, they were guaranteed a tryout for the football team. In the previous three years, nine of his boys had made it, and those who didn't had still come away with a sense of accomplishment. Rafe, however, had never tried out.

"Three sets of ten," he called out.

Amid grunts and groans of exertion, the boys lunged with varying degrees of agility. Up on the hill beyond the bleachers, a car remote beeped in the parking lot. The woman climbed into a bright blue hatchback.

He hoped she was the mom of one of his guys. Because Gray sure as hell wanted her back on his field again.

THE TWINS WEREN'T AT THE CURB WHEN LOLA PULLED UP behind a line of parental vehicles a little after one on Friday. She waited, tapping the steering wheel.

On Tuesday morning—because of the time difference, her sister talked to the twins in the morning, *every* morning—Andrea had emailed a list of instructions on what the boys could and couldn't eat. Not *should* not but *could* not. Of course, what Harry and William wanted wasn't on the approved list. And since half of what *she* ate wasn't on the approved list either, Lola was damn near ready to chuck it. The twins didn't have nut allergies. They didn't have a gluten allergy or lactose intolerance. So why cut all that stuff out completely? And really, what was wrong with good old-fashioned iceberg lettuce? Her sister was a food Nazi. She was also a movie Nazi and a TV Nazi. Lola would have felt sorry for the princelings if they hadn't been so annoying. What had come over Andrea? Was it Mr. Penfrey-Jones? Was *he* the real Nazi?

An overweight boy of about fifteen shuffled to a minivan, his stick-thin mother holding his arm in a vise-like grip. Her mouth was moving a mile a minute, and she shook her finger right up until he hauled himself dejectedly into the front seat. Through the minivan's back window, Lola could see the finger-shaking continue once the woman climbed in beside him.

Lola's was now the last vehicle at the curb. She wasn't supposed to leave her car unattended in the pickup circle, but no one else was around so she shoved the gear into park and got out to see what was holding up the twins.

Harry and William were seated on the bench, the coach standing tall over them, a dark-haired boy watching the proceedings from nearby. He was the twin's age, maybe a year or so older, and if they'd been standing next to him, he probably would have topped them by three or four inches. With their plain brown hair—worn very short per Andrea's edict—and their undistinguished height, Harry and William took after the Penfrey-Jones side. Andrea's husband was not a tall man. In fact, he was a bit Napoleonic in both stature and demeanor, in other words, a short dictator.

Coach Barnett talked, the twins listened. Across the expanse of red-brown track and short green grass, she was too far away to hear. He was intent, focused, and spoke with little animation, his hands on his hips, legs spread. His white shorts emphasized his deep tan.

He raised his eyes as Lola entered his periphery, his gaze dark, only shades lighter than his hair.

He seemed to study her as her stride brought her closer, then finally said, "I'm going to talk to your mother for a minute."

"She's not our mother," Harry—the younger by five minutes, which was why he was named Harry instead of William—said with a snotty edge in his voice. "She's our aunt."

Coach Barnett stared him down, his eyes narrowed. "Watch what you say."

"What?" Harry asked with feigned bewilderment. "All I did was explain that she's not our mother."

"First, you use your aunt's name, not *she*. Second, your tone is disrespectful. Now apologize to your aunt."

Harry stared at him stonily. William watched the exchange, posture erect, as if the outcome held some sort of significance. The dark-haired boy, a few yards off, simply observed, his expression unreadable.

Lola still wasn't sure why the three boys had been kept after the day's activities had ended.

"Do you understand?" Coach Barnett enunciated sharply, his voice harder this time.

Lola was so used to the boys' snotty attitudes that she'd barely registered the edge of derision in Harry's tone.

Harry and the coach locked eyes, the big stare-down going on, and, amazingly, it was Harry who gave in. "Sorry, Aunt Lola."

Lola had long since stopped expecting respect from them. She didn't even ask for it. She didn't care whether the twins gave it to her or not. Ages ago, she used to exert a certain amount of discipline, but Andrea didn't like anyone disciplining her children except her or Ethan Penfry-Jones. And since Andrea was incapable of discipline herself, the boys were out of control when their father wasn't home.

But the coach had gotten Harry to comply. Lola decided it was only polite to acknowledge her nephew's effort. "Thank you, Harry." Then she shaded her eyes. "You wanted to talk to me, Coach? I'm Lola Cook, by the way."

Up close, he was more than merely hot. With a tanned face, that sexy stubble along his jaw, and pectoral muscles defined by the polo shirt he wore, he was movie-star handsome. The strands of silver in his black hair only added to the effect. The coach made her downright breathless.

"Gray Barnett," he said by way of introduction. "Let's have our discussion in my office." He flourished a hand toward the locker rooms down by the end zone, then turned to the dark-haired teen. "I'll be back in ten, Rafe."

She saw the resemblance then, the same aquiline nose and cast of the eyes. The kid had to be his son. Not much doubt.

"What's the problem, Coach?" she asked, one step behind him.

"In my office," he said again. The deep timbre of his voice heated her insides.

She definitely enjoyed a good view, but she didn't normally have a physical reaction. This man was just too attractive. His stride was long, and a couple of times she had to skip to keep up. Passing beneath the goalposts, he crossed the track, then opened a door between the men's and women's locker rooms.

"After you," he said politely, holding the door for her.

She sidled past him, drawing a deep breath of some barely there scent, maybe soap or shampoo, laced with the aroma of pure masculinity. His proximity was dizzying, his height giving her a taste of how it would feel to be petite like Charlotte.

He rounded the desk and stood behind it. To his left and right, the blinds were lowered over windows she assumed looked into the locker rooms. Trusting. A male coach could peek out the blinds on the women's side, and vice versa for the men's side, or boys' and girls', as the case may be. Obviously the school hadn't had a problem.

God, what a thought. In her opinion, people were actually too distrusting these days, thinking there were peepers and sexual predators around every corner.

"Have a seat," he said.

"Thanks, but we have to get going." She had the boys scheduled for their driving lesson this afternoon, which was ultimately another way to get them out of her hair. But Lola also didn't want to be in the one-down position with this man. At least not under these circumstances.

"Fine. I'll get right to the point." He didn't smile, simply held her with a steady, dark-eyed gaze. "Harry and William don't want to be here." He referred to them as Harry and William, too, instead of the princely order, just the way she did. Harry was always dominant. "They don't want to play football," he went on. "They aren't team players."

She wanted to sag down onto one of the two folding chairs in front of the desk. She should have known the camp was too good to be true, that Heckle and Jeckle—no *oops* about that at all— would ruin it in less than a week. She didn't, however, show her weakness, and went for a light, mystified tone. "Why ever would you think that?" *Duh.*

"They refuse to follow instructions. They seem to delight in asking stupid questions just to be disruptive. I've had to force them to leave their iPhones in their lockers because they kept texting during practice." He shook his head slightly with disgust, the first glimmer of emotion she'd seen. "I swear half the time they're actually texting each other."

Well, that was just like the twins. She wondered how many times they'd sneaked the phones out to the field with them despite what the coach said.

"Yesterday they pretended to have heatstroke."

Her heart pounded. "Are they all right?" She hadn't noticed any ill effects when she'd picked them up.

"It was nine-thirty in the morning. There wasn't a thing wrong with them. But I had to take the time to send them to the school nurse, who declared them perfectly fit."

"Well, to be honest, they don't get a lot of exercise, so they might have *thought* they had heatstroke."

The coach cocked a brow.

Okay, she knew she was stretching. "Look, I'll make them leave the phones behind at home." She should have thought of that.

"It's past that point."

Oh God. She didn't want to hear the rest. She closed her eyes, then snapped them back open. "What?"

"Today they got Stinky Stu to urinate in the drink cooler."

"Stinky Stu?" she mouthed, thinking of the overweight kid dragged out by his mother. It was worse than she could have imagined, though at least they hadn't set the school on fire.

"First, I don't like the name they gave him."

So why did *he* use it? She didn't antagonize him further by asking the question.

"Second. I don't like that they pick on the weaker boys."

She didn't like it either, but what to do about it? It was exactly their modus operandi to get someone else to do their dirty work.

"Look," she said, hating the sound of pleading in her voice, "I'm sorry about this. But I'll have a talk with them, and I promise it won't happen again." Despite everything, she couldn't let Coach Barnett toss them out. What else was she supposed to do with them?

"I've had a talk with them already. I'm not willing to have them disrupt the team. The other boys are here to learn."

It was football. How many rules could there be to learn? Yet again, she decided against antagonizing him. She fell on his mercy. "I think the football camp is the perfect place for them to learn to play well with others."

"Those two boys have no desire to play well with others."

"Look, Coach Barnett, their mother's in Europe for the summer and couldn't take them with her. I'm not sure how else to keep them entertained while she's gone."

His jaw tightened. "I'm not a baby-sitter, and this is not day care."

Okay, wrong thing to say. "That's not what I meant," she said quickly. It was exactly what she'd meant. What, what, *what* would work with this man? Because she simply couldn't have them all day long and finish the Fletcher project on time and on budget. She decided on flattery. "I just feel you're the most capable man when dealing with kids who have a few issues. You can snap them into shape. If anyone can make them follow orders, you can."

The dark look didn't show an ounce of softening. "Discipline starts at home, Miss Cook," he said gravely.

She was losing. He was going to kick them out. She'd screw up the Fletcher job. Her life would be over. "Isn't there something I can do to convince you to keep them on?"

She held her breath while he stared at her. Until finally she had to take in a lungful of air. Then she realized her question had been suggestive. *Isn't there anything I can do, Officer, to make you forget about that nasty old ticket?*

While she hadn't intended the question that way, there was a small part of her that suddenly warmed to the thought.

He glowered so darkly she thought he'd throw her out on her butt. But suddenly he smiled, a big, white-shark-tooth smile. "I will let them stay on one condition."

"Great. Okay." She couldn't keep the enthusiasm out of her voice. Because honestly, he *wouldn't* think of asking her to sleep with him.

"Every time they misbehave and need to be disciplined," he said softly, "I will discipline *you* in their stead."

Lola's mouth dropped open.

2

LIKE THE COMMERCIAL SAYS, THE LOOK ON LOLA COOK'S FACE WAS priceless. Her sexy brown eyes widened. She gaped, the glimpse of pink tongue making his mind race with salacious images. Her short denim skirt revealed those deliciously coltish legs, and the sparkly spangly things along the neckline of her tight black tank top drew attention to her small but pert and definitely mouth-watering breasts.

"What do you mean by that?"

Oh, he so wanted to show her right here and now. But he'd save that for later. "I mean," he stressed, "that every time *they* do something wrong, *you* will come to my house, or wherever else I direct you"—because he could imagine other places he'd like to have her—"and *you* will take their punishment." He quirked one eyebrow. "That sounds simple enough, doesn't it?"

She had a long face with symmetrical features and full lips. Flecks of gold sparkled in her irises. Her hair was straight, and he imagined braiding it like rope and using it to bind her to him.

She wasn't young, but judging by the bewilderment in her gaze, he figured she was a neophyte where his tastes were concerned. His hand itched to introduce her to the pleasures of a light spanking, a little bondage play. It had been a while since he'd indulged himself with a woman beyond a quick sexual liaison. Since the day she'd sat in the bleachers, he'd imagined indulging with her. Today, she'd offered him the perfect opportunity.

"It doesn't sound simple at all," she said.

"Quite simple. On the one hand"—he flipped out his left palm—"the boys stay. On the other"—he flipped out his right palm—"they leave."

She shot out a breath. "That's blackmail."

"No," he said simply. "Someone needs to be punished. I'm merely giving you a choice as to who it will be." He smiled. She was quite beautiful when she was all riled up. What would she be like when he punished her? There was a world of delightful possibilities.

She threw her hands out in exasperation. "I can't believe you're suggesting this."

"I'm perfectly willing to have you take them off my hands. They're disruptive as hell." He shrugged. "It's up to you."

She pursed her lips, glared at him. Then she tossed her hair over her shoulder, paced the small office, and finally stopped to glare at him again. He imagined her glaring at him like that as he tied her to his bed.

"Tell me exactly what you mean by punishment," she demanded.

"What does one normally do with a naughty child?" he asked mildly.

"Send them to the corner."

He laughed. That gave him a very interesting idea. "Think something more hands-on."

She gaped. "You're going to spank me?"

"For a start." He raised a brow. "If they continue to misbehave, I'll have to get more creative."

She cocked her head. "What else? I can't agree if I don't have any idea how far you'll push me."

He liked her phrasing. It suggested a willingness within limits. "We're not bargaining here." He lifted one corner of his mouth. "But I won't do anything that makes you cry."

She snorted. "I don't cry."

"Then you'll be fine."

She cocked her head, folding her arms beneath her breasts. The bead of her nipples stood out against the tight material of her tank top, and he detected her subtle womanly aroma. She wasn't unaffected, despite her arguments.

"I need specifics," she insisted.

He rounded the desk, standing just outside her personal space. "The punishment must fit the crime. And since I don't know what your nephews—"

"Heckle and Jeckle," she said.

He laughed out loud, remembering the naughty birds from the old cartoon. In addition to that sexy, willowy body, she had a sense of humor.

"Or the little princelings, if you prefer," she added.

He had her. He knew she'd agree. He couldn't wait.

HIS SCENT WAS INTOXICATING IN THE SMALL OFFICE. LOLA FELT each breath in and out of her lungs, the elevation of her heart rate, and the rise of her skin temperature.

His edict was outrageous, but he set a fire burning deep inside. She'd never been so blatantly propositioned—if that's what you called it. A spanking? And what else?

Her whole body was abuzz with the need to know. She wanted to play his game because he attracted her, because he offered her something new and exciting in a rather routine life so far. She'd had a bad marriage in her twenties, and while she hadn't sworn off men, having had her fair share of affairs in the ten years since her divorce, she was cautious. She was a big talker, but she had to admit she did more looking than doing.

"All right," she finally said. God, she'd been standing there like an idiot for at least thirty seconds, her mouth hanging open in astonishment. "I'll do it. But you have to let them stay as long as I hold up my end of the bargain."

"Agreed." Up close, his dark eyes appeared almost black, a fire burning in their depths.

"You're not going to use a cane or a whip or anything, are you?" She wasn't a complete doofus; she'd seen movies and read stuff on the Internet. *Caning* just sounded bad, like something done to slaves on a plantation, not in a civilized society.

His mouth turned up slightly. "Just my hand," he said softly. And his voice wormed inside her, heated her.

"No marks," she said equally as soft.

"Maybe just one or two to show possession."

Her breath caught in her throat. The situation had moved from blackmail and discipline to something completely different. Something sexual. Her body tightened with need.

He stepped closer. She had to raise her gaze, up, up, up, despite her own taller-than-average height. "Your first punishment will be tonight," he said.

Tonight. He stole her ability to think. She could only nod in agreement.

He trailed a finger up the side seam of her denim skirt. "Wear this."

She just might faint he made her so dizzy with desire. He

circled her, breathed deeply, as if he were drawing in her scent. Then he leaned close, his breath against her hair.

"I might actually start hoping they'll disobey me just so I can punish you"—his body heat scorched her—"over and over."

Oh God, yes. She'd never wanted the twins to misbehave so badly in the more-than-fifteen years since the day they were born.

"YOUR AUNT HAS MANAGED TO TALK ME INTO KEEPING YOU ON," Coach Barnett said when they were back out on the field.

The twins made faces, scowled, mumbled something unintelligible. Behind his sunglasses, the coach was completely unreadable. He didn't threaten or make some sort of dramatic statement about it being their last chance. If she kept playing his game, they had innumerable chances.

"Rafe, grab your bag."

The tall, dark-haired boy dragged a workout bag from beneath the bench and hoisted it over his shoulder. His expression was sullen. He stared at the twins; they stared back, like gunfighters at the O.K. Corral. Then the boy glared at Lola. Maybe he was pissed they'd all kept him waiting. Observing him, she was again sure they were related, father and son, their mannerisms the same as well as the dark eyes, dark hair, square jaw, and sharp features.

"Tomorrow morning, eight. Don't be late." The coach shot the twins a look, but his head shifted slightly toward her, and she received his silent message. He'd ordered her to his house at seven o'clock that night and written his address on a note she'd shoved in the back pocket of her skirt. Without another word, he marched off the field, the teenager trailing him, listing slightly under the weight of his bag.

"Let's go," she growled, fixing a suitable scowl on her face.

Harry and William hefted their gym bags. After the first day, she'd bought them the necessary equipment and the duffels to carry it all in. "I'm very disappointed in your behavior," she said sternly as they followed her out to the pickup curb. What was she supposed to do with them tonight? True, they were long past fifteen, far from the age that needed a baby-sitter—at fifteen, she'd earned all her spending money from baby-sitting. But this was Harry and William. No way was she leaving them alone in her condo. God only knew what mischief they'd get up to.

"We didn't do anything," Harry said.

She beeped the car remote and they all piled in, Harry in the backseat.

"What about Stu?" She glanced at him in the mirror.

Most people couldn't tell the two apart. They had the same short brown hair, identical brown eyes, average height. Even their weight was about equal. But Harry had a small scar at the corner of his right eye from an encounter with a low-hanging tree branch when he was six.

And though the younger of the two, Harry was more outspoken. "Stinky Stu was afraid of having to do another lap around the track, so he blamed it on us."

As she turned out of the parking lot, she looked sideways at William in the front seat. "Is that right?" She knew he'd side with his brother.

"Coach Barnett is a tyrant, Aunt Lola," William said, his voice a tad whiny. "He makes us run until we almost have heatstroke."

"Been there, done that, William," she said. They'd already pulled that one on the coach, and she wasn't buying it either. "First of all, you shouldn't call other kids by derogatory names. Second, I saw Stu"—she'd almost said stinky—"and he didn't look like an instigator."

"And third, you believe the coach," Harry said snidely. "Adults always stick together. What took you so long in there with him anyway?"

She stopped at a light, willing herself not to blush. She was far too old to blush. "I was saving your butts from being kicked out of the camp."

"Oh, thank you very much," Harry drawled sarcastically under his breath.

"That was the deal," she said. "You do the camp and you get the driving lessons." She'd had to email the permission slip to Andrea, who'd freaked naturally, but she'd finally signed and agreed to pay for the course, plus additional hours because there was no way Lola was letting the twins practice with her car. They were exceptionally good with the driving instructor since it was something they wanted to do.

"It's not a fair deal," William grumbled. "We have to do five days a week with Coach Hannibal and all we get in return is three days of driving."

Lola ignored him except for one thing. "Hannibal?"

She sensed his eye roll without even turning her head. "Hannibal Lecter."

Her laugh was difficult to stifle. The nickname was quite amusing, almost as good as Heckle and Jeckle. But of course, with the boys, she had to keep a straight face, especially since she'd just admonished them over Stinky Stu's moniker. "You're exaggerating. He was very reasonable when I talked to him." If demanding that she accept the boys' punishment could be called reasonable. "He agreed to give you another chance." If she allowed him to spank her. "I don't want to have to report to your father that you got kicked off the team." It was the threat of threats, and the boys shut up.

She turned the corner into the mini-mall that housed the driving school and rolled to a stop in an empty parking spot. "I have to go out tonight and Charlotte's coming over to hang out with you."

"We don't need no stinking baby-sitter," Harry quipped. They weren't classic movie buffs, so she had no idea where he'd come up with the line.

She leaned around the seat to look at him. "She's not a baby-sitter. All she's going to do is hang out for a while."

Harry snorted.

"You got a hot date?" William chimed in.

"No, I do not have a hot date. It's business," she snapped, not feeling guilty in the least since it wasn't a hot date; it was something she had to do to keep *them* in football camp. "I'll pick you up at five."

As soon as they were out of the car, she backed up, then hit the speaker phone. "Call Charlotte."

The phone rang five times. Maybe Charlotte was either in a session or a meeting. She didn't get summers off from her guidance counselor duties, spending two or three days a week counseling kids on college applications, SATs, courses to take to enhance their eligibility for getting into a good school, et cetera. Charlotte's recommendation was that students attend a junior college first. It was cheaper on the parents' pocketbook, and there were several highly regarded colleges in the Bay Area.

Charlotte answered on the last ring before voicemail picked up. "Have you been committed to the asylum yet?"

The twins were enough to drive Lola to insanity. "I'm signing the papers tomorrow, but for tonight I'm free. Are you busy?"

"I happen to be dateless." The sad fact was that they'd both been dateless for months.

"Favor?"

"Sure." Charlotte always agreed and felt no compunction about backing out if she found she didn't like the terms.

"I've got a hot date tonight and I wondered if you could stay with my adorable little princelings."

"Ooh, a hot date. Tell all. Who with?"

"The coach."

Charlotte gasped. "Oh my God. No way."

"Oh yeah." Lola ran through the tail end of a yellow light, making it just in time. "He propositioned me after camp today."

"I'm in awe. How did you manage that?"

"I didn't. My darling little nephews pissed him off, and he said he'd only let them stay if I took their punishment."

Charlotte was silent for five long seconds. "What exactly does that mean?"

"It means I'm going over to his house tonight to receive a spanking."

"Get out." Charlotte's laugh rang through the car.

Lola smiled to herself. She was liking the idea more and more.

"Is he a freak or something?"

"I'm not sure what he is. But it's hot. And I'm going." She turned up the big hill toward her condo complex. "Will you help me?"

"You could just let the boys stay by themselves."

"We're talking about Heckle and Jeckle. Who knows what they'll do while I'm out."

"True. But I'll only do it on one condition."

"Name it." Lola would agree to anything.

"I want dirty details."

She pulled into her complex and zipped into her carport. "How dirty and what level of detail?"

"Ev-ery-thing," Charlotte enunciated.

Despite Charlotte being her best friend, Lola wasn't one for sharing every little thing, especially about sex. Charlotte knew the major details about her marriage, and Lola knew about Charlotte's five failed relationships (no marriages), but they'd never shared all the *dirty* details. Of course, one would wonder why a therapist who specialized in relationship and sex counseling could have *five* failed relationships, but Charlotte always said it was easier to tell other people what to do than to fix your own stuff.

"How about I tell you in euphemisms?" Lola suggested.

"Hmm," Charlotte considered. "Throw in a Hawaiian pizza and you've got a deal."

The boys hated Hawaiian. They wanted everything. Probably because their mother never let them have pizza, *neh-ver.* "Deal." She felt rather giddy breaking one of Andrea's rules.

"What time do you want me there?"

"Six." She could pick up a you-bake pizza on the way back from getting the boys. "Thanks a bunch. You're a lifesaver."

She'd barely unlocked the door when her cell phone rang again. She juggled the two gym bags off her shoulder, dumped them on the front entry tile, and kicked the door shut behind her so the cat wouldn't get out. Then she upended her bag, grabbing the phone.

"We're going into testing mode ASAP." Frank, one of the engineers she worked with at Fletcher Cellular, answered her *hello* in his usual monotone.

"Not today. You told me Monday." God, today could run into tonight. And she could *not* miss her date, or the coach would throw the boys out. But if she missed the testing, she'd get fired. It was her job to document the procedure for the manual.

"The powers that be want it done *by* Monday. That means weekend work. And I don't get paid by the hour like you do. But George still has a couple of things to tweak."

George was Fletcher's second engineer on the new product release for a GSM base station transceiver. In layman's terms, it was a global system for mobile communications, that is, cellular transmission. She'd worked closely with both of them to understand the product in order to effectively write the instruction guides. This particular manual was for installation and commissioning and was the last in the series she'd been working on.

"Won't be today, though," Frank went on. "But be on standby."

Lola almost groaned with relief. "Just give me a heads-up when you're ready."

"Sure thing, dude." Frank liked to pretend he was a California surfboy, but as far as she knew, he'd never even been on a surfboard.

She had enough time for some work before she headed out. The condo was a three-bedroom, two-bath unit. She justified the extra expense because she used one of the bedrooms as a home office, which was tax deductible. The twins were using the spare room, and Andrea had actually sprung for bunk beds for their stay so they wouldn't have to sleep together on a pull-out couch.

Knowing the basics, Lola prepared the test-procedure document so that all she had to do was drop in the diagrams and the exact specifications, then tweak what she'd already put together. Glancing at the clock on her computer, she had an hour before she had to pick up the boys. She wanted to shower and shave her legs before they got home because she certainly didn't want them to see she was primping.

She was in the bathroom when Ghost appeared on the closed toilet lid. Ghost was white and small, under seven pounds, and she moved on soundless paws. She was forever scaring Lola, who would turn around to find the cat simply there, sitting on a chair, the desk, the sofa, the TV stand, the bed, staring at her. Like an apparition. Lola had adopted her from the shelter the week she'd moved into the condo two years ago. With apartment living, the only pet she'd had up till then was a goldfish named Morty, who'd disappeared about six months after Ghost arrived, despite the fact that Lola put his fishbowl on the top shelf of the bookcase where there was no way the cat could get to him. A sad mystery. Ghost's claws had been removed by her previous owner, so she was indoor-only—necessary because Lola's condo complex backed onto a wooded hill that stretched down into a canyon where packs of coyotes roamed.

"You're giving me the Ghost eye," she said as she removed the skirt and her tank top.

The cat blinked and curled her paws beneath her, settling in. Lola, who wasn't into fussy things, had installed a fluffy cover over the toilet lid for Ghost's comfort.

She ran the shower taps until they were hot, then stepped beneath the spray. Letting the needles pound her back and buttocks, she thought of the coach's touch on her. Would it hurt? She found herself getting wet as she imagined the experience, and it wasn't the shower. The rush of the running water became the coach whispering in her ear, telling her that he hoped the boys kept on misbehaving so he could keep on punishing her.

She hadn't even had a taste of it, and she wanted more, too.

3

SHE WAS PROMPT. GRAY'S DOORBELL RANG AT EXACTLY SEVEN o'clock. He'd managed to get home only half an hour ago. With coaching in the mornings, more often than not, he didn't leave the office until nine at night. He'd rushed his CFO out tonight in order to be home for Lola.

She stood in a pool of sunlight, the sun falling low enough in the sky to reach beneath the overhang. Shafts of light shone through her black hair as it cascaded over her shoulders. His pulse picked up. She'd adorned her features with a hint of makeup and a light pink gloss, and he imagined those lips on him.

Holding the door wide for her to enter, he said nothing, as befitted the one who was in charge. She needed to learn to take nonverbal cues.

Her gold sandals slapped lightly on the tile, then she stopped in the entry hall as he shut the door. He circled her, giving her the once-over, then the twice-over.

"I'm glad you know how to follow instructions." The black-and-gold pattern of her T-shirt matched the gold sandals, and the denim skirt hit her midthigh, leaving a long expanse of leg bared for his inspection. He was a leg man, and he imagined hers wrapped around him.

"Here are the rules," he said, because what was a little dominance play without a few rules to make things interesting?

"Look, I said you could spank me—"

He covered her lips with his palm. "First rule, you only talk when I give you permission or when I ask you a question."

Her eyes deepened to the color of rich coffee. Then she licked him. He felt it like a stroke along his cock from base to tip, and he was instantly hard. It put him off-kilter; he should have known she'd have this effect on him. He'd fantasized about her for a week, dreamed of having her in his house, at his mercy.

"And no licking me unless I order you to," he added, maintaining control.

"Order me to," she whispered against his hand.

Christ. He wanted it now, but this was far too fast. He'd thought to savor things with her, build up slowly. "If you're not careful, I'm going to have to punish you for your own bad behavior, not just the twins'."

Her lips moved beneath his palm as she smiled. Then she grabbed him by the wrist and pulled his hand down. He felt marked by her lip gloss. "You haven't punished me at all yet."

Recognizing her excitement in her quickened breath, there was an answering rise in his heart rate. "Rules first," he said. "No talking or I'll have to gag you."

"I've never been gagged before." Then she slapped her hand over her mouth. "Oops."

Holy hell, she was going to be a handful. He'd used scarves, ropes, zip ties, ball gags, and anything else that was handy, but he usually led up to that kind of thing.

He stepped closer, breathing in the sweet scent of shampoo. "You will not back talk," he said menacingly. "You will follow every instruction without question. You will not flinch or move away. You will take it all." He dropped his voice to a whisper. "And you will love it."

Her eyes seemed to light from within. "Yes, sir," she murmured, her lip gloss smudged by his palm.

He ran his thumb beneath her lip, the heat of her skin rushing through him. "I don't need to be called sir or master."

"What should I call you?"

Anything. Everything. "Gray."

"I like Coach."

"Coach will be fine. Now go into the living room." He pointed to the left, around the wall.

The house wasn't huge. After the divorce, he hadn't needed more than three bedrooms, one a home office, another for Rafe. Straight ahead was the kitchen, with far more appliances than he could ever use, a breakfast nook to the left, and the family room on the right across the kitchen island. A small formal dining room lay adjacent to the breakfast nook, and it in turn circled round to the living room he'd directed her to. He rarely used the room except in the winter when he enjoyed a fire on a rainy evening.

He almost bumped into her when she stopped just on the other side of the living room's threshold. A straight-backed wooden chair faced the wall in the far corner. As a mischievous boy, he'd often been forced to sit in a chair just like it. *Face the wall, Gray.* He knew about being bad. He knew about accepting punishment. And he knew how to make a woman enjoy the punishment he meted out.

"The naughty corner," he whispered against her hair, breathing in her heady womanly scent. "Assume the position." His heart kicked into high gear. He enjoyed games. He was kinky. He liked the feel of a woman's hot skin against his palm. He got off on the moan of pleasure they inevitably gave in to.

He wanted to hear Lola moan. He wanted to feel her ass against his hand, the sting radiating up his arm. He wanted the heat of her to make him sizzle.

She was looking at him wide-eyed and innocent. "The position?"

"Bend over and put your hands on the back of the chair." When she didn't move, he lightly swatted her ass. A delectable precursor. "Do it now."

She skirted the sofa, wove between it and the coffee table, then around an end table, her sandals silent on the rug until she hit the hardwood on the other side.

Then she leaned over and braced herself on the back of the chair, her shapely ass beckoning him.

He needed his hands on her flesh.

LOLA FELT SHIVERY WITH DESIRE. SHE'D NEVER BEEN KINKY. SHE had no idea why the thought of his hand slapping her bottom turned her on. Maybe it was the months since she'd had a man. Maybe it was just the coach. Maybe anything he wanted to do to her would turn her insides to liquid. His rules heated her. His voice in her ear made her breasts swell with need. The salty taste of his palm when she'd licked him still tantalized her. With her back to him, she couldn't see him, could only feel the warmth of his body, and her rump in the air made her feel deliciously exposed.

"Very nice." His voice was low, a little hoarse, as if the sight excited him.

She had so many questions. Was he a dom? She wasn't naïve; she'd heard the term. She'd just never been with a man who was into this sort of stuff. Did he always do this to women? Had he done these things with his wife? *Why* did he get off on spanking? But of course she was supposed to be silent.

"To start, we're going to need to raise this delightful skirt." He leaned over her backside, hands on the hem, body nestled against her from abdomen to groin. Good Lord, he was hard. Her body answered with a rush of moisture.

If she'd had any doubt this was sexual, the idea was banished completely.

He raised her skirt inches at a time, his fingers hot and slightly rough along her thighs. "Has anyone ever spanked this luscious ass before?"

She was allowed to answer his questions. "No, never." Her voice was so husky she almost didn't recognize herself.

"It's good to be a woman's first," he told her as he stepped back to ease the skirt up over her butt. Comparatively cool air washed over her skin.

"Christ," he muttered on a breath. "You're gorgeous. Spanking a beautiful ass like this is a man's wet dream."

His compliments heated her as much as the brush of his fingers across her flesh. Oh yes, she liked the words, she *loved* the words.

"You're smooth like the soft skin of a peach and the color of cream." He cupped one cheek in his palm. "No naked sunbathing, I assume."

Who had time for sunbathing? Especially with the fear of skin cancer. Besides, her deck was too small and not at all private, and she never made it down to the condo's pool. But with the note of reverence in his voice, she was glad she covered up in the sun.

"I like the red thong. I want to make your ass match that exact shade," he whispered, and the soft caress of his breath bathed her flesh with warmth.

She was hot and turned on, yet her pulse raced with a lick of fear as well. Would it hurt? She'd never been spanked. Her parents hadn't believed in it. She didn't like needles. Or having her teeth drilled. Or pain in general.

He slapped her so unexpectedly that she squeaked, a little-girl sound that escaped her without warning.

"Don't tell me that hurt."

It hadn't. Despite a slight stinging, it actually felt . . . well . . . good, especially when his hand remained, caressing her butt cheek. But he hadn't asked a question, so she didn't say a thing.

"The imprint of my hand is so pretty on your flesh."

This time she was prepared for the sharp swat. It reverberated up through her cheeks to her back. What she wasn't prepared for was the stroke of his fingers right down the crotch of her thong. Her muscles tightened in reaction, intensifying the rush of pleasure. Yes, pleasure. Erotic, sensual, sweet pleasure. She gripped the back of the chair harder.

"Hot," he murmured. "Sexy."

His hand connected again, then slid once more down the smooth crotch of her panty, his fingers probing gently.

Oh God. She closed her eyes, the sensations luscious and overwhelming. Her body throbbed, not with pain but with pure pleasure.

He slapped her again, then again, another time, over and over. Her knuckles turned white on the chair. Her breath puffed from her mouth. Her ears started to ring. And always, there was the incessant stroke of his fingers, back and forth, up and down, pushing in.

"Spread your legs wider," he demanded, his voice harsh, far off, as if from somewhere deep in one of her fantasies.

Slap, stroke, caress. Lord. She'd never felt anything like it. The sting, the pain, the pleasure, they all became one single sensation. Incredible. Out of this world. Certainly out of her experience. She couldn't breathe. She could only feel and want and need.

She was on the edge of orgasm when he stopped. Lola groaned. She wanted to beg. *Please, please, please, don't stop.*

"Do you like it?"

She gasped, then the truth simply fell from her lips. "God, yes. Yes, please. More."

THEY WERE THE WORDS GRAY NEEDED TO HEAR. HE'D WANTED to make her beg. He'd used a cupped hand to spank her, causing the least amount of pain, yet her ass was a succulent shade of red. He'd done all he'd intended for her initiation. Short and sweet and delicious, enough to ensure she'd come back for more, a taste of what he could offer her.

But she drove him to *need* more. Her soft moans and sighs had wormed their way beneath his skin.

"I'm going to give you what you crave." What *he* craved. He'd spanked other women. He'd spanked his wife, but that was long ago, before his son was born. None of them had taken to it like Lola.

"We need to remove your panties." If she had any objections, she could most certainly voice them now.

She sighed her permission.

Slowly, lingering on each separate action, he hooked his index fingers in the elastic at her hips and drew the material over her sweet, burning ass. The crotch clung to her pussy a moment before pulling free.

Christ, the sight was enough to make him come. She was moist, her cream dampening the panties, the fragrance of her arousal filling his head, mesmerizing him.

Without prompting, she shifted so he could slip the silky material down her legs. As he bent, he pressed a kiss to the juncture of her thighs. She moaned, a wisp of sound.

Her taste, sweet and salty, enflamed him. His cock throbbed in his pants, and a wild urge rose in him. The need to take her was almost irresistible.

Yet he had so many plans for her, things he'd been dreaming of. He wouldn't spoil it all by rushing. She was too perfect not to savor slowly.

But he would take more than he'd planned. That sweet kiss. And her climax.

Rising, he put his hand to her pussy, steeped himself in the feel of her. "You're wet, you dirty girl. You loved what I did." She made no reply. "Didn't you?" His voice rose on the question, giving her permission to speak.

"Yes," she said with that same breathy sigh that tightened his balls.

"Does your bottom sting?"

"Yes. In a good way." Her long hair fell down over her shoulders, obscuring her face.

"Do you want to come?"

"God, yes." Need laced her voice.

"I'm going to make you climax like you never have before." Stepping aside, he opened the side table drawer and withdrew a string of three brass balls. He'd never used them. They'd been sitting in his bedroom cabinet, but they'd come into play in a particularly graphic and very satisfying fantasy about her, and tonight he'd retrieved them even as he'd told himself it was too soon.

Rounding to the front of the chair, he leaned back into the corner. Holding the end, he let the balls fall down on their chain. "Ever used Ben Wa balls?"

She shook her head, her hair swaying across her face. Reaching out, he tucked the locks behind her ears.

"I'm going to put them inside you where they'll stroke your G-spot."

Something flickered in her eyes. "They won't get stuck?"

He allowed her the question, even though he hadn't expressly permitted it. Wiggling the chain, he said, "This will be outside."

She eyed them a moment longer, then nodded.

"Shall I warm them or do you want them cold?"

"Which is better?"

Hell, the woman was perfect. "They're two intensely different sensations." He cocked his head. "We'll do them cold. Stay right where you are. Don't move."

In the kitchen, he grabbed a few pieces of ice. With the balls and the ice in his hand, he held them over the sink until water dripped through his fingers and his palms were slightly numb.

Back in the living room, he put his hand on her ass. She squealed and jerked away.

"Oh yeah," he drawled, "perfect."

Then he slid the balls inside her. She gasped, throwing her head back, and he lingered, testing, playing. Jesus, she was wet. And hot.

"This is going to be good, baby." The length of chain dangling from the pink lushness of her pussy was truly one of the sexiest things he'd ever seen.

He pulled her hair together in his hand, wrapped it once around his palm, the silky length like a rope to hold her in place.

Then he swatted her ass, his fingers landing squarely on the crease between her thighs.

Lola moaned, and her body began to tremble.

He had no clue how he would stop himself from coming right along with her when she reached her climax.

INTENSE SENSATION ROCKETED THROUGH HER JUST THE WAY he'd said it would. Lola gasped for breath, her entire body tensing, tightening, shuddering.

It was the slap on the outside, the heat of his fingers on her, and the rock and roll of those deliciously cold, dirty little balls inside her. It was like a cock hitting her G-spot except that the balls moved separately, eliciting completely different and totally incredible sensations.

"Oh God, Coach." She wasn't supposed to speak, but there was no way she could stop.

He smacked her butt and caressed her pussy simply with the angle of his hand. Over and over. He never entered her, never stroked her clitoris. But he drove her mad. Until she honestly couldn't remember her own name. Until she could no longer cry out his. Until she was panting and moaning, pushing back against him, increasing the pressure inside, forcing his slaps to be harder, more potent, mind-altering.

When he pulled on the chain, setting the balls into greater motion, she thought she'd faint. Then he swatted her again, and they went deeper, slip sliding over her G-spot.

Her climax was like a wave crashing over her head, dragging her down, tumbling her around, over, under. Her eyes leaked tears, her pulse pounded in her ears.

Then she found herself on the hardwood floor, her body

slumped against his, her face smashed to his chest. The balls lay on the floor beside them, still wet with her orgasm.

"Oh my God," she whispered.

"That was punishment," he answered.

If it was, she knew she had to make sure the twins were very, very bad.

4

PROPPED AGAINST THE SIDE OF THE SOFA, HE BASKED IN THE HEAT of her body and the afterglow of her climax.

"Can I speak now?"

He should probably say no. "Yes." She didn't move, simply lay boneless against his chest. He liked her there.

"Why do you enjoy doing that?"

Women always wanted to know why. Sometimes there was no answer, at least not one he could explain properly. "Did you like it?"

She'd already admitted it verbally and physically. Why try to deny now? "Yes."

"That's why I enjoy it. Because it's pleasurable."

"But there are plenty of other things that are pleasurable."

True. "I like the power in it. It's like when a woman sucks a man's cock, she holds all the power, and it's sexy as hell."

She snorted and leaned back against the support of his arm to look up at him. "Women don't have power when they give a man a blow job."

He enjoyed the pucker of her lips when she said the word. "Like hell they don't. When a woman has a man's cock in her mouth, she owns him. He'll do anything she wants." He'd proposed to his ex-wife while she was sucking him. Not that it was a bad thing, but she'd gotten what she wanted with her skills as a cocksucker.

At the advanced age of forty-five, however, he'd learned to control a woman even when his cock was in her mouth.

Lola tried to follow his logic. "So when a man's spanking a woman, he owns her."

"It's the one doing the spanking who holds the power. The hand can hurt or it can bring pleasure. And a little of both can be immeasurably satisfying."

She digested that for a time. "I still don't see how spanking is the only way for a man to get power. If that's what you're really after."

He shifted slightly, easing the pressure on his tailbone. "It's not the only way, just one of them. But more than power, I simply enjoy things on the kinky side. Tying up. Blindfolding. Having my wicked way."

"What about whipping and caning and"—she stopped, blinked—"and all that other nasty stuff."

"I don't use whips or paddles or floggers. I want to feel your skin heat beneath my hand. I want my fingers to sink into your wetness."

He'd started this by telling her he wanted to punish her for what her nephews did. Now he was admitting it was all about the punishment. It was time to let her go, before she figured out that tonight, with her perfect reaction and her magnificent orgasm, it had suddenly become all about *her.*

He rose, pulled her with him. She shimmied her skirt down, her eyes slightly bewildered with his abrupt move.

"Make sure they behave tomorrow," he warned.

"Yes, Coach."

He sensed there was more on the tip of her tongue, but she bent to retrieve her thong. He was there in a flash, grabbing it before she could.

"Mine," he said, one brow raised. He wanted the lingerie wrapped around his cock when he came tonight.

And after the next time her nephews misbehaved, he wanted her lips wrapped around his cock when he climaxed.

HE'D THROWN HER OUT. SORT OF. LOLA WASN'T QUITE SURE what had happened. One moment she was probing his psyche, the next he'd withdrawn and was showing her the door.

Except that he'd kept her panties. It meant something when a man kept a woman's panties, didn't it? And all those compliments. His sweet words rang in her ears just the way the spanking still burned exquisitely on her skin.

She was surprised to find it was dark outside. She hadn't realized how long the whole episode had taken. Her butt tingled as she drove, an incessant reminder. And her body still hummed with sexual satisfaction. *Yum*. That was the only word for it. She'd heard of bondage and submission and sadomasochism and all that stuff. Nipple clamps and other clamps. She shuddered at the thought. She'd been afraid to mention those devices just in case he decided to use them on her.

But then he'd tossed her out. If he hadn't kept her panties, she'd have been worried that he might not demand she come back for another punishment.

And she wanted to go back. Badly.

It was crazy. But it had been so good. He'd talked about enjoying his power over her. She'd enjoyed being at his mercy. And those brass balls, good God. They'd made her lose her mind.

Oh yes, she wanted more. She wanted him to send her to the naughty corner over and over. Who would have thought she would adore being . . . well . . . abused? Especially after the way Mike, her ex-husband, had treated her. Though *abuse* wasn't the right term for all the things he'd said to her. He'd just picked. And picked. And *picked*. Nothing she ever did was right.

The coach's house wasn't far from her condo, and all too soon she was pulling into her carport. With the door open, she checked her hair and face in the mirror. Her lip gloss was gone, her cheeks flushed. She fixed the gloss, smoothed her hair, and made sure there were no telltale signs. Except for the missing panties. Not that the twins would suspect anything about *that*.

Music, voices, and the sound of bodies crashing emanated from the condo's living room as she entered. Charlotte and the twins were obviously watching some sort of action movie.

The front door opened onto a small tiled entry, the bedroom hallway straight ahead. A louvered sliding door slightly to the left hid the closet where she kept her coats, umbrellas, towels, and linens. The condo was compact but had room for everything if she utilized each square inch efficiently. She padded past the kitchen, into the living room. Ghost was nowhere to be seen, probably hiding under her bed. Harry—well, that could have been William—was sprawled on the carpet, a pillow beneath his head. Charlotte hugged one corner of the couch, and William—yes, that *was* William—slumped in the other, his feet propped up on a small hassock. Like good boys and girls, they'd all removed their shoes, but the pizza tray sat on the coffee table alongside paper plates soiled with sauce, bits of pineapple, and stringy cheese. One lone piece of pizza was left to congeal on the tray.

Lola's stomach rumbled. She'd powered down a bowl of cereal, that was all, before she'd headed out. But though the pizza called to her, she wasn't going to eat it. As objectifying as it sounded, when you met a new man, you had to start counting every calorie.

On the big screen, a girl dressed in a violet miniskirt tossed a spear through a bad guy.

She gasped. "Oh my God, you're watching *Kick-Ass*."

Charlotte glanced up, smiled. "I love this movie."

But it was violent. And the girl doing all the damage—not to mention the bad language—was only twelve or so. Maybe she was even younger; Lola had never been sure.

"They can't watch this." Wasn't it R-rated? "That kid kills people."

"Only bad guys," William said, his gaze glued to the TV screen.

"Yes, but—Charlotte," she hissed. "Violence."

"Everything has violence these days. Kids are used to it."

"Yeah, Aunt Lola," Harry chimed in. "And we know it's just fake. It's not like we're suddenly going to put on superhero suits and start killing people."

"Or jump off skyscrapers," William added, "because we think we can fly." He glanced up at her. "We're not stupid. We understand the difference between reality and fantasy."

"At least there's a message in *Kick-Ass*," Charlotte said, siding with the boys. How could she, for God's sake? She was a guidance counselor and a therapist.

"What message?" Lola demanded.

"That you have to stand up for weaker people who can't stand up for themselves," Harry said. "Even if you could get hurt yourself."

Right. So that's why they'd been picking on Stinky Stu.

Harry rolled onto his stomach and looked at her. "If the movie is so bad, why do you have it in your collection?"

Because, well, she loved the movie, too. But it wasn't a kids' movie. Or maybe she was just afraid that Andrea would hear about it and have another hissy fit. "Do *not* tell your mother when you talk to her tomorrow." Andrea insisted on Skyping the boys every morning, and Lola usually managed to be absent. Though sometimes she was dragged in. Maybe tomorrow she'd have to listen just to make sure.

"Come on," Charlotte murmured—like a devil on her shoulder—"have that last piece of pizza and enjoy the movie."

Lola gave in, grabbing a paper plate and flopping down in the one vacant chair, her bottom tingling in a delicious reminder. Why not add pizza and a violent movie to all the other naughty things she'd done this evening?

Charlotte nudged her foot when the credits finally started rolling. "It's time for a nice glass of wine out on the deck."

Lola knew what that meant. Charlotte wanted her payback: details.

Harry rolled to look at her. "Thanks, but Mom's totally against us drinking until we're twenty-one."

Charlotte kicked him lightly as she walked by. "You poor kids, you're so deprived."

In the kitchen, Lola pulled the bottle of wine from the fridge. "Don't encourage them," she said softly. They liked Charlotte, a hell of lot more than they liked Lola.

"They'd probably be a lot better if Andrea would lighten up a little," Charlotte whispered back as she got down the glasses.

Lola poured. "It's too late for that."

Harry and William were playing video games as Lola and Charlotte crossed to the sliding glass door. Her deck wasn't large, more like a balcony, but had enough room for plants and a couple of chairs. Her condo was along the back of the last row of buildings and overlooked the canyon below. The forest lay in darkness, but on the far side, another housing development lit up the crest of the opposite hill.

They propped their feet on the railing, sat back in the chairs, and gazed up at the stars.

"Dish," Charlotte said. "Every naughty detail."

"He's kinky," Lola said, weighing how much she could keep to herself and still satisfy Charlotte. Sex talk actually embarrassed her.

"So he spanked you?" Charlotte was a therapist, more specifically, she was a sex therapist, and while she never revealed anything a patient said to her, Lola knew she'd heard some amazing things. Facts slipped out in phrases like *Did you know some people actually do*—insert kinky act—*or they try doing*—insert an even kinkier act? Charlotte knew all about kinky acts.

"He made me hold on to this old-fashioned wooden chair. You know, the kind they used to have in schools ages ago. Hard and straight-backed."

Charlotte raised an eyebrow. "Must be something from childhood. Like he had an old nun as a teacher who used to paddle him, and he's re-creating the experience."

"He said he likes the power of a good spanking." Lola immediately regretted the words. Gray's history wasn't her business, and she shouldn't share it.

Charlotte, however, moved on. "Did you like it?"

Lola tipped her head. "Have you ever been spanked? As an adult, I mean?"

"No. But I've heard it can be quite satisfying. And if *you* agree with that, I might have to try it." She shrugged. "As a therapist, I should probably try everything."

"I—" Lola started, stopped. "It—" She stopped again. Then she let herself go. "It was absolutely amazing." She lowered her voice as if the boys could hear through the closed door and over the sound of video gunfire. "I actually had an orgasm." Her face heated in the darkness. She hoped Charlotte couldn't see. And she didn't mention the brass balls.

"Oh, you dirty little bitch." Charlotte laughed. "You're a closet submissive. Would you let him do it again?"

In a heartbeat. "Yes, I think I would."

"Did you have sex after he spanked you?"

Lola shook her head.

"Did he come, jerk off"—Charlotte lifted her shoulders— "blow job?"

Lola shook her head. "No, he just spanked me." Was that bad? Did it mean he didn't want her? Or that he was impotent? Except that he certainly hadn't *felt* impotent. He'd been hard and throbbing against her.

"Hmm," Charlotte mused. "He's probably a control freak. Like he won't let himself come in your presence because it diminishes his power."

"Really? Do you have patients who are into this kind of thing? Like doms?"

She didn't confirm. "Are you seeing him again?"

"If the boys misbehave."

Charlotte snorted. "Oh, like that'll never happen." Then she smiled, batted her eyelashes. "He could be the man for you."

Lola rolled her eyes. "It's just sex."

"Which is very, very good," Charlotte agreed. "But you need more. You need a man in your life."

Lola shook her head emphatically. "I don't need a relationship. Men are too much work."

"*Mike* was too much work. You haven't had a real relationship since he burned you."

Her ex-husband was one of those men who wanted perfection and was woefully disappointed when he discovered Lola wasn't perfect. Unfortunately, being an idiotic, starry-eyed twenty-three-year-old, Lola didn't understand that until *after* they were married and Mike decided she needed a few more *adjustments*. He tried to instruct her on the proper way to behave, the proper way to dress, to wear her hair, her makeup, even her proper weight, how to cook, to treat his friends, to . . . well, how to do *everything*. And nothing she did was good enough. So, after five years, he found perfection in another woman. Lola had pitied her.

But she'd learned she wasn't relationship material, and ten years later, she was happy on her own. "I like being in control of my own life."

"I'm in control of my life, but that doesn't mean I don't want a man around. I just haven't found the right one yet." Charlotte had fallen hard five times. She'd practically been on the church doorstep, but she'd never taken that final step. There'd always been something that came between her and her man. Maybe it was being a therapist; she analyzed everything too much.

Lola didn't say that, though. She'd said it too many times in the past.

"He could sense exactly what you need," Charlotte went on. "A take-charge man who sweeps you off your feet and orders you to be his woman." A fire lit the depths of her green eyes.

"It's just sex." Lola flapped a hand. "He likes to spank

women. The twins are a convenient excuse for him to play his kinky games. Don't get carried away with this whole relationship thing. I don't need any entanglements." But what the coach had given her, well, yeah, she could have that again. More than once. A *lot*. She'd felt not only physically satisfied—huge understatement—but special as well with every sweet word he'd said.

"You just don't like *entanglements* because in a relationship something is required of you, and you're not sure you can give it. So you reject every man before he can reject you."

"I do not reject them," Lola defended. "I choose men who aren't interested in a relationship either."

"What about Ben?"

"He got too serious." Ben was the last man she'd dated, euphemism for the last man she'd had casual sex with over the period of a few months.

"He wanted a relationship. He asked you to live with him."

"Which meant I would have had to sell the condo or he would have to sell his house. It was too complicated."

"He was a nice guy."

"They're nice when they don't live in your house and can't tell you what to do."

Charlotte shook her finger. "See? You rejected him before he could start treating you the way Mike did."

"That's not true." All right, maybe a little. She just wasn't interested in giving a man sway over her life. She didn't want to feel like she needed to become someone else, someone better. "I like my life the way it is." And then she tried a little redirect, because honestly, she didn't want to argue the same old argument with Charlotte. "And I can't wait for the twins to misbehave so I can get my next punishment."

The distraction worked, thank goodness. "Ooh," Charlotte enthused. "You did like giving up a little control for a while."

"If it's sexual, then yes." Because it only lasted for a few hours. And boy, had those few hours been totally worth it.

5

SATURDAY MORNING, AS HE SHOUTED OUT COMMANDS, GRAY reflected that running a multimillion-dollar conglomerate was easier than coaching sixteen boys five days a week. Especially with his son and Lola Cook's nephews as three of the sixteen.

Rafe was sullen, but then he usually was around Gray. As the adult, Gray should know what to do to repair their relationship, but he was clueless. Everything he tried just seemed to push them further apart. It was far easier to order a subordinate to fix a problem than it was to divine the workings of a teenage mind when he hadn't been one in twenty-five years.

Harry and William were a different story. They delighted in flouting authority. He'd forbidden cell phones, so they'd brought small gaming devices that he'd never even seen before. They distracted the other boys until Gray had to take those away, too.

That conversation had gone the way every conversation did with those two.

"You can't take that," Harry said militantly. "It's a prototype from my dad's company."

"Yeah." William added a glare.

"You will get them back at the end of the day," Gray answered.

It had been his inclination to tell them to grab their toys and take a hike, but he'd made a bargain with Lola. And they'd certainly given him more than enough ammunition for getting her back into the naughty corner.

So he'd locked the devices in his office and made them run two laps. But throughout the morning, he could hear the whispers.

"Your *dad* made that?"

"Yeah. He's real smart."

"Can I get one?"

Even Rafe, who generally disdained games like Angry Birds, whispered with the other boys until Gray broke them into groups and had them perform some passing drills. None of them liked learning rules or doing agility exercises, but give them a ball, and suddenly their interest was piqued.

"Good job, Stu," he called encouragement. He couldn't run the ball well or kick, but Stu had an arm. And he could certainly block.

And his son was a damn decent kicker. "Great job, Rafe," he called. The praise earned him nothing more than a bored glance.

Harry and William weren't proficient at anything—except talking—but he began to wonder if that, too, was an act.

He'd loved coaching the football camp the last three years, but at the end of the day, he had to admit this first week had ground him down. Sending the boys off to the showers, he turned to see Lola at the gate.

The sight of her crossing the field wearing ass-hugging black shorts revived him. Her legs seemed endless. The sleeveless top, on the other hand, wasn't tight but tied at the back and flared over her hips. She appeared dainty and feminine. When she drew close, he noted the necklace dangling provocatively between her breasts. It had the effect of making him want to lick her right in that exact spot.

"In my office," he instructed as sternly as he would issue an order to one of the boys.

"Yes, Coach," she said with a cheeky lilt to her voice.

He didn't close the door behind her. Though the blinds inside were drawn, he had no doubt that one of her nephews, or anyone else for that matter, could put an eye to the end of the slats and see *something*. He wasn't about to compromise her that way.

Unlocking the desk drawer, he pulled out the gaming devices and handed them to her. "Another infraction," he said darkly.

Her lips moved slightly, as if she'd only just managed to stop a smile in its tracks. "Does it deserve punishment?"

"Most definitely." And he wanted it bad. "Quite frankly, I don't care if their father made these things or not, I don't want to see these devices back here. Understand?" A little overbearing authority seemed necessary.

She looked down at the devices in her hands. "Their father? What do you mean? He didn't make these."

"They claimed they were prototypes he'd produced." Obviously they'd made that up.

"Andrea sent these things from a store in Germany. The latest thing. Personally, one gaming toy is the same as another, but whatever."

"So they lied."

"Yes, they did." She nodded. "Definitely sounds like a punishment is in order."

"I agree completely. Tomorrow afternoon. Two o'clock." It wasn't his weekend with Rafe, and he had to take him back to his ex-wife's as soon as he got out of the showers. Bettina was talking about getting Rafe a car. Of course, they'd disagreed about it since Gray was the one who would pay for it, but Bettina was insistent. After all, *she* was the one who had to drive Rafe everywhere or let him use her car.

"Yes, sir," Lola said, her eyes sparkling.

He wondered why the hell he was letting Bettina occupy his thoughts for even a second when Lola was right in front of him. Despite the open door and the scent of earth and grass, he could smell *her.* Sweet, seductive woman.

He had the evening to determine the perfect punishment. And he would make it good.

"YOU CAN'T JUST *TAKE* THEM," HARRY WHINED. "THAT'S OUR PERsonal property."

"Yeah," William chimed in. "You can't take our stuff."

Lola wondered if William was capable of original thought. Though he was older by those five minutes, he always seemed to parrot whatever Harry said. She locked the Game Boys—or whatever the German versions were called—in her bottom desk drawer. Why the hell had Andrea sent them? Did she *want* to cause trouble?

"If you can't follow the rules, then you don't get to play with them." Sure she'd been hoping—praying—the boys would misbehave so she could see Gray again, but there still had to be consequences for their bad behavior.

"They're not toys," Harry huffed, affronted.

When she straightened away from the desk, she was taller than him. She glared down. "You can go one night without them in punishment for using them improperly. There's a time and place, and football camp isn't it. That was rude to the coach and the other boys who are trying to learn." She narrowed her eyes on them. "And to top it off," she added, "you lied."

"About what?" William groused, even though she'd been looking at Harry.

She pointed at the desk drawer. "Those things aren't prototypes. Your father's company manufactures cardboard cereal boxes." And other packaging materials. But that probably wasn't glamorous enough for the twins.

"You just don't get it, Aunt Lola," Harry said, obviously unrepentant if that twinkle in his brown eyes said anything. "People want illusion. They want to think something is bigger and better, and no one else has it. They want something new and exciting. All we did was make them feel special by giving them exactly what they wanted."

Lola stared at Harry a long moment. "How old are you?" she asked. Because honestly, the kid was kind of profound. He could read people, understand their needs. Most adults weren't even able to do that. The problem was he sounded like a con artist.

He wasn't exactly a handsome boy. His face was too round. Maybe that would change as he got older. By the time he was eighteen, girls might be falling at his feet. But there was something in his eyes, something that set him apart even from his identical twin.

"You know exactly how old we are, Aunt Lola," he answered haughtily.

Yes, she did. And despite the fact that she was two-and-a-half times their age, she wondered if they actually had the upper hand.

"I have work to do," she said. She was still waiting for that phone call from Frank. With her luck, they'd call just before two o'clock tomorrow. "Why don't you two go over to the pool?"

Harry smirked. "Are you sure we're old enough to swim on our own? There's no lifeguard, you know."

She didn't rise to his baiting tone. "Just make sure you wear your sunscreen." God, now she was sounding like Andrea.

When they were gone—after much noise and fuss—Ghost came out from behind the desk where she'd been hiding and climbed onto Lola's lap.

"Do those big, bad teenage boys scare you?" she asked, scratching the cat's chin. Ghost began to purr.

Lola rolled her chair up to the desk—the cat curling into a tiny ball of fur—tapped a few times on the mouse, and brought up the diagram she'd been working on. She had two monitors so she could compare documents and drawings, referencing without having to toggle back and forth between windows. She'd purchased state-of-the-art software and spent hours viewing online seminars to learn the latest tips and tricks.

Yet instead of digging in, she sat for long minutes contemplating Harry and William. And Gray. He was something new and exciting. He said all the right things. He made her feel special. Was she simply letting him con her into submission the way Harry conned his friends?

IN THE END, LOLA DECIDED IT DIDN'T MATTER WHETHER GRAY was conning her. She wasn't looking for a relationship, and she'd loved the things he'd done to her. She wanted more. Simple.

By Sunday afternoon, Frank still hadn't called, and neither he nor George had answered the messages she'd left. She was dubious they would get to the testing until Monday despite the edicts from *the powers that be*. She didn't have to worry about Harry and William either. They were going to the movies with a friend, then burgers afterward. The boy was older, and his mom was letting him borrow the car for the afternoon. Perfect. Andrea would probably freak, but she wouldn't know. It was daylight, for heaven's sake. She had to give the boys some leeway. Or maybe it was just a good excuse to get rid of them.

Lola wore a flirty little skirt and a short-sleeved sweater that buttoned down the front.

Gray didn't compliment her with words, but when he opened the door, his gaze was all she needed. His smoky eyes drifted all over, from the ponytail she'd tied high on her head to the thin, tight sweater, the skirt that could be flipped up over her butt oh so easily, and her bare legs. She felt like an ice cream cone licked from bottom to top.

"Go into the bathroom and take off that bra." He pointed down the hall.

Her nipples immediately peaked against the offending bra. His blue shirt was open far enough to reveal a dusting of hair, the jeans seemed to cup and enhance his private parts, and his chin was covered with a sexy five o'clock shadow.

Following his direction, she passed a home office with built-in cabinets, shelves, and desk. A large leather chair sat before an open laptop, a screen saver of geometric shapes flitting across the monitor.

The main bathroom was opposite double doors leading to the master bedroom. Before turning in, she caught sight of a large bed, burgundy comforter, and sturdy wooden headboard with bedposts of mahogany.

The main bathroom also had a door into a smaller bedroom. Pennants, pictures, and posters on the walls told her this was his son's room. Obviously the boy was at his father's house enough to require his own room.

She closed that door for no other reason than feeling uncomfortable stripping off her bra while looking at his son's bed. It gave her an odd sensation of guilt, as if she were trespassing.

"Are you done yet?" his voice boomed.

Lola smiled, shoved her bra in her bag, and just before opening the door, slipped off her panties, too. Let's see what he did
with that.

He stood at the end of the hall in the entryway, his face a stern
mask. Obviously he'd decided to play the hard-ass this time. At
the last moment, he stepped aside and pointed into the living
room. "Give me your purse and go to your naughty corner."

A thrill swept through her. People wanted illusion. They
wanted something bigger and better, something new and exciting, something that made them feel special.

Gray made her feel all those things. And he made her wet.

She handed him her bag without the least compunction. He
laid it next to his keys on a table to one side of the door. If her
phone rang, she should be able to hear it even from inside her
purse.

"I said," he snapped, his face tense, eyes narrowed, "go to
your corner."

The chair faced the corner like before, but this time he'd set a
long, standing mirror in front of it. This was new. She glanced
back at him.

"I like to watch," he said. "You're going to give me a show."

She was completely breathless, but she opened her mouth to
speak.

He put his fingers to her lips. "Not a word. Just do what
I say."

Then she saw the table beside the chair and her heart started
to race.

HER EYES WIDENED. HIS PULSE KICKED UP IN RESPONSE. HE'D SET
out a smorgasbord of toys: a ball gag, blindfold, scarves for tying,
a vibrator, a butt plug. Some of them would terrify her. Some

would excite her. He'd already decided which implement he would use. And exactly what he was going to do with it.

Instead of making her sit, he took the chair. "Get on my lap, your back to my chest."

She glanced at the mirror warily.

"Now," he reiterated, adding force to his voice.

She straddled him, sitting straight and stiff. Her ponytail swished across his face. "Take your hair down," he ordered. "You are always to wear your hair down around me." Though the nape of her neck called to him, he resisted as her silky hair tumbled down over her shoulders. He had a plan for her. And it wasn't *his* capitulation. True, after their last punishment session, he'd told himself he'd have his cock in her mouth the next time, but he'd changed his mind. He wanted to hold out a bit longer, to savor the build of his sexual tension.

She'd asked why he liked to punish and spank, why he was kinky. He didn't know why. Or perhaps it was more truthful to say he'd had a couple of experiences that might have led him here, but he couldn't be totally sure. He rather thought he had a predilection for it. Like a prodigy simply knows how to play a piano or a novelist begins making up his stories almost from the moment he learns the alphabet.

All he knew was that when he had her in his power, when she did whatever he told her to, his cock began to throb and some inner need took over.

It was taking over now. "Spread your legs and lift your skirt for the mirror."

She hesitated. "There isn't some hidden camera behind there or anything, right?"

"If I'm going to film you, I will tell you. Nothing is secret between us." He laid his hands along her thighs in an attempt to soothe her.

While it might appear that he held the power, all she had to do was say no. All she had to do was walk away. He could never force her. He could only demand, but in the end, she was the one who had to agree. She had to *want* this.

His tension released when she leaned back against him, parting her legs, resting her thighs along his. He held her at the waist. Then slowly, so very slowly, she began to tug on the skirt.

Over her shoulder, he stared full into the mirror. She'd braced the toes of her sandals on the floor, his jeans-clad knees between hers. He widened his legs slightly, forcing hers farther apart. She was all dark and light in the mirror, creamy white skin, black hair, black skirt, white sweater. The effect was mesmerizing as she raised her skirt for him. A little more, then more.

His heart ceased to beat altogether. She was trimmed to barely more than fuzz, the lips of her sex pink, plump, inviting.

"Holy hell," he said softly. "That's the prettiest pussy I've ever seen." He felt her laugh—or maybe it was a snort—vibrating against his chest. "You're utterly perfect," he whispered. "Touch yourself."

"Wha—" She never finished adding the *t*.

He put his hand over her mouth. "Do what I say. Don't argue. I'm dying to see your fingers in all that sweet cream."

Even in the reflection, he could see she was wet and ready. The sweet, aroused scent of her sex rose around them. "Touch yourself for me," he demanded.

She could still balk.

Yet Lola laid her head back against his shoulder and slipped her fingers down, down, down. His heart had started again, pounding against the wall of his chest.

"How often do you touch yourself? How often do you make yourself come?" He needed to know.

"Every night," she murmured. Her fingers moved, circled, swept down, up.

He wanted to take her right then. Open his jeans, shove deep inside her. Watch his cock impale her in the mirror. But not yet. No, they needed to build to that.

Her nipples beaded against the thin sweater. His mouth watered. He might go crazy if he didn't lick her, touch her. But it was the need, wanting her but not letting himself have her, that pushed him higher.

"Put your finger in my mouth." It was the only way he would allow himself to taste her. For now.

She raised a hand, rubbed her index finger teasingly along his lower lip. Then he sucked her in. He licked and laved, tasted the sweet saltiness of her cream. Heavenly.

He let her hand fall away, immersed in the taste of her. "Undo the top four buttons on your sweater to just below your breasts."

The mirror distanced her. He couldn't read her expression, only the slight hesitation as she held her fingers aloft just inches from his lips. Then she exhaled and began working the buttons loose.

Her breasts weren't large, but the creamy skin she revealed with each popped button made him salivate. He brushed her hair aside, then hooked a hand around her abdomen and hugged her closer in order to look over her right shoulder. Her nipples were hard, enticing beads against the sweater.

"Pinch your nipples," he whispered.

She slipped her right hand inside the open sweater. The material fluttered, and she gasped, her bottom tensing on top of him as she arched slightly.

"Is it good?" He wanted to hear her say the words.

"Yes. The pain. Like when you spanked me, it hurts so good."

He placed his palm over her hand, forcing her to squeeze her breast tightly. "Let me feel you do it again."

The mirror reflected their coupling, his large hand on hers, his knees between hers, parting her legs, and the sweet, tempting triangle of her sex.

Then she pinched, gasped, tensed, and Gray felt his body ride the edge of climax, not tipping over, but ready, so goddamn ready for her, he might actually go mad if he didn't have her.

6

LOLA ARCHED AND MOANED, HER NIPPLE SENSITIVE, TENDER, electric.

She'd masturbated, but never for a man. And certainly not every night as she'd claimed. Terrified of the twins sneaky ways, she'd tossed out her vibrator. And she hadn't touched herself since they'd arrived. Maybe that was part of the reason she'd become sex crazy the moment she saw Coach Gray Barnett.

But oh God, the feel of him against her back as she spread her legs, his hard ridge of flesh against her bottom, the heat of her own touch accompanied by his gaze, his mouth, warm and wet, suckling her finger, then his hand on hers as she tweaked her nipple hard, harder. It set her on fire.

"More," he whispered.

He was big and broad, his hot hand engulfing hers, urging her. Lola pinched herself again, twisted lightly until the pain became unbearable pleasure. She arched, rolled her bottom slightly. His cock seemed to throb beneath her, and he groaned.

This wasn't punishment. It was exquisite torture. She wanted him to touch her, his fingers on her nipple, his hand between her legs. His cock in her.

"Hell, that is so good, baby," he crooned in her ear. "Cup your breasts, keep pinching both nipples." He dragged the lapels of her sweater aside and placed both her hands over her breasts. "Yes, just like that."

In the mirror, she saw him reach for something on the table beside the chair. The blindfold? The gag? There'd been so many different toys lying there in wait for her.

It took her a moment to identify the light electric hum and recognize the cylindrical device in the mirror. The vibrator. He widened his legs, spreading hers, clamped a strong arm across her abdomen, and set the buzzing vibrator to her clitoris.

Lola cried out. The view in the mirror was mesmerizing, the sheer wantonness of it. She was spread out for him, exposed, her body twisting, rolling, arching against him. The heat was over-whelming, her whole body on fire, hot, wet, sizzling.

"Pinch," he ordered.

She could barely react to the command, her mind whirling in time with her body. But her fingers moved with a mind of their own, tweaking hard, pleasure-pain streaking down to her clitoris.

Oh God, oh God.

Maybe she'd cried the words aloud because he answered with, "That's good, baby, you're so beautiful, perfect. Take the vibra-tor, love it."

She did love it. His punishment was bliss. In that moment, she was completely his, totally submissive. She'd have done anything for more of his sweet words, his hot touch.

Then he told her the next thing he wanted. "Rub yourself for me, baby, while I put the vibrator inside."

"Yes, yes, yes," she chanted. "Please, please, please." Her body quivered and quaked as he entered her with the vibrator. She was so wet it slid deep easily, filling her. Oh God, she wanted it to be him. She wanted the fingers on her clit to be his. She wanted his tongue.

She gasped and moaned. Her body writhing, riding the vibrator, riding her fingers, rising higher, higher, twisting, turning, rolling. Inside her, the vibrator shimmied and shuddered over her G-spot.

And always there was his voice in her ear. "You like this, don't you, dirty girl, sweet filthy slut. You love touching yourself for me. You love seeing how beautiful you are in the mirror. Oh yeah, baby, fuck the vibrator, yes, fuck it for me." His speech got dirtier the more she rocked on him, his cock hard and throbbing. She moved her hips, working him as she worked herself.

Then she simply couldn't watch anymore, couldn't keep her eyes open. There was only sensation rocketing through her body. She panted, no words, just sharp little cries. Then, the explosion. Her eyes squeezed tightly shut, she curled over, bearing down on the climax.

On her own, she would have pulled her hands away, the pleasure too great, but he rolled with her, holding her tight with his arm, working the vibrator inside her, until she tried to wriggle away from him, from the intensity.

Finally, she lay curled in his lap, completely spent. She couldn't move, couldn't open her eyes. The solidity of his arms around her was the only thing holding her up. Otherwise she would have been boneless mush on the floor.

"You called me a slut," she said softly.

His chuckle rumbled beneath her ear. "It's a term of endearment."

Oddly, in his sexy voice, it had felt like an endearment, but she said, "You're joking." She couldn't be bothered to raise her head.

He stroked her hair. "A little dirty talk is sexy."

He was introducing her to a lot of firsts. Sexy, dirty talk. Touching herself for a man. Watching in the mirror. Giving him free rein with a vibrator. Other than spanking her, he hadn't touched her up to this point, hadn't kissed her, yet everything was utterly sensual. Intimate. Special.

"It's time for you to go now."

Now *that* was dumping the proverbial bucket of cold water on her.

"Oh, okay." She scrambled off his lap. Where were her panties? Then she remembered. They were in her purse along with her bra. She hesitated. Should she grab her purse and go to the bathroom? Should she put them on in front of him? Or should she just leave and stop somewhere along the way?

She took one look at him sitting in the chair—all satisfied and smirking as if *he'd* had the orgasm—and knew she needed to get out as fast as possible. "Well, thanks, that was great," she said, fumbling with the buttons of her sweater.

"It was perfect," he said.

Perfect? She'd never been perfect. But if she was, then why was he kicking her out? Lola didn't ask. She straightened her skirt, smoothed her sweater, adjusted her toes into her sandals.

He set the vibrator back on the table amid all the other dirty little toys, and she realized he'd been holding it the whole time she'd cuddled on his lap after . . .

Lola felt her cheeks burn, both sets. What they'd done didn't embarrass her. His quick recovery did. *Done, see ya later, goodbye.* Like it meant nothing.

"I'm sure I'll see you after training on Tuesday," he said.

She hadn't needed to interpret and analyze what a man really meant in a long time. Mike had been gone for ten years, and she was too old for that kind of adolescent ruminating. But really, what did Gray *mean*?

She absolutely would not ask. "Thanks"—which sounded odd under the circumstances—"talk to you later." She almost ran for the door, but forced herself to move slowly, calmly.

"I want your email address and your cell phone number."

His voice behind her stopped her dead before she hit the front entry tile. She turned. "What?"

"Your punishment doesn't simply end when I let you walk out the door. Sometimes you will need to be at my beck and call over email or on the phone." His face was impassive, his tone neutral, his eyes dark, but there was a sense of command about his rigid stance. He'd have made a great dictator. "And no, I'm not joking," he added.

She didn't get it. He didn't have sex with her, well, he *did*, but it was this weird one-sided thing. "Do you *only* like to watch and spank and do things over the phone and email?"

He laughed. "We're just getting started. Don't rush things."

She cocked her head. "What if the twins don't misbehave?"

He raised one brow. Her question didn't require a verbal answer. Of course, they'd misbehave.

So did this mean he wanted her? "Do you have a pen and paper?" she asked.

He stepped around her, entered the kitchen, grabbed a pad off the counter by the phone, and returned to hand it to her.

Lola scribbled everything down and shoved it back at him. "There. Satisfied?"

He smiled. "Extremely." Then he cupped her cheek, held her with his gaze. "You are absolutely perfect, my dear. And I will have you again." Then he handed her the purse off the table, opened the door, and ushered her out.

Perfect. He had her with that one word.

* * *

GRAY CLOSED THE DOOR. HIS HEART HAD STOPPED POUNDING, but his cock was still rock hard and throbbing. It was only with his last ounce of willpower that he'd managed not to undo his jeans and take her.

She obviously had no clue how close to the edge he'd been. Which was good. He still retained the upper hand.

Returning to the living room, he began clearing away the evidence of his debauchery.

Rafe had called this morning to say his mom was letting him use her car to go to the movies with some of his friends. He wanted to stop by afterward. Gray knew why. Rafe was angling for a car of his own, and most likely the visit was for a little buttering up. Gray didn't con himself into thinking his son actually wanted to spend time with him.

If Rafe hadn't said he'd stop by, Gray probably wouldn't have been able to let Lola go.

But he had her number, in more ways than one. And he would use it to his advantage when the time was right.

DAMMIT, SHE'D LEFT HER PHONE ON THE CAR'S CONSOLE. HOW the hell had she missed stuffing it in her purse? The whole time she'd thought she had it with her, but obviously not. Now it was flashing with messages. Instead of listening right then, she backed out of his driveway and drove half a block down. She didn't want Gray to think she was waiting for him to come out to her car.

"We're running the test in fifteen minutes." Frank. Giving her a fifteen-minute lead time. Just like an engineer not to consider that it would take her at least fifteen minutes to get there. The time stamp on the message was twenty minutes ago.

The next message. George. "Where the hell are you, Lola?" Ten minutes later. She could strangle engineers.

Frank. The third message. "Dammit, Lola, we can't wait all day. It's Sunday, for Christ's sake."

She narrowed her eyes as if the two of them were right in front of her. She'd left all those messages for them, not one answer, then suddenly it was an emergency. Twenty minutes earlier, she'd been sitting on Gray's lap with a vibrator in some very erogenous zones. Even if she'd put the phone in her purse, she wouldn't have heard it ring. She wouldn't have heard a jet landing on Gray's front lawn.

She dialed back on one of the missed calls. Frank answered, "Yo."

"Don't start without me." She used Gray's you-will-do-what-I-say-or-else tone. "I'm on my way."

"Three minutes," Frank said.

"Fifteen," she countermanded. They were just yanking her chain.

There was no time to stop to put on her bra and panties. She'd pop into the ladies' room at the Fletcher plant before she went to the lab.

She didn't speed, but her foot was heavier on the accelerator than it should have been, and she punched it at an intersection in order to get around a slow-moving truck.

The twins would probably return from the movie before she did, but what the heck, they were almost sixteen. They could stay home alone. And maybe, for fear of her wrath if they damaged anything, they might be good. Did they have to earn trust before being given it? Or should she give it to them, which in turn would teach them to be trustworthy? That was like the chicken and the egg question.

By the time she arrived at the plant, the afterglow of really hot sex had completely dissipated. Now she was just a slut with no panties or bra. *Slut*, in this case, was *not* a term of endearment.

She swiped her card key, pushed open the employee cafeteria door, her purse—with her panties and bra inside—under her arm.

Frank was pouring coffee from a pot that reeked like it had been sitting there since the morning.

Double damn. No chance to duck into the ladies' room.

He turned. "What took you so long?"

Lola didn't have time to hug her purse to her chest and cover her sweater. The cafeteria was cold. And her nipples knew it.

So did Frank. His eyes dropped, then just as quickly popped back up.

She would not let her attire—or the state of her nipples—undermine her. "I asked you to give me notice."

"I called," he said mildly.

"Fifteen minutes is not *notice*."

Tall and lanky, he had brown hair that was too long—and slightly greasy, as if he'd been here for the last forty-eight hours. A yellow splotch on his rumpled white T-shirt looked like mustard. He was past thirty and should have long since stopped pulling all-nighters as if he were still in college.

"Fine," he groused. "You're here, we can get started."

She resented the implication that she was holding them up. They were only working this weekend by edict.

She thought about going to the restroom first. But he obviously knew she wasn't wearing a bra. What would he think if she suddenly put one on? Surely he'd wonder why she'd been carrying her bra in her purse.

Lola decided it was none of his business. Her nipples were none of his business. She wasn't going to scuttle away like a woman who had just done something wrong. She'd had consensual sex with a very sexy CEO, and she was *not* going to let

Frank—or George, for that matter—bring her down. She marched ahead of him, head high.

In the lab, George was hidden in a warren of test equipment, wires, and computer monitors. A couple of years older than Frank, he was the stereotypical engineer. His black hair was short enough to qualify as a buzz cut, and a blue pen had leaked ink in the pocket of his white button-down shirt. When he saw Lola, his eyes widened, the effect made even greater by the thickness of his horn-rimmed glasses. She thought they'd discontinued the style back in the sixties.

"Hi, George." She took her seat on the stool between them. She didn't apologize for being late or for the sweater effect. They would just have to deal.

Pushing the stool back slightly so they could reach the equipment without interference, she turned on her word processor. She didn't use her laptop for note-taking. The small word processor didn't need to boot up, and it nestled on her lap easily. She could type quickly and download when she got home. It was much more efficient. She'd also brought a folder of printed diagrams to doctor up.

They were staring at her, not the equipment. For a moment, she thought they might actually have X-ray eyes and knew she wasn't wearing panties either. The oddest feeling swept over her, something very sexual, almost predatory. She was alone with two men, sandwiched between them like the cream center of an Oreo cookie. No underwear, just a thin sweater and a short little skirt. And half an hour ago, she'd been sitting on Gray's lap with her hands between her legs. In front of a mirror.

There was something so utterly powerful about that, the knowledge of what she'd been doing, the sexiness. And these two men suddenly salivating over her.

She didn't want them. She didn't care about them beyond this project. But Gray was right. Sex was power.

And she wanted more of it with him.

Next time she was going to make some demands of her own. And she knew exactly what would give her the power, even according to Gray.

7

"I'M SORRY, DAD, BUT THE GUYS WANTED TO GET BURGERS AFTER the movie. How was I supposed to say no?"

Cell phone to his ear, Gray hung his head. "Going to dinner was fine. Not calling me to let me know isn't. I was worried, especially when you didn't answer your cell phone."

Rafe gave a disgusted snort. "I told you I left it in the car."

Gray realized this was another form of punishment. Rafe had used hostility and indifference; now he was employing the tactic of getting Gray's hopes up, then dashing them. "Well, you better call your mother. She's worried, too."

"Only because *you* called her." The hostility was back. And something else, a noise.

"You're not driving, are you?"

"No," Rafe snapped. "I'm parked on the street."

Three teenage boys in a moving car was a frightening prospect, but the driver talking on his cell phone at the same time was enough to stop a father's heart dead. Gray knew he was nagging, but he'd laid down a strict rule, no talking on the phone while driving. It didn't matter that his ex-wife's car had Bluetooth, it was the distraction, not just the hands-free.

"Stop nagging, Dad"—elongated with a sarcastic drawl—"I know the law." He meant Gray's law.

Gray kept his sigh to himself. "Call your mother. I'll see you at training on Tuesday."

Rafe cut off with a mumbled word which might have been *good-bye*, or *fuck off.*

He sat in the family-room chair staring at the blank TV screen. His guts ached. Teenagers could make a strong man feel weak. When they were babies, you held them in the palm of your hand, so small, so needy, so perfect. Your guts ached with how much you loved them, and you wanted to keep them safe, give them everything. You struggled to make all their dreams come true. Then you lost them and you weren't even sure when or how. The goal had been to allow his wife to stay home with Rafe, and yes, Gray had worked a lot, he'd had to travel. He'd missed some important events. But he hadn't missed every single one. He hadn't consistently shortchanged Rafe. Just a few times. Obviously, enough times. He wasn't a bad man, but somehow he'd failed his son. Now he didn't know how to pick up the pieces.

Gray arched his neck, flexed his shoulders. The kinks remained.

Yet for a time this afternoon, with Lola, he'd been able to forget everything else. She made him forget. And he wanted her to help him forget a lot more. He planned to, later tonight, when the lights were off and she would be alone in her bed.

AT TEN O'CLOCK, LOLA SENT THE BOYS TO BED. AT LEAST SHE tried to.

"But there's no football on Monday," William whined, "so we don't have to get up early in the morning."

"Yes, but I do."

"We'll turn down the volume." Harry always had an answer for everything.

Lola was tired of fighting. Besides, she might actually get some work done in the morning while they were sleeping. "All right. But do not make me come out here and tell you to be quiet."

Harry grinned. He had an infectious grin when he won, especially if he won over an adult.

From the bedroom, she could barely hear the TV. The master bathroom was between the living room and her bedroom proper. Despite what she'd told the boys, by the time she laid her head on the pillow, she wasn't tired. Her body still hummed from this afternoon's interlude. Gray still hadn't taken her, entered her, come inside her. But he was getting close, closer, closest. Soon. She felt it. She was already wet with the thought of it.

Her cell phone vibrated on the bedside table. Glancing at the lighted screen, she didn't recognize the number. But she knew. Oh yes, yes, yes, Coach Barnett was hot for it.

"Are you alone?" The deep, sexy timbre of his voice made her nerves twitch. Just like that, she was ready for him.

"Totally alone, Coach. I'm in my bed."

"Very good. Wearing sexy lingerie?"

"No, Coach, I'm not wearing a thing."

He laughed softly. "Have you been touching yourself, Lola?"

"Not since I was with you this afternoon."

"Do you want to touch yourself now?"

After two amazing punishment sessions, she was a slave to the feelings he evoked. "Yes, Coach." *Make me do it again.* She glanced at the door. She'd locked it. Maybe she was paranoid, but she felt like she was living with two spies in her house.

"Ask me what I'd do if you were here with me right now?"

She liked his games. The men she'd dated hadn't been particularly inspired. And the games her husband had played were more like mindfucking. "What would you do to me?"

"If you were here . . ." His voice dropped a couple of notes. She felt it low in her belly. "I'd roll you onto your stomach and spread-eagle you across my bed. Then I'd tie your hands to the headboard and your feet to the bottom."

With his words, his voice, she actually writhed against the mattress imagining herself tied to those sturdy mahogany bedposts. "No one's ever tied me up before," she murmured, a little breathless.

"I'd pin you to the bed with my body and enter you slowly."

She needed to feel it. Rolling to her stomach, she spread her legs wide for him and propped a pillow under her chest so she could still keep the phone to her ear. "I can feel you now," she whispered, wishing she hadn't thrown out her vibrator.

"I would fuck you so slowly, over your G-spot. Then I'd tuck a pillow beneath your belly so I could rub your clit."

"Oh. Yes." Her hips rotated on the bed without her conscious thought.

"Touch yourself, Lola. Tell me how wet you are."

She shifted and reached between her legs. Her clitoris throbbed beneath her fingers. "I'm absolutely dripping, Coach."

"Do you feel how hard I am inside you?"

"Yes, Coach."

"Let me fuck you, Lola. Let me make you scream. Tell me how good it is."

"Coach." Her voice was barely more than a breath. She couldn't stand it anymore, and she flopped onto her back. "I'm so wet for you, Coach. Make me come, Coach. Please." Her fingers circled and swirled around her clitoris.

"That's it, baby. Come for me. Tell me what you're doing."

"Rubbing. Touching. Oh God. Coach." She let the words spill out with little thought. "I wish I had my vibrator. But it wouldn't be like you. Wouldn't be as good." She concentrated on her clitoris, circling fast and hard. She sighed and groaned softly, her hips rising, rocking.

"Come for me, baby. I want to hear you moan."

She bit her lip. "Coach." Low, harsh. "Coach." Then her body contracted, and she curled into the sensation, locking her legs around her hand, intensifying the quakes streaking through her.

When it was over, she unfurled slowly until she was limp against the mattress. She'd been quiet. No one but Gray could have heard.

He was talking to her. "Baby, baby, that was so sweet."

"Are you hard?"

"Fuck yes." His voice was suddenly harsh.

She loved the intensity vibrating across the airwaves. "I want to hear you come. Just like I came for you." She thought about power. When he was talking to her, making her touch herself, bringing her to orgasm, the power was his. She wanted some of that for herself. "Stroke yourself for me. Groan for me." She dropped her voice. "Come for me."

"Witch," he growled.

"You're dying to come," she seduced him. "You wanted to come this afternoon when I was on your lap. You could barely hold back."

He rewarded her with a deep groan. "Yeah."

"You thought about taking me in front of that mirror. Watching as you slid deep. Every inch inside me."

"Fuck." His breath shot out. "Yes, I wanted it. I wanted *you*."

"You still want me. You've been fantasizing all day about

tying me to your bed. Spreading me. Even biting my neck like lions do when they're mating." She was seducing herself with the images.

"You can't know how badly I want it." He was gruff, his pitch deep, each word an effort.

And her heart sang. He hadn't taken her. But he'd wanted to. He was holding back to keep his power. But she had it all now. "When you finally have me, I'm going to feel so good. So tight around you. So wet."

"Jesus, yes." His breath sawed, harsh pants of need.

"You'll pound me down into the mattress. You'll love my moans. And you'll go so deep, so far. Until you can't even remember your name." She hissed out a breath and said in a whisper, "Then you'll come. Come now."

No more words, just one long groan that reached deep inside her. And she knew he'd climaxed. "That was good, Coach, so good. You're going to dream about it tonight. You'll wake up hard in the night and have to stroke yourself again."

"Jesus, you really are a witch."

"I am, Coach. And I've got you under my spell," she quipped. "Now rub it in."

"What?" He sounded slightly dazed.

"Your come. Rub it in. I want you to sleep with it on you. I want you to wake up with the scent of it and think of me."

She pushed End.

Now *that* was power.

SHE'D BEWITCHED HIM. BECAUSE HE DID EXACTLY WHAT SHE SAID, rubbing the evidence of his orgasm into his belly, then waking deep in the night with a throbbing hard-on. The scent of sex and come swirled in the room, and the phantom echo of her voice whispered in his ear as he stroked himself to another bone-melting climax.

Christ. She'd turned the tables on him. And he liked it.

BANG, BANG, BANG.

Lola shot up in bed, heart in her throat, pulse racing. What on earth?

"Aunt Lola, wake up," Harry shouted through the door. "Mom's on Skype and she wants to talk to you."

"Coming," she called, adding, "Good Lord," under her breath. Andrea must have forgotten the time difference. Then she glanced at the clock. And had another heart attack. Eight o'clock? It was unheard of. She *never* got up this late.

It was sex. It was that orgasm. It was the way Gray made her feel. So good, so relaxed, so special, she'd slept an extra two hours. Damnation.

Jumping out of bed, she grabbed her robe and threw open the door. Harry and William—still in their pj's—were at the dining room table, not that you could really call the corner nook off the kitchen and living room a dining *room* since it could handle only a table, four chairs, and the breakfront.

"Where is she?" Andrea screamed. Her sister thought she had to yell over Skype as if it were a bad phone connection.

"We got her out of bed, Mom."

"Out of bed?" her sister screeched. "Didn't she make you a healthy breakfast?"

Lola nudged Harry out of the chair. "They're capable of making their own healthy breakfast." Although she'd let them buy Cap'n Crunch cereal on the first grocery expedition. Of course they'd complained of "crunch mouth" the next day. She was a bad aunt.

"Lola," Andrea said peevishly, "you look like crap."

"Thank you very much," she answered dryly. "You wanted to speak to me?" During every Skype call Lola hadn't been able to get out of, Andrea had a list of instructions for her. Most of which Lola ignored.

"I most certainly do." Every muscle in Andrea's face pulled into a scowl. "How on earth could you allow them to drive with a newly licensed teenager?"

"He got his license a year ago," William piped in.

"If you live for eighty years, twelve months is nothing," Andrea snapped. "Do you know that 95 percent of accidents involve teenage drivers?"

"Wow. I've never heard that statistic." Lola didn't believe it. Andrea was simply pulling it out of her . . . hat.

"Teenage drinking and driving is the leading cause of highway deaths."

Lola didn't roll her eyes. It would only make things worse. "It was the afternoon. They went to a movie. There was no drinking." She certainly hadn't smelled anything on their breath.

The twins hovered over her shoulder, getting into the picture. "No way, Mom," Harry defended. "We were not drinking."

"I'm talking to your aunt Lola. And it isn't what actually happened but what could have happened that's the issue."

Lola thought of that old philosopher—she couldn't remember which one—who'd once said something to the effect that he'd had many tragedies in his life, most of which never happened. That was Andrea, dwelling on things that never happened.

"Yes, well, they're fine, Andrea."

"And who is this kid anyway? Did you meet his parents?"

"Uhh . . ." Meet his parents? Maybe that was a mom thing; the idea had never even occurred to Lola. It was a good thing she'd never had kids of her own.

"You didn't." Aghast, Andrea's mouth dropped open. "What's his name?"

Harry jumped in before Lola could further incriminate herself. "Arby."

Arby? Like the fast food restaurant? Whatever.

"Did you even meet him, Lola?" Andrea glared, the look hot enough to melt the computer screen. "You didn't," she finished when Lola failed to answer immediately. She leaned into the webcam, her face filling the entire screen, which gave her the bloated cheeks of a puffer fish. "What if he isn't really sixteen? Or he's older and he's some sort of child molester? Do you realize what might have *happened*?" Her voice was rising to hysteria.

First teenage drinking, now child molesters? Okay, she *wouldn't* make good mom material, but honestly, Andrea was over the top. "You're catastrophizing, Andrea."

Her sister's face looked ready to explode all over the screen.

"Oh wow, Mom, you're getting fuzzy." Harry waved his hand in front of the webcam. "I think we're losing the signal. Mom, Mom, can you hear us? Mom?" He hit a button on the keyboard and Andrea disappeared.

Thank God. Maybe Harry possessed some redeeming qualities after all.

"Can we go to the mall today?" William asked as if he hadn't been hovering over her shoulder for the entire conversation.

"Not a good idea," she said. "Because I'm not sure how I could possibly meet every teenager you might come in contact with, not to mention potential pedophiles." Okay, she shouldn't employ sarcasm about their mother. Andrea had a point. Lola had let them get in a car with a kid she didn't even know. It wasn't catastrophizing to ask what she'd have done if they hadn't come home on time or answered their cell phones. She'd had no phone number to call, no parents to contact. It was negligent.

Harry rolled his eyes at her militant look. "Come on, Aunt Lola. We're going stir crazy. We'll keep our cell phones on at all times, and we won't get in a car with any strangers."

They were closer to sixteen than fifteen. She and Andrea had prowled the mall for hours when they were fifteen, and even fourteen and thirteen. What was being overprotective versus letting kids have some fun?

"All right, you can go." She glared and gritted her teeth at them. "But do not get into any trouble." Really, how much trouble could they get into at the mall?

Stores. Spending. Andrea's credit cards.

"And do *not* use your mother's credit cards."

They gave her identical eye rolls. "We're just going to the arcade," Harry said.

She contemplated their singularly innocent faces, sure they were planning something. "Fine. I'll drop you off after we've showered and had an extremely healthy breakfast." The mall should be open by then. "And don't forget your driving lesson. I'll pick you up at one."

Jeez. Being an aunt was hard work.

8

Bettina was his *ex*-wife, but Gray didn't correct his secretary. He hit the intercom button. "Send her in."

Mondays were his only full day in the office during the summer while he ran the football camp. His weekly executive staff meeting was at ten-thirty. He glanced at his watch. Bettina could have five minutes, which was all the time he could spare.

She strolled in garbed in a black dress with red piping along the collar and a full skirt. She accented the outfit with red lipstick, choker-length red beads, and red high heels. When they were married, her attire of choice had been sweatpants.

"You look nice," he complimented. "A lunch date?"

She sat in the chair opposite, spreading the skirt out elegantly. "I'm going to a poetry reading at a local teahouse. It's high tea. We need to dress the part."

Not a date, then. Bettina had not dated since the divorce five years ago. She'd gotten the house, he'd gotten the mortgage. Her lifestyle would be maintained unless she remarried. He could only hope, but he didn't believe she was interested in men anymore; she hadn't been interested in sex since Rafe was born. But she was a great mom.

"Rafe needs a car," she said, her words clipped. "I can't keep driving him everywhere or letting him borrow my car. It just isn't workable anymore."

When Rafe was born, they'd both decided she should be a stay-at-home mom. Division of labor, anything outside the house was his bailiwick. So he'd done the yard work every weekend and gone to the office every day, traveled as necessary, climbing the corporate ladder in order to buy a bigger house, the cars, save for the college fund, pay the bills, and provide health insurance. Bettina had done everything else. Taking Rafe to his various activities had been part of *everything else*.

Nothing had changed since the divorce except that Rafe hated him and Bettina held him in contempt.

"He has a bike," he said mildly, sitting back, clasping his hands over his stomach.

She snorted. "Oh, be serious." She tossed her highlighted blond hair over her shoulder. Rafe's black hair had come from him, a dominant trait.

He smiled slightly. He'd known it would piss her off. He wasn't sure whose idea it was to have him buy Rafe a car. Was she pushing Rafe, or was he pushing her? "When I was his age, I had to earn money to buy my first car."

Bettina gave a long-suffering sigh. "And your father had to walk five miles in the snow to get to school every day."

Gray's family was all back East. It was *her* father who had loved that old saying, even though he'd been born and raised in the San Francisco Bay Area where there was no snow except in the mountains, and even that was rare.

"He shouldn't be handed everything, Bettina."

"He's not." Her lips pursed and her nostrils flared.

She was still as angry with him as the day she'd told him she was getting a divorce. Yet he'd done his best for her and Rafe. She'd been a good mother, and he'd been a good provider. The divorce had nothing to do with the few sexy spankings he'd given her in the early years. She'd never complained. They'd had fun. Then she'd changed after Rafe was born. Sex became a duty for her, no longer a pleasure.

It was his traveling that finally did their marriage in, though. She never considered how grueling it was for him, especially coming home to her harping. Then she'd started accusing him of sleeping with other women while he was away. He hadn't, though he could never figure out why she cared anyway since she was no longer interested. When she'd divorced him, it was almost a relief. Except that he'd lost his son as well.

"Do you know how much homework kids have these days?" Bettina went on. "Not to mention all the after-school activities like soccer and—" She stopped, glared at him. "Oh, I forgot, you can't make the soccer games."

It was an old fight. Gray cut it off. She did have a point about activities, and a car would be easier. Why was he fighting so hard? Bitterness? Was he punishing Bettina? Perhaps it was time he got over it, for Rafe's sake. "All right," he sighed. "I'll take him out this weekend. I'm sure we can find him a good used car."

"You're such a cheap bastard, Gray." She narrowed her eyes at him. "He's a teenager. He needs something flashy and fun. Like a Mustang. Or a big truck he can impress his friends with. Don't get him something girlie or old man."

"I'm not buying him a car just to impress his friends."

She rose quickly, leaned over the desk, poking her finger close to his face. "Do not make me a laughingstock in the neighborhood by buying him an old, used beater car." Having the last word as always, she left in a swirl of skirt, her perfume still hanging in the air.

He sat for a long moment. He didn't want to buy off his son with an expensive new car. He wanted Rafe to learn the value of money and hard work. But he wouldn't buy him an old piece of crap either. He wanted reliability. Bettina should know that.

His secretary buzzed him. "Mr. Barnett, they're waiting for you in the conference room."

The staff meeting, he was late.

Gathering his folder, he thought of Lola for no particular reason. Hell, there was a very particular reason. She made him feel good. When he closed his front door, all the crap fell away. He wanted her tonight. But he'd have to wait until tomorrow when Harry and William used their cell phones, played their video consoles, or picked on Stu. Because they would do something. They always did. And Lola would be his.

Despite Bettina's visit, Gray was smiling as he joined the meeting.

ON TUESDAY, THEY WERE ANGELS. WHAT WAS UP WITH THAT? Gray wondered if he should provoke them.

"Use your body to shield the ball from the opposing team, William."

The opposing team consisted of several tackling dummies and his brother, Harry. He had the boys performing a fumble-recovery drill. He'd chosen Harry and William for the first demonstration, employing the slide technique because they were of equal size.

Having played high school football, he knew all the drills. As a wide receiver, he'd had a fair degree of skill, but he hadn't chosen to go on to college football.

"All right, this time let's have Stu and—" He glanced around. The problem was none of the other boys were Stu's relative size. He thought about putting Rafe up against him, Rafe being the oldest of the boys. Instead, he chose one of the slighter players. "Roger, you try it."

The reality was you were going to face guys who were bigger, but sometimes the little guy had more agility. The drill would help Roger work with that. He waited for some sly comment from the twins about the difference in size and weight. They simply watched as Stu and Roger took their positions.

He tossed the ball, simulating the fumble. Before Roger even moved, Stu leaped and fell on the ball, capturing it firmly. The boy had more in him than Gray had originally thought. His skills were improving.

He clapped twice. "Good job."

The other boys cheered, even the twins, and pounded Stu on the back when he rose. It was perfect.

Something had to be wrong. They were *too* perfect. Maybe Lola had had a talk with them. Maybe she didn't want another punishment. *Nah*, he told himself with an inward smile.

After the fumble recovery, he moved the boys into a zigzag-agility drill. This one was more difficult. Setting up a line of cones, the player was required to move forward, backward, and sideways through the cones as another player passed the ball to him.

No one, not even the twins, laughed when Stu tripped. He wasn't the only one tripping and dropping the ball.

"Great job," he called to each kid in turn. He believed the effort should be as recognized as the result.

As the morning progressed, Gray encouraged and challenged, applauded and beat the air with his fist over each and every boy's triumph. The field was scuffed, full of divots, the boys hot, sweaty, dirty, grass-stained, but smiling. At a quarter to one, he sent them all to the showers, but Rafe sidled up to him.

"Mom says you have to drive me home. She's got an appointment."

"All right." He realized it was a ploy on Bettina's part, but he'd take the extra time with his son. "Go get showered."

Once Rafe had jogged off the field, Gray pulled out his cell phone and punched in Lola's number.

He didn't let her get a word out beyond *hello*. "My house, six o'clock. Be prepared."

"Dammit"—she sighed—"what did they do now?"

"Unnecessary teasing," he said sharply. "This is going to be big-time punishment." He was already anticipating, gearing up.

"Yes, Coach," she said, and he detected a note of amusement.

"Don't be late." He ended the call, again without letting her say another word.

A case could be made that he was getting a little obsessive about her, but damn, it felt good. He wanted her. He was going to have her. And the twins lack of misbehavior wouldn't stand in his way.

FRAMED IN THE DOORWAY, THE SUN SHONE THROUGH HER BLUE flower-print sundress. Two thin straps were tied in bows at her delectable shoulders, and the elasticized bodice hugged her small yet perfect breasts. Her legs were bare and enticing. Gray's mouth watered.

She flipped her hair over her shoulder. "Is my chair ready, Coach?"

"In your naughty corner."

Tossing her purse on the hall table, she flounced through the living room, then flopped down on the chair. Next to her on the small side table, he'd laid out many of the same implements and devices as before. Her legs slightly spread, one hand between them, she glanced over her shoulder to ask, "No mirror this time?"

He rounded the chair to stand in front of her. "I haven't decided what I'm going to do to you yet. There are so many possibilities." He folded his arms over his chest, stared down at her, contemplating. He'd had numerous fantasies since the last time he had her at his mercy, but he was so close to her now that her scent rose to mesmerize him. All he could think about was dragging her to his bed, falling on her, taking her.

But that wouldn't do. Not yet.

She raised one eyebrow. "A spanking?"

"Been there, done that." He stroked his chin, rough with stubble. There hadn't been time to shave when he got home from work.

She tipped her head. "Tying me up and blindfolding me?"

"And then what would I do with you?" What did she want him to do? He needed a clue to the inner workings of her mind.

"You're the master here. I'm just the submissive. I'm at your command. But if you really haven't decided . . ." A slow smile grew on her face and her eyes twinkled. "I've got a few ideas."

"Do tell." His blood pumped faster through his veins, and his cock throbbed with desire.

Tucking two fingers into his waistband, she hauled him closer. She sifted through the toys on the table, pushing aside the vibrator, the ball gag, the butt plug.

Then she held up a red silk scarf. "Use this on me."

"Where?" To tie her up, gag her, blindfold her? They were all heady possibilities.

"Tie my hands behind my back." She bit her bottom lip, blinked rapidly. "But first we'll do this." She tugged on his belt, pulled it free, then yanked on the top button of his jeans.

All four popped free, and his cock bulged hard against his briefs. "Oh, look at that," she whispered, glancing up. "You look ready for something, Coach. Something very big."

Christ, he was ready. "But you're the one who needs punishing."

"And that's just what we'll do, Coach." She fluttered the scarf at him. "You'll tie my hands behind my back." She demonstrated, and the sight of her in that position made his blood roar through his ears.

"Then what?" He was surprised his voice didn't crack.

She lowered her voice almost to a whisper. "Then you'll force me to suck your cock." She fluttered her eyelashes. "Isn't that a perfect punishment?"

Hell, yes. Because it was what he was dying for. Her lips wrapped around his flesh, her tongue on him.

"Do you want to blindfold me, too, Coach?" she asked, her voice sweet with childlike innocence.

"No. I want to see your eyes. And I want you to watch as I feed my cock to you."

"Then you better tie me up really quick, Coach, or I might just take matters into my own hands." She stroked down the front of his briefs, her fingernail grazing him from tip to base.

He grabbed her finger. "Uh-uh-uh. Not until I say. After all, this is *your* punishment." He was supposed to be in charge, yet he liked the turnaround. He liked the games she wanted to play.

Tugging the scarf from her grasp, he circled to her back. She already had her hands in position.

"You want to try everything, don't you?" he whispered at her ear as he secured her wrists.

"Yes, Coach. I like being dirty with you. It's fun."

He wanted to see her eyes, and he leaned to the side, pulling her chin toward him. A fire burned in the depths of her gaze. He felt an answering spark. "There are so many things we can do," he murmured.

It sounded like a promise.

"Make me take you, Coach. Now."

When he was in front of her again, he fisted his hand in her silky black hair, twisting it around his palm once, and pulled her face down to his cock. She nuzzled him, her warm breath heating him.

"Make me taste you, Coach. You know you want to. You need to."

She was the seductress. And he needed it bad. In this moment, she became the master and he was her slave.

9

YANKING DOWN HIS BRIEFS, GRAY LET HIS COCK SPRING FREE.
Lola licked his length, and a tremor ran through his body. He
barely suppressed the groan that rose up in his throat.

Running her tongue through his slit, she swiped away a drop
of pre-come. "You taste good, Coach."

He tugged on her hair. "Suck me, baby." He did not beg; he
ordered, trying to at least show some sense of control, even if he'd
totally lost it.

"Yes, Coach." Her lips engulfed the head, and she sucked
hard.

He swore and tipped his head back, savoring the smooth feel
of her tongue on him. But then he needed to watch her.

And she was watching him, triumph burning in her eyes. He'd
told her a woman held all the power when a man's cock was in
her mouth, and now she reveled in that power.

"Suck me all the way." The words were a command, his tone
hard, but of course she knew she had him. She knew he'd do

anything. He'd denied letting a woman have the power like this in a long time. But he gave in to Lola. Easily. Swiftly.

She took him deep down her throat, sucked hard on the way up.

"Fuck." He couldn't help the word, the need in his voice. "Don't stop. Faster."

She gave it to him, hard and fast. His hand fisted in her hair, he showed her the rhythm he wanted, needed. But he wasn't fucking her mouth; she was taking him. Owning him.

She slowed, grazing her teeth around the ridge, then drove him crazy with a deep suck on his crown.

"You sweet, perfect, dirty slut, just do it. Suck me. Make me come."

Her mouth was supple, warm, wet, her tongue working all his erogenous zones. And her gaze beguiled him, her eyes so dark, so penetrating, seeing everything, knowing that she had him on the edge.

"Don't stop. Fuck. Make me come." He threw his head back, his hips pumping. But she wouldn't give it to him, simply kept him riding that wild, crazy edge. "Fuck. Please. Lola. Godammit. Please."

With those words, she set herself to the rhythm of his hips and took him to heaven. He lost it all then, his essence, deep down her throat, pumping, gushing, filling her. He pulled her close, held her head, kept her there, his legs trembling beneath him, until the last shock waves died away.

Lola looked up at him. She was definitely the cat that ate the cream, every last drop. She licked her lips. Then she licked his cock, cleaning him.

"Was that good, Coach?" She fluttered her eyelashes.

"You fucking know it was." He was still throbbing, sensation rippling across his skin.

"I see what you mean about the woman having all the power."
She laughed. "And I even did it with my hands behind my back."

"You sound a little smug." He stepped back, tucking himself
back into his jeans and fastening the buttons.

"Because you loved it."

"And you think that means you've turned the tables on me."
He buckled his belt. She'd most definitely turned them on him,
but she was enjoying the power way too much.

She stood up and licked her lips once again. "Look who has
all the power now," she whispered.

He was on her in a second, lifting her high, and tossing her
down on the couch, forcing an *oomph* of air from her.

"What are you doing?" She struggled to rise, unable to get leverage with her hands tied. He grabbed two implements off the table.

"We're far from done. I still haven't punished you." Then he
fell on her, pushing her down into the couch cushions.

She bucked beneath him, but without the use of her hands,
she couldn't throw him off. "Let me up."

"You gave me an idea earlier." He shoved the ball gag in her
mouth and secured it. "Gagging." Then he slipped the blindfold
over her head and patted it against her eyes. "Blindfolding."

She wriggled, furious noises distorted by the ball in her
mouth.

"And now you're mine to do with as I wish," he whispered
close to her ear.

SHE WAS HIS PRISONER. HIS BODY PINNED HER TO THE COUCH, HIS
legs flung over hers so she couldn't even kick him. The taste of his
come was still on her tongue. It had been so good. She'd been in
charge, had made him quake with release. Yes, it was power and
it was heady.

"Did you like that little taste of power, Lola?" he murmured against her ear.

She screamed. Nothing much came out. She'd loved taking him in her mouth, making him come, swallowing him. But she'd wanted to walk out still holding all that power.

He shifted and the spaghetti straps of her sundress fell away. He tugged the top down over her breasts. Air brushed her flesh. His hot mouth took a nipple. He licked, sucked. Then he bit her. She screamed, the gag muffling the sound, and a wave of exquisite pleasure rushed down between her legs.

"Look how hard your nipples just got. And I do believe you're wet." He nuzzled her ear and whispered, "I can smell how wet you are." His warm breath sent a shudder through her.

She couldn't say why being unable to see or speak or move should intensify every sensation, but it did. Her bound hands had splayed out beneath her, supporting her bottom. She felt his jeans rough on her skin, his cock still hard against her, his breath sweet and warm. His voice strummed a chord inside her.

Still pinning her, he yanked her dress up to her waist. She was naked now except for the band of material. Then his hand was between her thighs. Oh God, oh God.

"See how wet you are." He caressed her with slippery fingers.

She was no longer fighting, her body moving with his touch, begging for more. She arched into him. *Please take me, please, please, please.* How easily he made her beg.

He moved again, his hand on her breast, his fingers swirling around her nipple. He pinched hard. She bucked and writhed against him, her body on the cusp of climax. She couldn't see, couldn't talk, there was just his voice, and his magic fingers working her.

"You love the sweet pain. It makes everything hotter, intense."

Yes, yes, yes. She shoved her head back into the couch and tried to rub herself against him. How had he done this to her so quickly? Zero to sixty.

He crawled down her body, spreading her legs, falling between them. She could have kicked him. But all she wanted was—

He put his mouth on her.

—that, oh God yes, *that*.

He suckled her clitoris as he reached up to tweak both her nipples. Licking, sucking, pinching, he made her stark raving mad with need. Beneath the mask, tears leaked from her eyes. Her body was cruising just below climax, reaching, straining for it.

He abandoned one nipple and, once again with the speed of light, entered her with two fingers. He was everywhere, her breast, her clitoris, inside her, a slow, relentless stroke across her G-spot.

Please, please, please.

It started with the small bang of a firecracker inside her, sweeping out, gaining momentum, turning everything molten in its path. She screamed around the gag, cried behind the mask, her body contracting, releasing, exploding. She was nothing but a mass of nerve endings and sensation.

Until finally she became aware of his weight on her, his rough clothes on her skin, his body heating hers, the scratch of his stubble on her chest.

God. It couldn't get any better.

But her arms were starting to ache slightly with the awkward position, her hands trapped beneath her.

His lips moved against her hair. "Look at who has all the power now," he said, throwing her words back at her.

He did. And it was just as good as when she'd had it.

Tugging the blindfold off, he tossed it, then removed the ball gag. Her jaw ached slightly, and she rotated it a moment.

"You okay?"

"Yeah." Her voice sounded hoarse.

"Very hot."

Then he kissed her, his lips wet with her juice. Her flavors mixed with his. His tongue stole into her mouth, played with her. Oh. Yes. He cupped her head, held her as he angled, opened a little wider, went deeper. Oh my. God. Until this moment, she hadn't realized that he'd never kissed her. But oh, how good he was. When he pulled back, she was dizzy.

And her hands were free. He'd untied her as he kissed her.

"I like the way you taste, Lola. I like the way you come. You're perfection."

She'd never met a man so sensual, so into touch and taste and kinky things, sexual without even getting inside her. The men she had known were all about the end result, intercourse, sometimes even skipping all the sexy foreplay. With Gray, foreplay was an end in and of itself.

"Somehow that didn't really feel like punishment," she said slowly, her voice dreamy.

"Punishment doesn't have to feel bad."

It most certainly didn't.

Then she realized her dress was stuck around her middle. She yanked it up.

"Here, let me. Since I untied them." With light caresses, he fashioned the straps into little bows at her shoulders.

She stood, and he smoothed down the skirt for her. Then, still seated on the couch, he shook his finger at her. "Naughty, naughty, you weren't wearing panties again."

"I took them off in the car."

"Such a dirty little slut." His gaze was shiny with laughter and the lingering heat of desire. No man had ever made her feel wanted the way he did. Intensely.

Lola wanted to touch him. She wanted to bend down and kiss him again, long and sweet. "I have to go." But he could have begged her to stay.

He stood and ran gentle fingers through her hair. It was probably a mess.

"Can I fix myself in your bathroom?"

"Of course." He held out a hand in invitation.

She couldn't go home with her panties in her purse. What if *someone* accidentally looked inside her bag and saw what they shouldn't see? Grabbing her purse off the hall table, she scampered down the hall, her sandals slapping on the hardwood.

She paused at the open door of his bedroom. And for one brief moment, she saw herself spread-eagled on the bed, hands tied to those dark wood bedposts. Her heart did a fast triple beat.

Then she closed the bathroom door. Two bright spots of color flamed in her cheeks, and her hair was a mass of tangles. She tamed them with a small brush. Being naked beneath the dress was decadent, sexy, and deliciously slutty, to use Gray's word. But she retrieved her panties from her purse and stepped into them.

She hadn't challenged him about whether the twins had actually misbehaved. What was it, *unnecessary teasing*? She hadn't questioned, didn't care. She wanted to be here. She wanted the things he did to her, craved the new sensations. A ball gag. It was so Betty Paige, the bondage actress from the 1950s, and so exciting. She imagined having Gray truss her up with ropes so she couldn't move, then spanking her until her bottom was red and she was creamy with desire. She wanted anything and everything he dished out.

This punishment thing might actually be getting out of hand.

Semi-satisfied with her reflection, she opened the bathroom door. And froze when she heard voices.

"I wanted to talk about the car, Dad."

Dear God. His son was in the house. Had he seen the stuff in the living room? The chair? The sex toys? The ball gag?

"It's not a good time right now, Rafe." Gray's low, modulated tone.

Okay, they were still in the front hall, not the living room. Lola hugged the wall just inside the bathroom door.

"Why not?" Rafe's surly voice.

"I'm busy right now," Gray said patiently. "I told your mother we'd look at cars this weekend when you're with me."

Of course. He probably had some sort of arrangement for when his son stayed over, the wife having one weekend, Gray the other.

"I want to talk about it now. Because Mom said you were going to buy some used piece of crap. She says she doesn't want a junker in her driveway so all the neighbors can see."

"Rafe," Gray said in his stern coach voice. "We'll talk about it this weekend. Right now, I'm busy."

Silence lasted five seconds that felt like forever. "You've got a woman here, don't you?"

"I said I'm busy." Each word was clipped, harsh.

"You're seeing some slut on the side, aren't you? Mom was right."

"Do *not* use that word in a derogatory manner about any woman."

Yes, only use the word when you're punishing some hot little slut on the couch while you have her gagged, tied, and blindfolded. Lola closed her eyes. It had been so good. His son's words turned it into something sordid.

"Your mother doesn't know anything about who I see or what I do. It isn't her business."

The boy's voice rose an octave. "It's *my* business. Because your women were always more important than Mom." He paused, added, "And me," like it was an afterthought.

"Rafe," Gray broke in. "I don't know where you're getting these ideas. I always have time for you."

"Not tonight. You told me to get out. And you're going to buy some piece-of-shit car because I'm not good enough for anything else." He was shouting now. "I hate you."

Then the door slammed with a reverberation that seemed to rock the entire house.

Her feet were frozen to the tile floor, her fingers stuck to the wall like skin on iced metal. She didn't want to hear this, didn't want to know it. She didn't understand kids. She didn't know how to comfort a man whose son had just told him he hated him.

And how many women did he really have?

"You can come out now," Gray called.

She was breathing hard. God, she didn't want to. But she had to at least act like an adult.

He stood at the end of the hall, a behemoth filling the opening.

"I'm really sorry," she said, almost stammering. "I parked in the street, not on your driveway, so people wouldn't think—"

He was suddenly there, his fingers over her lips. "Don't apologize. I'm sorry you had to hear that. I don't know what's going on with him." His eyes, usually so dark and commanding, were a soft, aching brown. "It's not your fault. It's mine."

"Maybe I shouldn't come here again."

"Let me worry about that." He cupped her cheek, his voice dropping to a sexy note that seemed to stroke her all over. "Tonight was excellent. You were perfect." He ran the pad of his thumb along her lips. "And I have a duty to keep punishing you whenever the twins misbehave. I can't break that bargain." He searched her face, looking for something.

"Of course. We have a bargain," she agreed. "You can't kick them out if I accept their punishment."

"Good girl," he whispered. "You'll have to keep coming back as long as it's necessary."

She would. She wanted his punishments. Oh hell, she *needed* them. From him.

GRAY WANTED TO PUNCH A FIST THROUGH THE WALL.

How could Rafe's timing have been so off? Actually, if he'd walked in ten minutes earlier, when Lola was bound, gagged, blindfolded, and Gray's head between her legs, well, that would have been worse.

Her face had been red with mortification, her eyes wide. Jesus, what a fiasco.

All he had to do was buy Rafe the fucking car, a new one, with all the bells and whistles. Bettina would be happy. Rafe would be happy. But then he'd be gone again. All Rafe wanted was the car. He'd say and do anything to get it. But all that crap about Gray's *women*? That was Bettina's poison. Gray had no way of combating it. He'd never introduced Rafe to any of the women he'd seen after the divorce. He didn't date. He had women he slept with, women he played with, but he'd kept all that private. He'd never chosen a woman over Rafe.

Until today. He'd sent his son away. He'd chosen Lola.

Grabbing the phone, he dialed Bettina. "Rafe was here," he said when she answered.

"Yes, he asked to borrow the car so he could drive over to talk to you man-to-man."

Right. Bettina had probably sent him. "You might have given me a little warning."

"Why?" Her voice was laced with sly innuendo.

"You know why, Bettina. Because *you* want a new car, and I'm getting him something used. Stop working him up."

"I am not. He's seventeen. All he wants is a little freedom to go out with his friends without having to beg me to drive him or let him use my car."

"I'm not saying that's unreasonable."

She went on as if he hadn't spoken. "And if you weren't such a cheap—"

He cut her off. He wasn't getting into this with her. Arguing only made things worse. "Look, he was upset when he left. Call me when he gets home so I know he's okay."

"Fine. Whatever," she snapped. They were usually at least civil to each other. He figured that once the car issue was settled, their relationship would return to normal.

He'd suffered through a sex life with Bettina that was practically nil for an excruciating twelve years. She'd kicked him out anyway. Nothing he did or didn't do ever made things better with Rafe. And the truth was his son was acting more like he was still twelve instead of seventeen.

Lola was the only thing that made life bearable at the moment. So hell, no, he wasn't giving her up.

10

"YOU KNOW, AUNT LOLA, IF YOU KEEP WEARING DRESSES AND skirts, we'll start to think you're going on a hot date instead of working." Harry always had to say the one thing that would set her off. It was like she had a button on her forehead screaming *Push Me*.

She wouldn't let it get to her, not after that horrible scene in Gray's house. She flared the sundress. "Oh, this old thing? It's just so hot in the labs, I didn't want to roast alive." The labs were actually freezing. She'd once again used work as an excuse to get out of the house.

In the kitchen, she found the expected mess. Tomato seeds had dried on the cutting board along with streaks of avocado and bits of wilted lettuce. The counter was covered with enough bread crumbs to feed a flock of blue jays. All she'd done was ask them to make a couple of sandwiches for themselves for dinner. Was that so hard? "How could you possibly use five plates and all this cutlery?" she called out.

Harry shouted back, louder than necessary. "We had more than one sandwich."

"You could have used the same plate." She took a glass from the cupboard to pour herself some seltzer water.

"Mom said it gets bacteria."

Their mouths probably had more bacteria in them than a plate could pick up in the time it took to eat two sandwiches. "I asked you to clean up after yourselves."

"We will," Harry answered.

"Before we go to bed," William shouted.

She marched around the corner of the dining nook and glared at the two of them. As usual, they were on the couch with their ubiquitous electronic devices deployed. "Now," she said.

His gaze riveted to his laptop screen, Harry's lips turned down. "But, Aunt Lola—"

"I'm not your *but*. Clean it up now." Then, when William opened his mouth, she added, "And I'm not paying you to do it either." They thought they should get paid for every chore, even if it was cleaning up the mess they'd made.

"Oh, man." Harry put his laptop on the coffee table.

"Jeez," William groused, his fingers moving a mile a minute on the mini-keyboard of his smart phone.

"Now, William."

"Fine, I finished my text." He tossed the phone on the couch.

She left them mumbling in the kitchen. She'd probably have to repeat their cleaning efforts, but she was not letting them get away with turning her into their maid.

The end of Ghost's tail twitched against the dust ruffle of Lola's bed. The cat thought that if she couldn't see you, you couldn't see her.

Closing the door, she climbed on the bed, plumped the pillows behind her, and sent out an emergency Charlotte text.

Can you talk?

Two seconds later, her phone rang.

"Did they set fire to the school?" Charlotte asked.

"No. But Coach Barnett has a kid, and he almost caught us."

"Doing what?"

"What do you think?" Lola fiddled with the fringe of a pillow she'd hugged to her abdomen.

"The price for my advice is dirty details."

"We were . . . um . . ." What the hell, Charlotte was her best friend and she'd heard it all. "He had me bound, blindfolded, and gagged. And he was doing things to me with his mouth."

"Wow." Charlotte extended the word on a long breath. "Did you like it as much as the spanking?"

Incredible, stupendous, and magnificent didn't begin to describe it, so she skipped all the adjectives. "Yes. Even better."

"Naughty, naughty Lola."

She laughed. In Gray's house, she hadn't been sure she'd ever be able to laugh again (only a slight exaggeration), but Charlotte could always bring out the levity in her, in anyone, for that matter. "It was kinda hot"—an underwhelming description of an overpowering event—"then his son dropped by."

"And you were A, on the couch bound, gagged, and naked with a man between your legs; or B, untied and naked; or C, fully dressed. Or none of the above."

"I was in the bathroom. His son never saw me. But he figured out his dad had a woman there, and he called me a slut and said he hated Gray."

"So now he's Gray?"

Lola could picture Charlotte's raised eyebrow. "Coach Barnett. But we are engaging in some sexual activity, so I do occasionally think of him as Gray."

"All right. First, how old is his son?

"What difference does that make?"

"The level of trauma, of course."

"Aren't kids always traumatized by the thought of their parents having sex?"

"Lola," Charlotte admonished.

"Okay, he's seventeen or thereabouts."

"Hmm."

"What does that mean?"

"Teenagers are a species of their own."

Lola sighed. "Tell me about it." The twins weren't just a different species; they were from another planet.

"What did the coach say to you afterward?"

"What a man normally says. That it wasn't my fault, yadda, yadda." There was a lot of banging and clanging out in the kitchen, but she wasn't going out to investigate. She'd given the boys a chore, and she wouldn't check up on them, at least not until they were done.

"Does the coach want you to come back?" Charlotte prodded.

"He says he needs to keep punishing me for the twins' misbehavior."

"Then what's the problem? He's a big boy. He can handle his son."

"Charlotte, they've got issues. I don't want to get in the middle of that and make things worse. You're a psychologist. Isn't that what you're supposed to say?"

"If I had Coach Barnett and his son in my office, I would be working on *their* problems. But I'm talking to you about your problem. And quite frankly, it's only a problem if *you* make it one. He doesn't want to stop. You're both adults. And you're both enjoying it."

"But I don't want to complicate the situation with his son."

"I would never counsel an adult to stop having a sex life simply to make their child happy. That isn't a solution. It's merely giving in to pressure. And the issue is almost always about something else."

"I have no idea what their issues are."

"If it will make you feel better, why don't you ask the coach?"

"No way." Ghost jumped onto the bed beside her, flopped down, and began to clean her paws. Lola scratched her ear.

"Lola, do not use his son as an excuse to stop seeing him."

"I'm not." On the contrary, she didn't want this to end. But she wasn't a kid person and she didn't know how to handle kid issues. And well, she was thinking about something else, too. "I just—" She stopped, not really sure how to verbalize it.

"Just what?"

"Maybe what we're doing isn't normal."

"Let me tell you, people come to me all the time with issues they think are abnormal. Ninety-nine percent of the time, they're absolutely normal."

"Spanking is normal? Tying me up? Using a gag and a blindfold?" Was it normal to like it as much as she did? After listening to his son call her a slut, well, *normal* versus *abnormal* was something she needed to think about.

"Routine sex games," Charlotte said. "Do you know how many people come to me because their sex life has become stale? And I tell them to try a few sex games, role play, experimentation. It might not be for everyone, but if you both like it, then go for it."

Lord help her, she did like it. She loved it. She wanted to keep on doing it. At least until she stopped liking it. "And his son?"

"Let *him* tell you when his son becomes a problem affecting *your* relationship."

"It's not a relationship. It's just hot sex."

"Deny, deny, deny," Charlotte singsonged. "For now, just enjoy. You know, you really analyze too much."

"Hah. That's pretty funny coming from a shrink." Especially one who overanalyzed her own relationships.

But Charlotte was right. Gray was an adult. His relationship with his son wasn't her business. It wasn't like he was her boyfriend or anything. She should allow him to take care of his own problems instead of sticking her nose in where it wasn't invited. And she should enjoy the hot sex, kinky as it was, as long as it was offered.

"Shrinks are practical, above all. Now tell me when you're seeing him next."

"When the twins screw up. Which will probably be tomorrow. And speaking of the twins, they're awfully quiet out there. I better make sure they haven't put regular dish soap into the dishwasher."

Charlotte laughed. "Go tell the twins to be especially bad tomorrow."

She had a feeling that if they didn't misbehave, the coach would make something up.

LOLA HADN'T CHECKED THE STATE OF THE KITCHEN. SHE HADN'T even gone back out to see what the twins were up to. She was dozing, her laptop listing to one side, when her phone chirped with a text message. Really, proofing documents in bed was the best way to fall asleep.

She grabbed her phone. She'd been expecting an email or a text, or even a phone call from either Frank or George giving a status regarding their comments on the test procedure she'd documented. They should have already sent her their red-lines— short for lining out inaccuracies and correcting errors, which used to be done with a red pen.

It was neither Frank nor George. Her heart did a silly leap when she saw Gray's number.

She opened his text and read.

U ok?

I'm fine, thank you.

She was a writer, although it was just technical manuals, and she still had a hard time using shortcuts, dropping pronouns, and ignoring proper punctuation even in text messages.

Sorry about 2nite. ☹

Don't apologize. I hope everything's ok with your son.

Fine dont worry.

He dropped his apostrophes and commas like a good texter. What exactly did that mean? *Call me.* Her fingers itched to type the words, but they sounded so needy. If she'd only wanted phone sex, that would have been fine, but she wanted to hear his voice, wanted to talk. Which was way more than casual sex.

Told twins to be good 4 U tomorrow.

There, she'd managed to use some shortcuts. He shot back with:

Need them 2 B bad.

That lifted her. He wanted to punish her again. Though she couldn't say that anything he'd done to her was true punishment. She'd liked it all too much. She responded:

You're bad.

He sent her a devilish face this time, and after that the phone was quiet. Maybe she should have texted that she wasn't wearing panties. Just to keep the conversation going. But that was needy, too. She was *not* going to be needy. No matter how good it had felt lying on his couch bound and blindfolded with his mouth on her.

She straightened the computer on her lap and proofed the page that was open, since she'd been drifting through the middle of it the first time around. She'd have to go into the plant tomorrow and find out what the heck was going on with those red-lines. Red-lines, they sounded inherently bad, but with technical writing—and probably any other kind of writing, too— numerous people in the process had input. Everyone corrected everything. Especially engineers like Frank and George, who had the technical expertise she didn't. Her specialty was saying things in terms that non-engineers could understand, including all those pesky little details that technical people took for granted. *If they're working with this equipment, they should already know that.* She couldn't count the number of times she'd heard that phrase out of Frank's or George's mouth. And it wasn't necessarily true.

There, okay, she was in control again, thinking about work, preparing for tomorrow, making a mental task list. Good. It meant she wasn't thinking about Gray Barnett and what he was going to do to her next, when he'd finally do what she was dying for, how he'd feel deep inside her . . .

Damn. She was thinking about him again.

"COACH, I NEED AN ORGASM TO HELP ME SLEEP."

Lola's husky voice over the phone did things to him. Having just climbed into bed after finishing the last of today's paperwork, he glanced at the clock's lighted numerals. The midnight hour, and she was bewitching him.

"So touch yourself," he said softly. "You don't need me for that."

"Oh, but I do, Coach. It's so good when you're watching me. And it's pretty darn hot when you're listening."

He couldn't resist her and threw the sheet aside. "You'll have to be very quiet, or the twins will hear."

"I'll be as quiet as a mouse," she whispered. "Now tell me what to do, Coach."

She was a seductress. A succubus. Maybe he was actually dreaming this. "Put your finger right on your clit."

"Ooh," she murmured.

"Remember what it was like when you sat in my lap and I used the vibrator on you."

"Oh, Coach." Her breath shot out in little pants. "It was soooo good."

"It certainly was." He joined her, stroking his cock. Rafe had left in a huff. Bettina had called when he showed up at home, her voice frosty and condemning. With Lola's voice in his ear, none of that mattered. There were only her sighs, her gentle moans, and the soft, dirty little words she whispered to him.

"You need to fuck me, Coach. I need you inside me."

Christ, he loved her dirty talk. He needed her just as badly. She soothed something inside him. And she was hotter than Hades when she played his kinky games with him.

"I'd like to tie you to a bed and fuck you while people watch us." It was one of his kinkier fantasies. He'd watched, but he hadn't yet played the exhibitionist. Part of him wanted that with Lola, while another, bigger part was jealous as hell of any man even looking at her. It was such a sexy combination.

"Do they get to touch me?"

"Nothing more than a breast or a buttock." The thought of another man—or even a woman—stroking her nipple, pinching her hard, it made him crazy, and his fist pumped faster.

"Oh, Coach. You make me so wet. Oh, oh." She breathed fast and hard, her breath harsh pants across the airwaves.

"Are you about to come, Lola?"

"Yes, oh yes."

It was time to take charge before she actually took charge of him. "Stop right now."

"What?"

He recognized the immediate change in her voice, from high and dreamy to hard and demanding. "You will not come until I tell you that you may," he said.

She was silent for the count of five. "So tell me to come, Coach. You know you want me to," she cajoled.

"You'll come when I say you can. Now circle your finger on your clit, but don't come."

"Oh." Her voice seemed to shiver. "Yes."

"Roll slowly around your sweet, little hot button," he whispered, then added more sternly. "But do not come."

"No, I won't. Not until you say, Coach."

"Good girl. You're so delightfully dirty." He'd never known another woman so willing to do whatever he wanted. "Dip deep inside, get your fingers all wet and slippery, then rub it all over your clit."

"Oh God." Her breath came faster, punctuated with a small moan.

"You're on the edge, Lola." He stroked with her, rising and falling with her. And he was on the edge, too. "Just the lightest touch will set you off. But don't you dare come yet."

"No, ahhhh." She sucked in a breath. "When, oh please, when?"

"Pinch your nipple hard for me."

He felt her gasp in the tip of his cock, as if there were a string between them, attaching them. "Make yourself shake with need, Lola. But don't you dare come until I say."

"Oh Coach, oh Coach," she panted.

His balls tightened in response to the sound of her voice. He was in as much danger of coming as she was.

"I'm going to count to ten, Lola. Then you can come. Right when I come."

"Yes, yes."

Between her sweet moans and the throb of his cock in his fist, he could barely remember how to count. "One, two"—Christ, what came next—"three, four, five"—he closed his eyes, gritting his teeth, holding his orgasm at bay—"seven, eight, are you ready, Lola?"

"Hell, yes. Oh God. Please, Coach, please."

"Nine. One more, Lola."

She growled and panted. He was cross-eyed with need.

"Ten."

She climaxed with a long, low cry that was barely more than a hiss. And he exploded with her, coming hard, cursing, shouting her name over and over.

And finally he was aware of her voice. "Oh, Coach. You have me all tied up and ready to do anything you want."

It took him three seconds after that to realize she was no longer there. The truth was the exact opposite: He was the one all tied up and willing to do anything for her.

11

"LOLA, I'M STILL WAITING ON THE FIRST-PASS CHAPTERS FOR THE configuration."

Lola froze in her tracks. She'd been trying to avoid Paul Robinson, the head of documentation and technically her boss. At least he was the one who signed her invoices.

The day hadn't gotten off to a good start. She'd overslept. That midnight session with Gray had been a bad idea. God, she still couldn't believe she'd called him. It was crazy. Probably she was half-asleep and didn't know exactly what she'd been doing.

But it had been so totally amazing. He knew how to turn her inside out with nothing more than his commands.

You have me all tied up and ready to do anything you want.

Her words were so very true. She was practically his sex slave. The twins, her work, everything was starting to become second to her need for him.

Okay, stop thinking about him. Concentrate, Lola. You need to get it together.

"I've just got a couple of details to solidify, Paul, then I'll have those files in your inbox." She wasn't about to lay the blame at Frank's or George's feet. First, she was asking for a quick turnaround on their red-lines—though that was because they were late with the testing—and second, they were her main information contacts. Piss them off and she was dead in the water.

"The product ships in four weeks, Lola." He gave her a stern glare. At a couple of inches over six feet, Paul would be considered tall and even commanding except for the fact that he stooped, almost as if trying to hide his height. His sandy hair was wavy, his eyes ringed by dark circles, and his skin pasty enough to make her worry about his vitamin D intake.

"I understand the timetable, Paul. Don't worry, it will all be done."

"I'm not *worrying*," he stressed. "But it is my ass on the line." He gave her a beady-eyed stare. "And if my ass is on the line, so is yours."

She held up a hand. "Everything is right on schedule." She had most of the manual written and formatted, but the diagrams needed work and there were a lot of technical details that still needed to be added. Of course, once she was done, there would be a final set of red-lines, and she was also responsible for getting the completed guides to the web designer so they could be uploaded as pdf's accessible by the customer. Things had been known to go wrong at that point, too, glitches in the download.

"It better be ready, Lola." Then he stepped around her, stalked down the wide hall, the heels of his dress shoes tapping on the linoleum tiles.

She decided to cut him some slack; everyone got worked up with a new product release. Poking her head inside the lab doors, she found the room silent except for the hum of test equipment and news talk radio.

Frank and George were probably in the factory working out the latest bug.

Pivoting on the toe of her sandal, she slammed into a male chest. Hands grabbed her arms, steadying her.

"You okay?"

George was way too close, invading her space, his hands still on her arms. As politely as possible, she shrugged him off. "I'm fine. You just scared me." She pointed at his shirt. "If you use hair spray on that ink stain as soon as you get home, it *might* come out." Though she wasn't sure hair spray worked on red ink.

"I don't have any hair spray."

George was the furthest thing from a hair spray kind of guy. He was more like a fifties hair-tonic man. "Then buy some on the way home."

He grinned suddenly, a piece of lettuce stuck between his front teeth. "Thanks for looking out for me, Lola."

She hadn't been. "Maybe you should pick up a pocket protector, too. Or don't put your pens in your pocket. I was looking for you."

"You were?" His face lit up. It was kind of scary.

"About the red-lines on that test procedure. I emailed it on Monday."

"I didn't see it until yesterday morning." He furrowed his forehead until his black eyebrows almost met.

"Yes, George, but I sent it Monday afternoon."

He ignored that part. "That's only a day's turnaround."

She didn't point out that it was thirty-six hours, not twenty-four. It wasn't her problem that he didn't look at his email. "I realize that," she said patiently. "But we"—always use *we* so that you're not placing blame—"didn't start the testing until Sunday, and we need to make up the time by making comments as quickly as possible."

"All right, Lola." He batted his eyelashes at her, which was also pretty scary. "I'll have it for you by the end of the day, I promise."

"Thank you, George. You know where Frank is?"

"Manufacturing."

"Thanks." She turned.

"Lola?"

She turned back. "Yes, George?"

His cheeks were sporting red splotches as if he'd suddenly had a hot flash. "I was wondering if you were busy on Friday night."

Oh no. Nonono. Don't do it, George.

"Actually, I am." First, you try an easy letdown.

"Oh." His chin dropped. Then he glanced up eagerly. "How about Saturday?"

She'd never figured out if telling a man you were busy until he stopped asking was wimpy or kind and face-saving. "Busy on Saturday, too, I'm afraid."

"Oh." He deflated. "I guess you're busy next weekend as well. And the one after that."

So George had already been through this, poor guy. "You're a nice man, George, but—"

He held up a hand in front of his face. "Don't say it. Because maybe you'll change your mind. So I wouldn't want you to say anything you'll regret. Gotta go." And he scuttled away.

The scene left her feeling crappy. He *was* a nice guy. Just not her type. In any way, shape, or form. She blamed it on Sunday when she'd shown up without her underwear. It sexualized her in George's eyes. Dammit, she should have gone into the bathroom and put *all* her clothes on.

Yet how easily Coach Gray Barnett had gotten her to take them off.

*   *   *

TRUE TO HIS WORD, GEORGE HAD SENT HIS RED-LINES BY THE END of the workday yesterday. Frank had sent his this morning. After football camp, the boys had hung out at the condo pool, leaving her a chance to finish all the corrections and adjustments from both engineers. She was only slightly behind schedule, nothing she couldn't make up.

For dinner she set out plates of spaghetti—with brown rice spaghetti instead of plain pasta. She was trying to prepare healthy dinners. The salad had everything from the usual avocado and tomatoes to carrots to tiny pieces of apple for a little sweetness.

"Are you sure you were really good for the coach the last couple of days?" she asked.

"Yes, Aunt Lola," the twins answered in unison, a hint of mockery in their tones. She realized they'd been calling her Aunt Lola since the day Gray had admonished them. It was *not* a sign of respect.

She and the coach had that glorious session on his couch Tuesday evening, not to mention the delicious phone sex later that night. Then nothing for two days. Not a call, not a text. Zippo. Nor had he kept the boys behind at camp. They'd been waiting at the curb right on time.

Gray must have rethought the situation with his son and decided it wasn't worth it.

The boys dug into the spaghetti and salad. At least she'd done something right this time.

"Can we go to the mall?" Harry asked.

"After dinner? Don't you want to watch a movie or something?" Terrible aunt that she was, she didn't feel like dragging herself over to the mall, once to take them, and again to pick them up.

"We're so bored, Aunt Lola. Come on, it will give you time to work without having us in your hair."

She eyed Harry. That kid really had her number. "Aren't you bored with the arcade?"

"We can go to the theater at the mall," William added. "See something *new*."

Baby-sitting by mall. Was it really such a bad thing? Or was it akin to baby-sitting by TV?

"Arby said he might be there, too."

Ah, so they wanted to hang out with their new BFF, Arby. Maybe she'd get a chance to meet the kid just like Andrea wanted. "All right. I'll take you. But you're not allowed to drive anywhere with Arby after dark. Stay at the mall arcade or the movie theater."

"Sure, Aunt Lola."

They agreed so readily, she almost believed they had some nefarious plan devised. She didn't trust all this good behavior. But she dropped them off at the mall half an hour later.

"Look and see what time the movie ends," she called as they scrambled out of the car, "so I know when to pick you up."

"But we don't know what we're going to see yet," William complained.

"Well, pick one and tell me the time," she said reasonably—at least *she* thought she sounded reasonable.

They both ran to the ticket window, jabbered back and forth, pointed. Two teenage girls—with too much makeup and too much breast showing in Lola's opinion—stood to the side, their avid gazes on fresh meat.

William jogged back and leaned down into the window. "Okay, it ends at ten."

"I'll be right here at ten then. Where's your friend Arby?"

"Don't know."

All right, she'd meet him after the movie when she collected the twins. "Have fun."

But William was already racing back to Harry. And the pretty teenage girls had edged a few steps closer. More power to 'em. She'd never been that courageous at their age.

Besides the lack of coach contact, it was a good day. And the evening was extremely productive without the boys around. She was back on track and almost ready to send Robinson the chapters he was so anxious for. Then she had to break to retrieve the boys from the movies.

Harry was on his phone when she pulled up three minutes late. She half-expected her cell to ring, but obviously he was talking to someone else.

"Have a good time?" she asked.

"Awesome. Cool." They both answered at once.

"What'd you see?"

Harry rattled off some Ninja title. She'd never heard of it and promptly forgot it.

"Where's your friend Arby?" She wanted to know before pulling away from the curb. She hadn't seen them with another boy, nor had she seen the two pretty girls.

"He called and said he couldn't make it," Harry supplied.

"Too bad." She was beginning to think the kid might be a mythical creation.

Back at the condo, the boys dashed to the front door. They were like toddlers, always running everywhere.

"Hey, Aunt Lola, you've got an admirer."

She closed in on them to see a tissue-wrapped bunch of flowers on the doormat. Her heart rate picked up the pace. Maybe the coach was sending her flowers. Although she didn't figure flowers were his style.

Harry held them up. "I guess your secret admirer doesn't like you very much."

Lola realized there was something wrong with the flowers. The petals were brown and the leaves on the stems withered. They were dead.

"Who sent it?"

"If there was a card, he wouldn't be a *secret* admirer," Harry quipped.

She shrugged. "It must be a mistake."

"Could be the wrong house," William offered.

A couple lived in the next unit. It could have been for them if the husband was pissed at the wife. Or vice versa.

Lola pushed past them and unlocked the front door. "It's a mistake or a joke or something." She flapped a hand. "Just throw them in the trash."

"Doesn't it bother you?" Harry asked. "It's kind of weird, don't you think?"

She glanced over. What was up with him? "Maybe they're from some girl you two met down at the pool." She narrowed her eyes. "Were you behaving yourselves?"

Harry looked at her a moment, as if he wanted to say something more. Then he shrugged. "Of course, we were good. And I'll do like you say, Aunt Lola, and throw out the flowers." He marched them into the kitchen and shoved them down into the can, the leaves crackling.

Lola stood in the hall in sight of the kitchen. Dead flowers on her doorstep. Hmm.

Just yesterday, she'd rebuffed George. No, he wouldn't drive all the way over here to leave her dead flowers. And he couldn't do it. He didn't know her address, for one thing. She used a PO box on her invoices. Her home address was on the contract, but he'd never seen that. Had he? No, why would he have? And he was too . . . nerdy? Wimpy? Beta? The reality was George wouldn't have enough gumption. Besides, he hadn't seemed that angry or upset. George was actually a nice guy.

The flowers were a mistake. Or they were for the twins, some girl trying to get their attention after they'd ignored her down at pool.

She was more worried about why Coach Barnett hadn't called.

12

IT WAS JUST AFTER TWELVE ON FRIDAY. GRAY'S TEAM, AS IT WERE, was engaged in an angle-tackling drill where one player assumed the role of defender and the other, ball carrier.

"Keep your head elevated, Peter," he called.

The point of the drill was not only tackling technique but also how to do it safely. In turn, he stood behind each defender and signaled the ball carrier the direction to run.

"Good job." At close to the end of the second week, each boy was showing marked improvement.

Each one, that was, except Rafe. He gave the bare minimum. He wasn't a bad player, per se, he just didn't try. Like now. When he was the ball carrier, he fumbled. When he was the defender, the other kid broke through. Any other child, he would have called the parent in and discussed whether the boy actually wanted to be involved. But he *was* the parent. He didn't even know how to motivate his own son. Maybe he should send him home, but he simply couldn't give up.

At twenty to one, he sent the boys in to the showers, turned on his Bluetooth, and hit a speed dial on his phone.

"You won't escape punishment tonight," he said softly when she answered.

"Who's this?"

She knew exactly who it was. "Your coach." He picked up cones and stacked them as he spoke. Cleanup wasn't his job, but he liked to leave things relatively neat.

"Oh," she said. "I didn't recognize your voice."

"My sweet, you are trying my patience." But he knew his transgression. He hadn't called. His reasoning had been specific. She was becoming too important. He was too needy. He'd had to show himself he could resist. And he had, for three days. But after football camp tomorrow, he had Rafe for the rest of the weekend. So he wanted her tonight. Rephrase. He *needed* her tonight.

Lola sighed for him, the sound reaching deep inside. "What did the boys do now?"

He was tempted to tell her Harry and William had done absolutely nothing. But they were his leverage, so he didn't have to admit he would have her no matter what.

"It's a technical football thing they refuse to do. You wouldn't understand. Suffice it to say, it's very distracting to the other boys."

"I understand football," she challenged.

"These are football *drills*," he stressed, a smile on his lips. She saw right through him.

"All right. Whatever. What time do you want me at your house?"

"Not my house. I want you to meet me in the Highway 280 Park and Ride on Edgewood." It wasn't far from either of them. And there was no chance Rafe would *accidentally* drop in.

"What are you going to do to me in a Park and Ride?"

He could imagine dragging her into the backseat of his car and having her right there. But that was a little too risky even for him. "Meet me there, that's all you need to know."

"I need to know what time," she said with a snarky little snap in her voice.

Her show of haughty bravado actually turned him on. "Eight."

She shot out a breath. "What am I supposed to do with my little termagants?"

"I won't keep you out past their bedtime."

"Well," she said, still snarky, "if I'd known, I would have had them go to the movies tonight instead of last night."

"Send them out again. Isn't Friday the new release day?"

She huffed.

"Don't forget our bargain and how much you owe me, Miss Cook."

"I haven't forgotten."

The boys were beginning to emerge from the locker room. Peter, Roger, Tom. Then Harry and William. Rafe came out almost on their heels. He had his mom's car today so Gray didn't need to drive him home.

"Yes or no, Miss Cook?" he said softly before Rafe approached him. "Do you agree to my terms?"

"All right, fine, I'll think of some way to get out of the house." She hung up on him.

Gray smiled. She wanted it. She just didn't want him to know how badly.

LOLA DIDN'T WORK HARD TO COME UP WITH AN EXCUSE. SHE looked up the new releases on the Internet, then simply told the twins that it was her treat. They lapped it up, especially when she gave them money for popcorn, candy, and drinks. Andrea would have a fit. Lola decided she would definitely be missing in action for the next Skype call.

The sun hadn't quite dipped behind the mountains, but it cast long shadows across the road, and darkness would fall soon. Gray's car was at the far end of the Park and Ride. Since it was so long after rush hour ended, the lot was close to empty. She pulled in next to him.

All he did was jerk his thumb at her, indicating she should get in beside him.

Her blood had been pumping hard since the moment she'd received his instructions. Of course, she'd sounded snooty, but she didn't care that he hadn't called for three days. He was back and he was hot for her. She knew it, felt it in her bones. And she was hot for him. How he made her feel was all that mattered. She wouldn't think about the future or the end of football camp.

She slid into the seat beside him. His jaw was deliciously stubbled. Why that turned her on so much, she couldn't say, but she'd loved the feel of it between her thighs. Her fingers itched to touch him.

"Where are we going?" She tried to use the same clipped tone she'd employed on the phone, but her voice came out slightly breathy.

He held up the long red scarf. "Cover your eyes with this."

She liked the intrigue. She could feel herself already getting wet for him. "Whatever you say, Coach," she answered, still with that clipped, haughty tone. She tied the scarf over her eyes. Made of some soft material that wasn't as slippery as silk, it slid into place and stayed where she patted it down.

"Don't peek," he instructed as he started the engine and backed out. The car swayed into the turn out of the parking lot. He was heading back toward the hills, away from town.

"You still haven't said where we're going."

"And I'm not going to." His deep voice trailed like a lick down her spine. "It's a special place where I will have my wicked way with you."

She thought of his fantasy, having sex with her in front of a crowd, and shivered. It had a frighteningly sexy appeal. She imagined him filling her, then pulling off the scarf to reveal an ocean of avid faces watching their every move. Her skin tingled with anticipation.

"Tell me more. Tell me everything you're going to do." There was the edge of pleading in her voice.

"Whatever happened to the rule about not talking unless I give you permission?"

"Oh, did we have that rule?" she said quickly. "I must have forgotten." She put her fingers to her lips. He certainly hadn't been good at enforcing it the last couple of times either. He seemed to pick and choose when the mood struck. But he was obviously in the right mood now.

He tugged on the bottom of her denim skirt. "What are you wearing under there?"

Ah, the rule. She was allowed to answer if he asked a question. "Nothing, Coach."

He stroked up under the material, his fingers hot on her skin. "Good girl."

He'd made a few turns, then they seemed to have reached a winding, rutted road, the car bumping along. The sun was falling behind the mountains, everything getting darker behind the scarf.

Then he pinched her nipple, and Lola squeaked. Oh God. How was he able to make her enjoy that? It should have hurt. Instead, it was like a direct current straight down between her legs.

"No bra," he said, and she could swear his voice was a tad huskier. "Good girl."

She wanted to say *Yes, I'm a very good girl.* But he hadn't asked a question, so she wasn't allowed to answer.

She squirmed in the seat, squeezing her legs together, intensifying the pleasure he'd begun.

"What are you doing, Lola?"

"Making sure I keep my libido up while we make this long drive." She wanted him to touch her. Was she allowed to ask?

Before she could say a word, he said, "Pull your skirt up."

Oh yes, yes. Just what she wanted. She wriggled until the skirt rode just above her hips.

"Spread your legs," he ordered, and there was a new harshness to his tone.

Lola pulled one foot up onto the seat, her knee falling to the side. And she was exposed.

"Now touch yourself for me."

She groaned. She wanted him to do the touching, dammit. But she was such an obedient girl, she tipped her head back against the seat and put her hand between her legs.

"Let me taste how wet you are."

She adored his carnal nature and held out her hand for him. Grabbing her wrist, he pulled her arm until she leaned forward, then he licked the tips of her fingers.

"How can you drive and suck at the same time?" she murmured.

He didn't admonish her for talking. "I can drive and do a lot of things. I can also drive while *you* suck." The car headed into a bend, came out, turned into another, bouncing into a rut. Where on earth were they going?

"Is that an invitation for me to . . . ?" She left the question hanging.

"No. Touch yourself. That's what I want." He let go of her wrist.

She was ripe for him, ready. He'd had her on edge since this afternoon when he'd called as she was on her way to pick up the boys. And she did exactly as he demanded.

"Do I have your permission to come, Coach?" she ventured, cocking her head in his direction as if she could see him from behind the scarf.

"If you can come in five minutes, because that's how long it will take to get where we're going."

She imagined a mansion in the hills. Only rich people lived on this side of the freeway, multimillion-dollar houses with fabulous views.

"Tick, tick, tick," he said softly.

Then all she wanted was an orgasm as he watched. She closed her eyes—since she couldn't see him anyway—and found her clitoris by touch. Giving him a sexy little moan, she bit her lip, sensation rippling through her.

She was wet, her skin hot, her nerves tingling as she stroked. "Can you see me in the dark, Coach?"

"I can see everything. Your dirty hand down there, your pretty little pussy. You are gorgeous like that."

They hit another rut, and the extra hard contact of her fingers shot an adrenaline rush through her.

"Make yourself come, baby. You're so goddamn beautiful when you come."

He always complimented, always rewarded. Even when he'd spanked her. Her fingers moved faster. Her body rose. She panted. And her orgasm shimmered on the horizon.

"Do it for me, baby. Because I love how hot you make yourself. You don't even need me to do it for you."

She needed his voice. She needed his eyes on her. She needed his desire.

"Christ, I want to pull over right now and do you here."

His words sent her over the edge.

* * *

SHE WAS MAGNIFICENT, HER SKIN ALABASTER AS THE MOON ROSE overhead, her lips parted on a sexy moan that wrapped around his cock, her body trembling with release. He loved watching her pleasure herself. He loved watching her inhibitions melt away. Because she was doing it for him. He freed her.

The wheels went off the road, bumping hard for a moment before he corrected. The track was not well maintained, the car dipping and bouncing. He hadn't traveled it for years, not since he'd brought Rafe out here to hike eons ago. Before the divorce, when his son still loved him. The county had let the area fall into disrepair, and not many people even knew this trail was hidden back here in the hills.

And here was where he wanted to have her for the first time. In the open air, trees and sky and stars above them.

She settled into her seat, her leg still crooked beneath her, skirt above her hips. Her scent filled the car, filled him.

"Did I do good, Coach?" Her voice was soft, a little dreamy, after-orgasm languid.

"Very good. You always please me. I am *never* disappointed"

She smiled.

He let the car roll to a stop. What had once been a dirt parking area was now a mere clearing, the weeds and scrub having reclaimed it. He could no longer distinguish the trailhead, especially not in the dark. The setting was excellent—secluded, private, yet still out in the open.

"Get out," he directed.

She put her hands to her skirt, starting to shimmy it down.

"Take it off. Completely."

She hesitated only a moment, then unzipped it. Planting her feet on the floorboard, she rose slightly to shove it down her legs.

His heartbeat sounded like a drum in his head. Her milky-white perfection stole his breath.

Opening the door, she was gloriously naked from the waist down, her legs long, her ass pert and beckoning. Luckily she'd chosen sandals instead of high heels. He hadn't thought to prepare her.

Outside, night sounds abounded, crickets, an owl hooting, a coyote's far-off howl. It was now full dark, and moonlight fell through the trees, illuminating the small clearing.

"Over here." Taking her arm, he guided her to a tree at the edge of the hard-packed dirt.

She was exposed. She was vulnerable. She was willing to do anything. And she was his.

Bracing her body with his, he put her hands on the tree trunk. "Hold on." Then he stepped away, grabbed her hips, and pulled her back until her bare ass was neatly presented to him.

"Do you know what I'm going to do to you?" His gruff voice left an ache in his throat. Need rode his belly. The drive had heightened his anticipation. Watching her come tied his insides in knots. He needed. He wanted.

"No, Coach."

He slapped her ass hard, his palm stinging.

She cried out for him.

"Do you want another one?"

She gulped a breath. "Yes."

He smacked her again, the erotic sound rising into the warm night.

This time she moaned. Her juices slicked his palm. He put his hand to his mouth, tasted her. Jesus. So sweet. So good. "Another?"

"Yes, please." She panted, then added, "More than once. Don't stop. You have so much to punish me for."

Holy hell, she was absolutely perfect. He swatted her over and over, his fingers connecting with her pussy, probing, stroking. Until her body trembled with need, and she was begging. "Please, please, please," a pant between each repetition, a sob in her voice.

"Do you like it, my sweet little slut?"

"Yes. You know I do. I love it. Please."

She was close, her scent signaling her readiness, her need. He smacked her once more, then quickly entered her with two fingers. And her body contracted around him, dragging him deeper. She screamed, deep, full-throated, ending with a long, sexy wail of pure pleasure.

Nothing had ever been so good for him. No woman had ever reacted so perfectly. No one was like Lola.

13

SHE CLUNG TO THE TREE, HER BODY SCREAMING, WAVES OF SENSA-tion rolling through her. Her legs trembled. Oh God. He was so good. *This* was so good.

There were sounds, insects, birds, and the rustle of clothing, the tearing of a condom package. Then warm hands at her hips. His body over hers.

She cried out as he entered her. The pain of intrusion was exquisite, rippling through her. "Oh God, yes, I needed this."

She'd been dreaming of his possession, lusting for it.

"You need a man inside you, deep, taking you, forcing you." His voice was rough, like the scrape of a razor over bristles. "You need possession, utter and complete."

She needed *him*.

He took her relentlessly, pounding against her, the slap of his body almost like the smack of his hand. Everything tingled, half pain, half pleasure. She barely managed to maintain her hold on the tree. Then she was pushing back on him, taking even as she was taken. Throwing her head back, she gasped, then cried out his name. Her whole being centered on their joining, the points of contact, the contractions, the thunder and lightning inside and out. He didn't put his hand between her legs. He didn't touch her beyond that hard grip on her hips and his cock deep inside her, yet he claimed every part of her. And everything suddenly imploded, drawing down to one spot inside, the nub of her femininity. And she flew apart in his arms.

Seconds, minutes, hours later—who knew how long—she was on the ground, surrounded by male heat, male scent, male strength.

Lola was incapable of moving. She wasn't quite capable of thought either. She could only drink in sensation and air to breathe, feel the hard beat of his heart against her and the puff of his breath in her hair until it slowed.

"Why do I like it?" she whispered.

"Because pleasure and pain are two halves of the same sensation."

"But I don't like it if I stub my toe or knock my elbow."

He laughed. "Stubbing your toe isn't sexual. My hand on your ass is extremely sexual."

Oh yes, it most assuredly was. Her butt still stung, yet the pain was definitely pleasurable. She could still feel the heat of his hand on her, his fingers caressing her with each stroke of his palm.

"Why do you like it?" she asked.

"Why do you always ask *why*?"

She asked why in her job all the time. It was natural. She had to know everything so that she could write it down in terms anyone could understand. But she couldn't write down in layman's terms why she kept coming back to him for punishment or why he needed to administer it.

"I like to understand things." It was the best she could offer.

"Because it feels good."

"Yes. But not everyone would think it feels good. Why do we?"

"I've never had a woman ask. They either say no, or they want more."

A tiny pang wormed its way beneath her rib cage. She really didn't want to think about all those other women. "Like I do?"

She felt the brush of his chin across her hair as he shook his head. "No. No one's been quite like you."

Something starving inside her wanted to hear more. Probably shades of all those years of living with Mike's incessant criticisms.

"But why do you like to hurt me?" She'd asked Mike the same question, but with Gray, the connotations were completely different. Because she loved what he did to her, no matter the why of it.

"It isn't about hurting you. Or about the pain." Then he was silent a long time. A coyote pack went wild in the distance, yapping, closing in on their prey. In the tree overhead an owl hooted. Lola wanted to remove the scarf, tip her head back, look at him. *See* him.

Then he spoke, and she let him have his say in the darkness. "I worked at a local movie theater when I was sixteen. The projectionist was a woman. She was twenty-five or something, a lot older than me, and pretty in a Lucy Lawless kind of way, all buffed from hefting those reels onto the projectors. I liked to go up in the booth when things were slow and watch her change reels. She rarely spoke, she just did her work and let me watch. One night when we were showing a sexy movie with some real hot stuff going on, she sat down in a chair, braced her feet on the projector, pulled her skirt up, and played with herself."

Lola bit her lip. She was wet all over again just imagining the emotions of a raging hormonal teenager while a sexy older woman let him watch. His surprise, heart in throat. Then his lower region suddenly going berserk.

She didn't want to interrupt his story, but she had to know. "Did you touch yourself?"

"I only watched." He laughed softly. "But I couldn't stop jerking off when I got home." He stroked her hair away from the scarf. "I went back again and again. Sometimes she would masturbate. Depended on the movie. Her mood. I don't know. But I was like an addict."

Beneath her, he was hard again. Lola didn't resist this time. Tossing aside the scarf, she climbed into his lap. He shifted so she could straddle him. Moonlight through the trees glittered in the dark pools of his eyes.

"She was working late one night. She had to pack up all the reels because a new movie was coming the next day. I stayed to help her after everyone else was gone."

Lola put her hand between her legs to stroke him. He still wore the condom. She pulled it off, wanting the feel of hot skin against her palm.

"One minute we were packing reels, the next she was leaning up against the projector, her skirt over her hips. I think that's why she wore skirts all the time, easy access."

His face was dark, his cock hard, his voice soft. And Lola wanted, needed. "Give me another condom."

One materialized in front of her. She ripped it open, rolled it on, then slid him deep inside, the fit tight, their bodies vacuum-packed together.

"Tell me everything," she whispered.

* * *

SHE SEDUCED HIM WITH HER BODY AND HIS OWN MEMORIES. Hands on her hips, he surged inside her, then leaned his head back on the tree to savor her features.

Her long black hair floated around her face, her brown eyes as dark as the night. Her lips were luscious and plump with the little bites of ecstasy and excitement she gave them.

Tell me everything. He'd never told a soul. Not even Bettina. He was sixteen. In California, it was technically statutory rape because of the difference in age. And there were the things she'd made him do to her, the things she'd done to him. It had been a secret he'd never wanted to share, a secret he'd held close on cold nights in Bettina's even colder bed.

Tell me everything.

He needed to tell Lola while he was buried deep inside her.

"All she said was, 'Spank me.'"

Lola rose slowly, twisted slightly, and took him deep once more with equal deliberation. She was achingly tight around him. His fingers spasmed against her hip.

"There was just this nicely shaped ass begging. So I swatted it."

Lola rotated her hips, squeezed her inner muscles. She put her head back, arched, drove him mad, came forward again, and gripped his chin. "Then what?"

For a moment, he couldn't remember. He swallowed. "She was wet. She got wetter every time I slapped her. I was so hard, I thought I'd come in my jeans. But she just wanted more. Harder. My fingers were all over her, slipping in all her cream."

Lola rocked on him, a gentle yet relentless rhythm that almost made his eyes roll back in his head.

But he kept talking. "She spread her legs, and I knew she

wanted me to go deeper. So with every swat, I slipped inside her, a little more every time."

His hips moved on their own, meeting Lola's, thrusting. Her fingernails dug into his arms as she anchored herself. Need forced a grimace to his lips. He didn't want to talk; he only wanted to fuck her, now.

"Don't stop," she ordered.

He had to obey, closing his eyes, jamming his head back against the tree so that he could concentrate on what she wanted. "She came hard, practically gushing all over my fingers. And she shouted dirty words I didn't even know existed."

Lola wrapped her hand around the back of his neck, held him, pumped him, her nipples grazing his chest as she moved.

He was here and now with her. And he was sixteen again, feeling the need, the uncontrollable emotions. "Then all of a sudden, she turned, threw herself at me, knocking us both to the floor. I don't even know how she did it, but she shoved my T-shirt up over my head, trapping my arms in it, blindfolding me with it." He remembered the utter helplessness, the fear. And all that pent-up desire he'd been feeling for weeks while she teased.

Just as Lola teased him, rocking, rolling, slipping, sliding against him.

"Her hands were tearing at my jeans. And she just fucked me like that, so hard my dick hurt the next day. And I came inside her."

His eyeballs ached. His cock throbbed. And he needed her, rolled with her, surfaced on top of her. "I was a virgin." He gasped with his first thrust, her legs high around his waist, taking him deep. "And I was so goddamn worked up, I just shot inside her in two seconds."

"Was it as good as this?" she murmured.

"Fuck yes." He pounded her into the ground without regard.

He was past caring. "I couldn't see." He grunted, drove deep again and again. "And it was so fucking hot . . . so exciting . . . so out of control."

He was gone, spending deep inside her, shaking with the intensity of it, eyes squeezed shut, shooting stars behind his lids, and the tight grip of her body making it last forever.

He came back to earth, his face buried in her hair, her words whispered into his ear. "What happened after that?"

"She did things to me all that year."

"Things?" Lola always needed more explanation.

"Kinky things. She had me tie her to the projector. She brought a paddle. I had to use it on her. Sometimes she wanted to tie me up. She liked to pretend she was raping me."

"That's kind of hot." She rubbed against him. "And?"

"She got another job, moved on."

Lola considered it all for a moment. "That's why you like what we do. Being in control and powerful, then out of control and powerless. The two together." Her voice seemed far away. "You were sixteen. It was a formative experience. You're always trying to re-create it."

Maybe. He'd never told anyone, not even his friends on the football team. To share it would have destroyed the pure carnal nature of it. To tell would have broken its spell.

But why hadn't he told Bettina years later?

And why had he made the revelation to Lola now? Gray wasn't sure he was ready to examine the question.

"I must be hurting you." He'd damn near collapsed on her during his explosion and had no idea how long they'd lain there before she'd spoken. Thank God, the thick layer of leaves had protected her back and butt as he'd taken her. Not that he'd thought about that in the moment.

"I like the weight of a man on me."

He couldn't see her eyes, her face. His body blocked out all the light. "It's time to go. You have to pick up the boys."

She snorted. "Heckle and Jeckle are more than capable of taking care of themselves."

They probably were. He wasn't so sure about himself. He needed to think about the revelations he'd just made, the things that had come to him as he was buried deep inside her. He wanted to understand why she, of all women, had drawn those things out of him. Why she made him lose control. And why she made him like it.

HE DROPPED LOLA AT THE PARK AND RIDE, WATCHING HER DRIVE away as he turned on his phone. Four missed calls and three messages. He listened to Bettina's rants about why he wasn't answering his phone, then erased them.

He called her back only to make sure Rafe was all right.

"Where the hell have you been?" she snapped. "I called and called."

When they were married, she'd gotten pissy if he didn't answer his phone right away. But they weren't married anymore, she'd kicked him out, and he owed her no explanations. "I was busy."

"What if something had happened to your son and I needed you?"

"Did something happen to Rafe?" It hadn't. Or she would have started with that.

"No."

"Then why did you call me four times?" He'd wanted to savor the memory of Lola, but the lassitude of magnificent sex had faded the moment he'd heard Bettina's messages. Now there was only his ex-wife's harpy tone in his ear.

"I wanted to remind you about your promise to get him a car."

He watched headlights flash along up on the freeway above the Park and Ride. "I don't need a reminder." It occurred to him that she was checking up on him, trying to see if he had a woman. Rafe must have said something to her about believing Gray had someone with him the other night.

The question was why Bettina should care.

Why, why, why? He sounded like Lola. Maybe he'd never really searched for answers. Sex between them before Rafe had been good, sex before marriage even better. She'd played a few of his games, though she'd never totally gotten into them. She was nothing like Lola.

"Well, you can pick him up in the morning and take him to football camp." Her voice droned instructions in his ear.

Normally Rafe would have been with him tonight, but he'd wanted to go out with his friends. There was always an excuse to spend less than Gray's allotted time every other weekend. He'd always hoped *this* was the weekend they'd make a breakthrough. It hadn't happened yet.

"Yes, Bettina." He no longer cared what he was agreeing to.

"Fine. Don't wake me up when you get here in the morning."

There was blessed silence in the car. Ten minutes ago, there'd been Lola, her sweet scent, her sexy sounds. Her questions.

She made him think, made him remember, made him ask. How had things gone so wrong with his marriage, with Rafe? Sure, Bettina lost her sex drive after childbirth. But they'd been civil to each other. They'd cared for Rafe. They'd been good parents together. She didn't like his traveling, of course. Then she'd truly gotten a bug up her butt during one of his London trips.

Bettina always picked him up from the airport, a habit they'd started early and never broken. He'd had a long flight from London, and he'd stood out in the diesel fumes and the noise and the crush of travelers for over an hour waiting for her. His cell phone had run out of juice in London and he'd forgotten his charger, but he'd sent her an email before he left. At SFO, he'd managed to find a pay phone, called a couple of times, left messages. She hadn't answered. He'd gotten worried. She could have had an accident. What if she'd had Rafe with her? His panic had risen. He'd taken a cab home, only to find her watching the evening news. When he asked where the hell she'd been, she'd said that if he couldn't bother to answer his phone while he was away, then she couldn't bother to pick him up. She hadn't believed that he'd forgotten his charger. Even when he'd shown it to her upstairs in the bedside drawer, she'd accused him of leaving it behind on purpose.

The London trip was the moment her anger with his traveling had boiled over. It was the first time she accused him of screwing other women while he was away. After that, it had only been a matter of time, eighteen months to be exact. Life fell apart, and his son stopped loving him.

Now, as CEO, he traveled far less. It was too late. He was still trying to pick up the pieces. He wasn't sure he'd ever be able to.

But tonight with Lola had reminded him how things were supposed to be, how much better they could be.

14

DAMMIT, GRAY HAD CLAMMED UP AGAIN. AFTER THAT FABULOUS sex, he'd shut her out. As if the fact that he'd revealed too much to her had sent him running.

Lola rolled her eyes. Men. She'd never understand them. She knew what Charlotte would say. *Just stop trying to understand them and go with the flow. Enjoy.* Of course, Charlotte was right. This wasn't a relationship, the sex was fabulous, and that's really all that mattered. She shouldn't want anything more. That made her too dependent on him, and of course, dependence led to disaster.

On the console between the seats, her phone chirped at her. There was a new voicemail. Dammit, she should have checked before driving off. It had to be one of the twins. She hadn't wanted to take the phone with her on Gray's little joy ride.

Few cars passed her on the road as she headed down the hill, and no one was behind her. All right, she'd have to be illegal for three seconds while she hit the voicemail key, then tapped in her pin. With that done, the car's Bluetooth took over, and the woman's electronic voice told her she had one message. It started playing automatically.

"Bitch. Bitch. Bitch. Bitch."

Lola almost slammed on the brakes, and her senses heightened with an adrenaline rush. The voice was deep, then it was high, childlike, then feminine, a man, then a woman.

"Bitch. Bitch. Bitch. Bitch."

The initial loudness of the voice had scared the crap out of her, but her pulse was returning to normal and she punched the Off button on the Bluetooth, shutting the message down in mid *Bitch*. The words had been almost unreal, different tones as if several people were shouting. Then again it could have been one person changing his or her voice.

Dead flowers. Now a message. Maybe it wasn't some girl the twins had harassed. And George definitely knew her cell number. Could he be *that* upset because she'd turned him down?

The light ahead turned yellow and she almost punched the gas to make it through, thought better at the last minute and slammed on the brakes. Her purse flew to the floor on the passenger side. The phone went somewhere under the seat. Dammit. She felt blindly with her hand until the light turned green again. Headlights appeared in the rearview mirror. She had to move.

Later that night, when the boys were in bed, she closed her bedroom door and listened again. She couldn't be sure, but she thought someone might have been giggling in the background. There was no caller ID. Whoever had left the message had blocked their number.

All right. Maybe it was George, maybe it wasn't. If she wanted to know, she was going to have to buck up and ask him.

LOLA WALKED ONTO THE FIELD THE NEXT DAY WEARING WHITE shorts that made Gray ache to lick her tanned thighs. Her tank top was tight across her breasts. He salivated for a taste of the slight swell of flesh above the scooped neckline. A gold ring graced the middle toe of her right foot and a silver chain circled her left ankle.

He noticed everything from the swish of her long black hair to the white polka dots on her black flip-flops.

She made him instantly hard. She drove him totally crazy. The similarities between his feelings now and his feelings at sixteen struck him. He was obsessive, addicted. And he liked it. He wanted more. Perhaps that was why he'd told Lola about his affair with the projectionist. Because she made him feel those same intense emotions, gave him those same crazy thoughts. The more he thought of it, the more he knew that was the answer. No one but Lola had made him feel that way since he was sixteen.

She was early. Usually she waited at the curb outside with all the other parents, but this time she'd parked up in the lot and walked down. She'd come for him. To see him. Maybe to touch him. And God help him, he wanted it. But Rafe would be coming out of the locker rooms at any moment, and while he wasn't ashamed of the things he did with Lola, he didn't want to put her in the middle. Rafe was already pissed off as it was.

The locker-room door opened with a whoosh, banged against the wall, and the cacophony of sixteen teenage voices and thirty-two pounding feet rolled across the field like a tidal wave hitting shore.

Lola stopped. Gray turned. Not sixteen. Probably only half his team. Boys made a lot of noise. Whatever she'd wanted to say to him would have to wait.

Rafe, half a head taller than the rest, was running, his muscles bunching, flexing. Gray hadn't seen him this excited since . . . months, maybe even years, maybe before the divorce. The ever-present sadness closed around his heart like a fist, yet there was also a kernel of hope. Sure it was the car, the expedition, the ability to drive away, freedom at the wheel of a car. But it was also a chance for them to bond.

His son slid to a stop on the green, leaving a divot he packed back down with the toe of his athletic shoe. "Are you ready, Dad?"

Dad. It had never sounded so good. Rafe rarely used the title, or if he did, it was accompanied by a sarcastic intonation.

He wanted to look at Lola, smile, drink her in, but he couldn't afford the luxury right now. Instead he turned his back on her and curled his arm around his son's shoulder. "Ready to go?"

Rafe shrugged him off. "Yeah."

A second wave of players crashed through the doors onto the field, heading for the parking lot or the curbside amid a chorus of *Bye* and *See ya later*. In the two weeks since football camp had started, relationships had sprouted, friends made, a semblance of cohesion established.

"Hey, Aunt Lola."

It was Rafe who turned to the voice—Gray wasn't sure whether it belonged to Harry or William—then pivoted in Lola's direction.

There was something assessing in his gaze, from bottom to top, then top to bottom. "She's too old to dress like that," he muttered.

The twins were frolicking around her, which was kind of an

odd sight since *frolic* was not a word Gray would ever have applied to those two.

"Dress like what?" he asked neutrally.

The twins grabbed her hands and pulled her in the direction of the parking lot on the hill. They bubbled with uncharacteristic excitement. Lola cast one last look at him, nothing more than a quick glance over her shoulder.

"Toe rings," Rafe said, "and anklets and short-shorts. Only sluts are supposed to wear anklets."

Gray's heart did a slow roll in his chest. "What did I tell you about that word?"

Rafe turned on him, his eyes dark. "I didn't *call* her a slut. I just said that's what kids say about wearing anklets."

What was wrong with Rafe? Okay, fine, he was pissed at his old man for never being around when he was younger. But where was this disrespect coming from? What was up with this denigration of women? Gray enjoyed kinky sex games, a good spanking, a little bondage, but he always respected any woman who chose to play. And Lola was not a *slut* in the crude sense of the word.

"A lady's choice of jewelry doesn't say anything about her character, Rafe. Don't make snap judgments, not about the girls at school or women in general."

"I'm just saying what other kids say."

"You don't need to follow the crowd."

"Fine." Rafe shot a last look at the retreating figures. "Can we go now? Doesn't it take forever to negotiate a car deal?"

Yes, it did. Probably the most they'd get accomplished today was choosing the make and model. Tomorrow would come the wheeling and dealing.

Three hours later, he wasn't sure they'd even get as far as making the right choice. They disagreed on everything.

"A Volvo is an old-man car, Dad. The other kids will just make fun of me. Mom thinks I shouldn't have to drive the same kind of car she drives. Since it's going to be in the driveway, she thinks I should have something that makes the house look upscale."

Fuck what Bettina wanted. Gray didn't say it, and he resisted closing his eyes, sighing, or putting his hand to his forehead. "Volvos are upscale, and they've got a great safety record."

"It's boring."

Everything that wasn't a Mustang or a four-wheel-drive pickup was boring. They'd been to seven lots, and all the cars were either too old, too many miles, uncool, old man, girlie, or unacceptable for some other unexplainable reason. God forbid if he suggested a minivan. Funny how Bettina had used some of the same words, almost like Rafe was quoting her.

"The Volvo is a great deal and the miles are low." The gas mileage wasn't bad, and the price was right, though he fully intended to deal down a bit.

"But, Dad—"

"I've seen plenty of kids your age driving Volvos."

"Yeah"—Rafe's voice rose—"and they're uncool because they're driving their old man's car."

"You've been driving your mother's car, and that was fine."

He gritted his teeth. "Don't you get that's why I need my own car? Because I was driving *Mommy's car*," he mimicked with derision, as if someone had actually used the taunt on him. "And she needs to do her own thing, not be tied to what I have to do."

Gray had had enough. He'd already heard Bettina's arguments. He'd agreed to buy a car. "This is the best deal." He spread his hands. "This is the one we're getting."

Rafe crossed his arms mutinously. "I'm not driving it."

He loved his son. He had never hit him. He never would. But saying that Rafe tried his patience was stating it mildly. What he really wanted to ask was *Why are you acting like such an asshole?* But he would not ask. His son wasn't an asshole. Gray was simply a shitty parent. Didn't the child's behavior always reflect on the parent?

The lot was by no means packed with car buyers, but he was aware of a few turned heads. A young couple, their child opening and closing the doors on different models of minivans, a matronly woman inspecting SUVs, the over-fifty salesman Gray had put on hold while he and Rafe decided—or argued. Activity stopped, voices fell. All that was left was the whoosh of traffic out on the freeway and Rafe's anger carrying across the lot.

"Look, Rafe, we need to compromise here."

"You're not compromising, you're dictating. Like you always dictated to Mom."

Gray shoved his hands in his pockets to avoid clenching his fists. "You're right. I'm opposed to a sporty car or a fifty-thousand-dollar pickup truck. But we've seen a helluva lot of cars today that suit the purpose. Tell me which one appealed to you the most and we'll go back and look at it. If you want to drive out of a here with a car today, then you have to compromise."

Life was full of compromises. Unless you were Bill Gates or Warren Buffett, you couldn't have everything you wanted.

He waited. Rafe shuffled his feet, grimaced, turned, shoved his hand through his hair, turned back. Then finally he said, "All right, the Subaru."

Gray didn't hesitate. "That's a good choice, son." The miles on it had been reasonable and the service record up-to-date. "It's actually kinda cool with the four-wheel drive."

"Yeah, I guess," Rafe muttered.

"And you can take it through the mountains without using chains unless the snow is really deep." The price had been good as well.

In the end, they were able to complete the deal, and Rafe pulled his new used car into his mom's driveway a little before dinnertime. Though it was Gray's weekend, Rafe wanted to show off for Bettina.

Rafe rang the bell as if he didn't have a key, and when Bettina answered, he grabbed her hand, pulling her down the front walk. "What do you think, Mom?" He actually sounded enthusiastic. And slightly nervous.

They were like any other normal family in a tree-lined neighborhood, the sun still bright and hot, a leaf blower breaking the quiet four houses down, a lawn mower blaring, a dad washing the car, three kids on bicycles. It had been his neighborhood five years ago. Then he'd been the dad mowing the lawn and washing the cars. When he wasn't traveling. Sometimes the grass had been inches thick and clogged the mower. But he'd done his part.

"Well, now," Bettina said, crossing her arms. She wore flowered capri pants and a white sleeveless top. She was so buttoned-up compared to Lola.

"It's got four-wheel drive, and I could even take it through the mountains without using chains." Gray smiled at the almost word-for-word repetition of his own sales pitch. Rafe rushed on. "It's not an old-man car or girlie. I think it looks good. Don't you?" He waited with a childlike need for approval.

Bettina looked it over, pursed her lips, opened the door, glanced at the instrument panel. "It seems very nice, dear."

"And it's got seat warmers. I can drive you in it sometime if you like." Rafe was almost pathetically eager for her approval.

Finally Bettina reached out to him, ruffling his hair. He didn't pull away from her. "I'm so glad your father finally saw reason and got you something you actually like."

Gray flattened his lips. She just couldn't resist a dig. He waited for Rafe to say they'd argued for three hours about what to buy, but his son said, "I told Dad I thought it was a pretty good deal with low miles and everything."

If he didn't know better, he'd have thought Rafe was defending him. It was more likely, though, that he wanted to take credit for the purchase. "Rafe made a fine choice."

"Well." Bettina gave a brittle smile. "That sounds just great, Rafe. Why don't you take it over to show your friends? I'm sure your dad won't mind giving up a couple of hours of his time with you." She backed up to the front path as if afraid Rafe might run over her toes.

When Rafe shot him a hopeful look, Gray held himself in check and nodded his assent, though he wanted to slam Bettina down. "Why don't you pick up a pizza for us on the way home?" Pulling out his wallet, he handed Rafe a twenty.

"Sure, Dad." Then he hopped in his cool Subaru, backed out, looking carefully both ways, and waved in the rearview mirror.

Gray would never truly understand teenagers, despite having been one himself. One minute, his son was pissed as hell, then bam, he was happy and excited, as if there'd never been an argument.

"Well, at least you weren't cheap," Bettina said.

He'd been reasonable. He couldn't say the same about Bettina, but he'd had enough arguments for one day. "Could you call the insurance company on Monday and get the car added to the policy?"

Bettina pursed her lips. "I'm busy. Can't you do it?"

He boiled over. "You wanted him to have a car. I got him a car. What more do you want?"

"I want a little consideration for my time. I'm not at your beck and call."

"I have plenty of consideration for your time, but you chose to be a stay-at-home mom so you could take care of Rafe. So please"—fucking—"take care of the insurance." He stepped back because being too close made him want to lash out.

She followed, off the front path onto the driveway. "My being a stay-at-home mom doesn't mean *you* get to foist all your parental duties on me."

The argument was so old and tired and worn out. "What is your problem, Bettina?"

She glared at him. "Just because you've got a new girlfriend—"

So she did know. And she wanted to grind him down. But he wasn't about to let her steer the fight to his private life. "This is about work, not a woman. I will be at work on Monday, and it would be extremely helpful if you would take care of the insurance half of this transaction for your son." He'd done his half today by purchasing the car.

Her face was red, her eyes wide and dark. "Fine. I'll do it. For him, not you. I need all the registration information."

Opening the car door, he grabbed the folder off the seat. "Here's all the paperwork. I appreciate your help."

She snatched it from his hand, turned, marched back into the house, slamming the front door. Without the leaf blower to cover it, the noise reverberated through the neighborhood.

What the fuck? He didn't want to sound like one of those guys around the coffee pot bashing his ex-wife, but Bettina had always been moody. Her moods had sometimes lasted days, even months. Divorce hadn't changed much. Last month she'd been fine; this month she was making up for it. Maybe it was having Rafe underfoot for the summer. Except that he spent the mornings in football camp. Whatever. Women and teenagers were beyond him.

But Lola, now she was a whole other issue. He wanted to call her. Now. But she'd have the twins hanging around.

Instead, he sent her a text, a dirty, filthy, sexy text. And he felt a hell of a lot better.

.

15

"I'VE NEVER SEEN SO MUCH STUFF." LOLA GAWKED.

It was Saturday evening, and she and Charlotte were wandering through the relatively empty lingerie department at Macy's. Or perhaps it only felt empty because it was so vast and had only five customers, including her and Charlotte. She found it utterly overwhelming, racks upon racks of bras, panties, stockings, garter belts, body shapers in all sizes, colors, styles, and brands. How did anyone actually choose?

A young blond woman at the counter asked the clerk for a particular designer, and, as Lola watched completely amazed, the salesgirl led her right to the rack. She wasn't sure how even the clerks could know where everything was.

Charlotte held up a leopard print thong. "This is cute."

Lola agreed. Animal prints always had sex appeal. "I've already got a couple of pairs. But they'd look great on you."

Charlotte shuddered and put them back. "I can't afford Macy's unless I'm looking in the 75-percent-off clearance rack."

That's where Lola usually looked, too. But she wasn't shopping to buy. She was looking, wondering, fantasizing. What would Gray like her to wear? She fingered the strap of a sexy red demibra overlaid with black lace. The cups were far too big for her, even in the smallest size. She didn't want to emphasize her lack of proportion.

She moved on to a rack of neon boy shorts.

Charlotte put a hand in front of her face. "Oh my God, they hurt my eyes."

Lola wasn't the shopping type, going to the mall only when she absolutely had to. When she was younger, different story, but now, there were too many choices, too much stuff she simply didn't need. She was only here because she'd taken the boys to dinner at Chili's, which was at the mall. She hadn't felt like cooking. She'd invited Charlotte to pay her back for the other night when she'd done the baby-sitting—though God forbid Lola should actually *say* that word in reference to the twins. Of course, the twins had wanted some arcade time before heading back home. So she and Charlotte were shopping.

Lola examined a pair of bikinis with a pretty pink flower at a strategic point. She didn't like bikinis.

"Way too boring for you, darling," Charlotte drawled.

Lola preferred a thong and no panty line.

The day had been kind of a bust. She'd gone to the plant all ready to confront George. Or at least test things out. He wasn't in. It was probably the first weekend he and Frank had taken off in weeks. Now she'd have to tackle him on Monday when everyone was there.

Then, of course, there'd been Gray. He hadn't even acknowledged her on the football field, as if the last thing he'd wanted to do was introduce her to his son. After that scene at his house the other night, she understood why, but that didn't stop the odd ache that had surrounded her heart. Not good. She wasn't supposed to get achy about the man. She wasn't supposed to get her feelings hurt.

She hadn't told Charlotte any of that. She hadn't told Charlotte about the phone call or the flowers or her problem with George. She hadn't even said she was looking at underwear that would impress Gray. And Charlotte didn't ask. She was waiting her out, knowing everything would eventually flow forth.

"Ooh, I found the perfect thing." Charlotte held up a thong with a small ruffle along the back elastic. Made of sheer lace, it was practically see-through.

Yes. Gray would love that. He'd pull it off her with his teeth. Reaching out, she flipped over the ticket. And damn near had a heart attack. "For a scrap of lace?" she gasped.

"It's cheap for hot sex that lasts all night long," Charlotte countered.

"I couldn't."

"Of course you can. It's only money. And when was the last time you paid more than a couple of dollars for panties?"

"Never." But Lola took the small hanger, stroked the ruffle, put her fingers behind the lace, and saw that it was indeed see-through.

"Live a little," Charlotte whispered, the naughty little devil on her shoulder.

She was thinking, she was deciding, she was almost there—

Her phone chirped with an incoming text message. It was probably the twins saying they were done. She hung the panties back on the rack, then retrieved her phone from her purse.

It was not Harry or William. Her heart beat faster. It was Gray. She glanced up at Charlotte, who was looking at her with a knowing gaze.

"Go ahead," Charlotte mouthed as if Gray might hear. "Read it."

Lola opened the message and absorbed his words.

I want to tie you facedown on my bed, blindfold you, and take
you with your legs spread wide for me.

A flush heated her entire body. He'd written a full sentence,
no shortcuts. As if he were whispering in her ear.

"Oh, you must tell me what that says," Charlotte hissed.

Lola hugged the phone to her chest in case Charlotte tried to
grab it.

"Tell"—Charlotte narrowed her eyes—"or I will never speak
to you again."

Lola didn't believe her, but she told Charlotte anyway. "He
wants to tie me facedown on his bed and have his wicked way
with me."

Charlotte put a hand to her chest. "Oh, I like this guy. He is
so hot. And I bet he'll do it, too, the next chance he gets."

He would. He'd already tied her up and taken her on the
couch.

"Okay, type back that I say he should put a pillow beneath
your hips and—"

"Charlotte," Lola snapped.

She shrugged. "Okay, fine, spoilsport." She grabbed the see-
through ruffled thong off the rack. "Take a picture of this and
ask him if he wants you to wear it for him."

"You're joking."

Charlotte sighed. "Clearly you are not used to sexting."

"Sexting?" she echoed.

"Sex texting. Now take a picture and send it to him." Charlotte extended her arm, and fluttered the hanger like a matador
waving his red cape at a bull.

Lola's pulse raced as she pushed the camera button and

framed it up, only the tips of Charlotte's fingers showing. She snapped the picture and hit Send, then typed a brief message.

Shall I buy this for you?

He was quick to reply.

Do I have to wear them or will U?

She laughed.

"What?" Charlotte hissed.

"He wants to know if I'm going to make him wear them."

"Oh yes, I really, really like him. Tell him he has to wear them for you, of course."

She could actually imagine all that masculinity trapped behind see-through lace. "Oh my," she said on just a wisp of breath.

"*Oh my* is right. Now tell him."

She didn't question that she was taking pictures of lingerie and sexting like a teenager—though she could only hope that teenagers did not sext; they were too young. It was fun, it was sexy. It took the edge off an otherwise not-so-great day. She typed:

What size are you?

Extra extra large.

Lola read back his answer, and she and Charlotte laughed together.

Then a second text followed the first before she had a chance to reply.

Buy his and hers.

They went into peals of laughter. The salesclerk glanced up. A woman six racks over turned their way. On the other side of the cash register, a man—balding, midforties, a bit of a paunch—examined a pair of silky boy shorts. She hoped they were for his wife or his girlfriend, but after what Gray wrote, she couldn't be sure.

"Oh, you have to buy two pairs," Charlotte said, wiping at her eyes.

But Lola was busy typing.

If you put on the panties, then I'm going to spank you in them.

"What are you saying?" Charlotte wanted to know.

Lola sent the message without telling.

U can spank me or make me wear women's panties, not both.

She bit her lip as she read his reply.

"What, what?" Charlotte elbowed her and tried to peer at the phone.

"He says I have to choose. I can either spank him, or I can make him wear women's underwear."

"Oh baby, you have to spank him. That is so hot."

Lola noticed the one man in the department had moved closer. He might actually have been trying to eavesdrop.

She typed without saying another word.

I choose spanking. When do I get to do it?

He typed quickly on his end because his answer was almost immediate.

Only after I have U in front of a room full of people.

She held the phone to her chest.

"What did he say?"

She couldn't tell Charlotte that one. It was too kinky. "He reneged. He said he likes spanking me better."

"Just like a man." Charlotte rolled her eyes. "Get you all worked up on sexting, then rip the rug out from under you. But"—she lowered her voice—"I love the spanking thing."

To Gray, Lola typed:

IF I do that, will you let me spank you?

When, not if. I will have U before an audience, my beautiful sexy little slut. R U sure U really want to spank me?

She felt wet on the inside, like the creamy center of a chocolate truffle. She wasn't truly sure she'd want to. Taking his cock in her mouth, *that* was the kind of power she liked. On the spanking spectrum, she preferred to be on the receiving end.

No, I like it mucho better when you do it to me.

After all, she was the one who got the orgasm.

Your wish is my command. Gotta go now.

"He's gone," she said, keeping the last exchange to herself.

Charlotte leaned on a rack. "Well, well, well, you have found yourself a live one. I like this guy."

She pulled Charlotte away, heading for the center aisle. "He's kinky," she said softly.

"Hey, wait, the panties. You have to buy them."

"He doesn't need them. He's going to spank me instead."

"For *you*. You can't get the guy all worked up with a photo, then not come through with the goods."

"They're ridiculously expensive."

"Splurge."

In the end, she splurged. As a sex therapist, Charlotte recommended that couples treat themselves. They should experiment. They should even get a little kinky. Though Lola figured that having sex with an audience might be too kinky even for Charlotte.

"WE BROUGHT YOU FLOWERS, AUNT LOLA. TO MAKE YOU FEEL better about the dead ones you got." Harry did both the speaking and made the offering.

They were by the fountain in the center of the mall where they'd agreed to meet.

"You got me flowers?" Honestly, she couldn't believe it.

"What do you mean *dead flowers*?" Charlotte asked, her tone harsh.

"Somebody left Aunt Lola a bunch of dead flowers on the front mat the other night," William supplied. "She seemed really bothered by it.

Darn it. She wasn't going to tell Charlotte about those. And William was exaggerating about her reaction. "Thank you, boys, that was totally unnecessary, but very sweet." And very scary because it was *so* unlike them. What did they want? They were planning something. What? It had to be something bad. Because she absolutely did not trust them. But of course it would have been impolite to question them after they'd bought her a present.

"I didn't see a flower vendor in the mall," she said conversationally, thinking, thinking, and ignoring Charlotte completely.

"Oh, Arby came by to show us his new—"

Harry socked William in the arm, cutting him off and finished the sentence for his brother. "His new iPad. And he drove us over to the grocery store. They've got a big selection of flowers over there."

Weirder and weirder.

"What dead flowers?" Charlotte snapped. William had already answered, but that wasn't enough.

"Somebody made a mistake. Or it was a prank or something." Then she shook a finger at the boys. "And you know, it's much more likely it was one of your friends playing a joke on *you*." Or them playing a joke on *her*.

"Guys don't give guys flowers, even dead ones, not even as a joke," Harry said soberly. "We know it bothered you, so we wanted to get you something to make you feel better."

She didn't get it. They were being far too nice. She hadn't needed to rag on them to clean up after themselves in the kitchen since the night they'd made sandwiches. All right, she was totally afraid to open the door to the hall bathroom, which they were using exclusively, but all in all, they weren't acting like themselves.

They were like Stepford kids.

She hoped she figured it out before she turned into a Stepford aunt. "All right, let's head home."

Charlotte held her arm. "What about these flowers?"

The boys bounded ahead, heading out to the parking lot. "It's not a big deal."

"Some weird dating ritual from the coach?"

Lola laughed, both amused and relieved. "Believe me, that's *not* one of his weird dating rituals." But he sure as hell had a lot of other ones, most of which she found quite exciting.

"Good. Because I like him. I think he can be really good for you, Lola. I haven't seen you this excited about a guy since"—she shrugged—"never."

Yeah, Gray was good for her. As long as things stayed simple. But in the long run, there were way too many impediments, his son being the biggest of them all.

16

IT WAS MONDAY MORNING, AND SHE WAS ON HER WAY TO HER
confrontation—no, call it fact-finding—with George. The boys
were knuckling down with their online driving instruction. They
were probably cheating and doing it together, but that actually
might help reinforce what they learned.

The Bluetooth rang with a new call. She pushed the button
and called out, "Hello?"

"Where are you?"

Gray's voice. She melted inside. Ahead of her, the light turned
yellow. She pulled to a stop and concentrated on him as she
waited. "Driving," she told him.

"I want you here in five minutes."

She bit her lip, smiled. The guy in the next car glanced at her,
looked away, did a double take. As if he somehow knew she was
just about to get sexual. "Where's here?"

"My office." He rattled off the address.

It was in Mountain View close to Shoreline. She'd done a job there, knew the area. "That's going to take twenty minutes."

"I'll be counting. And for every minute you're late, you'll get another spank on your pretty little ass. When you arrive, lock the door, walk to my desk, and bend over to accept your punishment."

The light turned, and he was gone. She blew away the car next to her and pulled in front so she could make the turn to the freeway.

Suddenly, going to Fletcher and fact-finding with George didn't seem all that important. And just for good measure, she'd be five minutes late so Gray would have to add that extra spank. Hey, wait. The boys were at home. They hadn't done anything wrong today.

That's exactly what Lola told Gray twenty-three minutes later, after his secretary had closed the door behind her. "You haven't even seen them today, so how could they have misbehaved?"

There was no question who *they* were. "There have been countless times they've misbehaved. I couldn't possibly call you for every single infraction." He narrowed his eyes. "This makes up for all those I missed."

The office was large, with a four-person conference table, framed maps of the world and the U.S. on the wall, bookcases, filing cabinets, and two chairs in front of the very large wooden desk behind which he stood.

"That's not fair," she complained. "You can't backdate punishment."

He slowly rounded the desk, his gaze on her. With each step that brought him closer, her skin heated, her heart fluttered, her breath puffed a little faster. When he dressed in shorts and a polo, the play of muscle and sinew as he moved raised her pulse. In jeans and a casual shirt, he stole her breath. But he was absolutely delectable in a dark suit, white shirt, and gray-and-black-striped tie, his chin freshly shaved and kissable.

"If I'm remembering correctly, I told you to lock the door." He pointed one finger. "You haven't done that yet. And if you want to be able to sit down when you leave here, you better lock it now."

She wanted that door locked because she needed his hands on her. It was the only reason she backed up, turned, locked it, and came back to him. He'd also told her to bend over the desk, but she stopped less than two feet away.

He didn't seem to mind. "Good girl," he said with exceptional softness. He held up his hand. "My palm has been twitching to have at you."

"You're diabolical."

He grinned, all white teeth and wickedness. "Yes, I am." He reached out, clamped onto her chin, drew her closer. "But there's something else I've been itching for."

"What?" She matched his soft voice. The touch of his hand immobilized her. His scent mesmerized her, not sweet, not spicy, something earthy and erotic, calling to her.

Then he bent his head and took her mouth. They did so little kissing that she parted her lips with surprise rather than desire. He delved deep, and God, he was sweet in her mouth. She grabbed his arms to steady herself as he took her. Then he bound her to him with an arm at her waist, angling his head, taking the kiss deeper. Lola spiraled down into him, where the only things that existed were his arms around her, the heat of his body, and his heady taste taking her to heaven.

By the time he set her back on her feet, she was dizzy, and he was so close that she saw two of him.

"Did you wear them?"

She shook her head slightly, trying to clear it. He morphed back into one Gray. "Wear what?"

He reached into his jacket pocket, pulled out his phone, hit a couple of buttons, and held up the screen for her to see. "These panties."

Oh. The ones she'd sent him the photo of. "Yes."

She had no clue why she'd worn the thong today. She'd dressed in a circumspect business skirt and a utilitarian white bra beneath a plain white blouse. And the sheer black thong with that sexy little ruffle. Because it made her think of him.

He backed off to lean against the desk, folding his arms across his chest. "Let me see them."

The door was locked. So Lola raised her skirt.

He perused her with lids at half-mast; all she could really see were his black lashes, slightly longer than a man's had a right to be.

"Exceptionally nice. Much better on your delectable body than in the picture."

They were sexy as hell, better than anything else in her drawer, with the flirty little ruffle just above her bottom, the see-through triangle of lace in front. Sexy and totally feminine.

He raised his eyes to hers, a fire burning in their depths. "Do you know what they make me want to do?"

She shook her head, that heated look stealing her breath.

His lips curved in a slow smile. "Then I'll show you."

In a move so quick, she startled, he grabbed her around the waist, lifted her high and walked her to the conference table. Her sandals slipped off, and with her skirt bunched at her waist, the wood was cold on her bare bottom.

She managed to find her voice. "I thought you were going to spank me." The moment the words were out, she remembered she wasn't supposed to speak when they were in a punishment session, a rule she forgot most of the time, and so did he.

He obviously didn't care about the infraction this time

either. "If you hadn't worn those panties, I would have spanked you. Lean back on your hands."

She did. It was so damn hot to be ordered to do something. Maybe it was the whole alpha male thing. A woman wanted her man strong and commanding.

He spread her legs, stepped between them. "Look at you," he drawled. "That pretty, trimmed pussy barely hidden by your dainty little panty." He rested his hands on her thighs, dropped his voice to a whisper. "Touch yourself for me. Through the panty."

She bit her lip, breathed in deeply, her nostrils flaring. Then she slid her fingers over her mound, teasing him with the slow move. The material was soft beneath her touch. She traced her nether lips.

"Yes. Just like that. Make yourself feel good for me."

His eyes on her, the hooded gaze, his total concentration, that's what made it good for her. She loved the way he had sex. It wasn't just a little kissing, a little fondling, then down to business. He savored every touch. He made each individual act an event in itself. He made her feel sexy, special, desirable, seductive, all the words she would never have applied to herself.

His fingers tightened on her thighs. "Does that feel good, baby?"

"You know it does." The soft caress, the slow build.

He glanced up, eyes dark. "Better than a spanking?"

"Different. Not better, not worse. Spanking is fast and hard and cataclysmic. You take me so high so fast that I'm just nerve endings, sensation."

He put his hand over hers, made her rub herself a tad harder, a beat faster. "But this is slow seduction."

"Yes."

He hooked a chair leg with his foot and pulled it closer, then sat in front of her, hands on her inner thighs. "Make yourself come. I need to see." Knocking her hand away, he peeled aside the crotch of the thong. "Jesus, that's gorgeous."

He leaned in quickly, blew warm breath on her. It was like adding cornstarch to a hot sauce, everything thickened and tightened inside her. The muscles of her thighs bunched.

"Now make yourself come," he demanded.

"Why don't you do it for me?"

He raised just his eyes, shadowing them with his lashes. "Because watching makes me hot. Because I can see every subtle change in your body. I can see exactly how you do it, what makes you feel the best. And because it's dirtier if you do it to yourself."

She liked his touch on the panty, holding it for her, as if they were doing this together. And she loved his words, the way he thought, his kinkiness, no inhibitions, no right and wrong.

She slipped her middle finger down the moist flesh and circled her clitoris.

"You're so damn wet. I can see the little jewels of moisture." He leaned in to flick his tongue across her labia.

Oh God. It was electric. Her buttocks clenched in reaction and her finger flew faster.

"Yeah, baby, that's it."

Raising her feet, she planted them on his thighs, let her legs fall open, then tipped her head back. Delving finger-deep inside herself, she came back to circle and massage with more of her own cream. So good.

Then she opened her eyes, looked at him. "Put your fingers in me at the same time."

"Yes, ma'am," he answered, easing two fingers inside, stroking her G-spot slowly.

"Oh God." She arched her neck, shot out a breath, moaned.

"Come now, baby."

With the fast thrum of her finger on her clitoris and his slow, smooth glide inside her, her body rushed to the precipice. A kernel of heat burst out, grew, then exploded, racing along every nerve ending.

She did not cry out, but bore the bucking of her hips silently, her teeth clamped on her lower lip. When it was over, she sagged back flat on the table.

He put his mouth to her, and this time she did cry out, softly, before she choked off the sound. He took her with that slow pump of fingers inside her, his tongue swirling over her sensitized flesh, and she did a high dive into climax all over again, jerking against him even as he held her down with both hands on her thighs.

Lord, it was never-ending. She put both palms over her mouth to keep from screaming.

Then he was there, hunched over her, his body blanketing hers, his lips half an inch away, tempting and seductive with her juice on them.

"Kiss me," he ordered, his voice harsh.

She loved the kissing, God, she loved it, because it was so rare with him. She took his mouth, savored the uniquely male taste mixed with her salty-sweet come. A delicious combination. Wrapping her arms around his neck, she went for a long, deep foray.

It wasn't nearly enough when he backed away, standing straight. He held up a condom packet. "I want to fuck you right here. I want the scent of you on this table so that in every meeting, I'm reminded of this, and with every subordinate seated here, I can think of how I fucked you right on this spot, took you, made you scream. And my body will burn from the inside out." The heat of his gaze set her on fire.

This wasn't punishment anymore. It wasn't submission. It was ownership. She grabbed the condom and ripped it open, then held it out, making her own demand. "Put it on. Now."

He didn't bother to unbuckle, simply unzipped, pulled out his cock.

"Jesus," she whispered.

He stopped mid-action.

"You're so big." And beautiful. Hard, thick, the crown shiny and purple with desire, a drop of pre-come pearling.

"You've seen me. You've sucked me before."

She wrapped her fist around him. "But this is so different. This is the big CEO taking me in his office. Throwing company policy to the winds. Your secretary guarding the outer sanctum while you have your wicked way with your dirty, slutty little slave." She squeezed, stroked to his tip and back down. Impossibly, he seemed to swell in her hand.

He was still, his breath puffing, his gaze lasering her. "Christ. Do you have any idea what you do to me?"

Yes, in this moment, she did. In this moment, she had all the power. More even than when she held him in her mouth.

"Fuck me, Coach," she whispered. "Make me take every inch." She squeezed once more, then released her hand one finger at a time.

"I will fuck you blind and make you scream for more." He rolled on the condom at light speed, grabbed her hips, and plunged, as if all in one motion.

Lola arched, gasped, raised her arms and curled her fingers around the opposite edge of the table. Gray leaned over her, bracing himself with his hands right next to her. He watched her face as he withdrew slowly, slid deep again with equal slowness.

She panted, the slow inexorable glide of his body over her G-spot making her body quake.

"Holy hell," he uttered on a breath, his eyes closing. "Do you know how that feels?"

"Do it again," she begged.

He took her with an exquisitely measured pace, his body flexing, driving deep, slipping away, coming back to do it all over again. It was enough to drive a sane woman completely mad, especially coupled with the high of being in his office. Anyone could suddenly knock at the door. His secretary could buzz him with an urgent call. Maybe someone had a key.

"Yes. Please." She raised her legs and locked her ankles at the base of his spine, trapped him in the center of her body. Then she contracted her muscles around him.

"Fuck," he growled. "You're killing me." Anchoring her head in his hands, he increased the tempo with each new thrust. His eyes blazed. For her. With need of her.

He wore all his clothes, even his suit jacket. His tie hung down, the collar of his shirt tight along the cords of his neck. It was complete decadence, taking him like this, in this place.

"Fuck me," she whispered. "I'm your slut. You ordered me here. Fuck me. Take me. Make me do every dirty thing you want." She was crazy. She didn't care.

His face reddened, his skin turned hot. He swallowed, then pounded her hard. The table creaked and wobbled. Harsh, panting breaths echoed in the room. Moans, groans, hers, his, and his soft chant of "Fuck, fuck, fuck."

She squeezed her eyes shut and just as before, everything came down to sensation, his breath across her cheeks, her parched throat, heated skin, the scrape of his clothing, the hardness of the wood against her back, and the rigid cock beating, pulsing, throbbing inside her.

She cried out, clutched him with her arms, her legs, her tight body, and came apart. It was so good, she would never be able to put herself back together again in quite the same way as she'd been before.

17

HE'D LOST HIS BREATH. HE'D LOST HIS MIND. HE COULDN'T MOVE. And he didn't care.

He'd never had sex in his office. He'd always wanted to, but no woman had been right for it. Lola was perfect. She made reality better than fantasy.

"I screamed," she said softly.

His face was buried in the crook of her shoulder, the fruity scent of her hair tantalizing. His cock throbbed. Leaning over her, the position was awkward, but Gray didn't care about that either. He realized it wasn't that he *couldn't* move, but that he didn't want to.

He also didn't care about the executive staff meeting he was ten minutes late for or the phone calls he had to make, or about his customers, his suppliers, his employees. There was just Lola and this moment.

"Mindy might have heard," he said, referring to his secretary. Though Lola's cry hadn't been as loud as a scream, there was still the possibility they'd been overheard, and the idea made him pulse anew. A proclamation. His stamp of ownership.

"I didn't mean to," Lola said. He felt her voice against him and inside him.

"You couldn't help yourself." God, yes, that was good. That's how he wanted her, totally lost to everything but him. Just as he was lost to everything but her.

"Are you going to get fired?"

He laughed. There was a rule against sex on the premises. He'd violated it. But Mindy wasn't likely to tell. Of course, if he made a habit of it . . . but he wouldn't. Some things should be done only once or they lost their impact. He couldn't duplicate what they'd just created.

There would be other moments, potent yet different.

After allowing himself several more indescribable seconds, he finally pulled away from her, straightened. She lay deliciously debauched on the table, hair in disarray, nipples peaked against the white blouse, skirt around her hips, pussy wet with her climax, his cock still in her. He burned the sight to the inside of his eyelids.

"Do you know how good you look?" He heard the awe in his voice and didn't care about that either.

"No."

"Da Vinci. Botticelli." Magnificent.

He held his hands out, and when she grabbed on to him, he hauled her up until they were chest to chest. Then he tangled his fingers in her hair and licked the seam of her lips. She opened. He caressed her tongue with the tip of his. The kiss was so damn sweet, his heart turned over. He didn't kiss her enough. He was always so busy with her body.

Pulling away, she licked her lips as if she needed one last taste of him. "I like you inside me."

He loved it. He didn't want to leave her. Still cupping her head, he said, "I like the feel of you around me."

"You planned this, didn't you? You had a condom."

He grinned. "Hell, yes, I planned it. I lay awake long into the night thinking about it." He rubbed her nose with his. "But it was even better than I imagined."

"Good."

Then he had no excuse to stay inside her. "Don't move," he ordered.

His body ached, having to leave her, to lose her. He disposed of the condom and the package—what would his janitors think when they emptied his trash?—then returned to her. She still wore the delicate thong. He smoothed it back in place. Lola shivered.

He put his hands to the hem of her skirt. "Lift." And he pulled it down, straightening it over her thighs. "Do you have a comb?"

"I left it in my car."

He used his fingers to untangle the silky locks, holding hanks of it close to her scalp so it wouldn't pull.

"There," he whispered when he was done. "Good as new." Hands at her waist, he hoisted her up and onto her feet.

She stood a long moment just looking at him, her gaze roaming his face. "That wasn't punishment."

"No," he agreed. "I don't believe it was."

They were beyond punishment. They'd moved into something else entirely.

LOLA WAS SLEEPWALKING. SUDDENLY SHE WAS AT HER CAR WITH-out truly knowing how she got there. Okay, okay, she remem-bered sliding her feet into her sandals, Gray unlocking the office door, opening it, ushering her out. She remembered the studious bent of his secretary's head as she pointedly ignored them, obviously having heard something more than Lola taking dictation. She remembered those things, but they were all dreamlike.

Retrieving the car key from her pocket, she chirped the alarm. The locks popped up.

She'd never had sex like that. No man had ever made her cry out when she knew she absolutely could not, should not. She was hooked, obsessed, crazy, totally in over her head.

And she was almost sure he was, too.

That was dangerous. It was no longer punishment. They didn't need excuses. All he had to do was call her up and order her to come to him. She'd drop everything and go. It didn't matter what kind of work she had to do. It didn't matter what prior plans she'd made.

Was this sexual addiction? Or addiction to Gray?

Lola started the engine. The dash clock flashed the time at her. She'd lost an hour. A whole hour. How could he have made her come for an entire hour? Yet that's how it seemed, her body simply riding from peak to peak. He was some sort of magician. Or a hypnotist. Or just all male. She couldn't afford this kind of addiction. Addiction was need, and need led to heartbreak.

She'd been on her way somewhere when he called. Oh yeah, she had to go to the plant. She needed to see Robinson. Then she had to find George.

Lola rested her forehead on the steering wheel. God. George. She so did not want to tackle the issue now. She wanted to savor that amazing hour with Gray. She couldn't lose it yet. There hadn't been any messages since that phone call on Friday. Maybe he was over it. Maybe she didn't need to say anything at all. Or maybe it was the twins and George had nothing to do with it.

She heard the voice of reason in her head saying that a problem only got bigger when you ignored it.

But when she got to the freeway, her car turned in the opposite direction, back home. She didn't have to see Robinson. She could call. In fact, she could do it now.

He answered on her second ring. "Hello, Paul Robinson here."

She liked his formality and knowing immediately that she was talking to the right person. "It's Lola, Paul. Did you get the files?" At this point, she had the document in separate files. She would collate them later when she was ready to do the table of contents.

"Yeah. But we've got problems."

"What?" Dammit, she should have called him from home so she could take notes. She tapped the brake as she closed in on a slow car in front of her. Changing freeway lanes now would distract her from whatever Paul said.

"They're corrupted. The software wouldn't even recognize them."

Corrupted? How the hell did her files get corrupted? It wasn't possible. "Did you try opening them with FrameMaker?" Which was the program in which she'd created them.

"Of course I did, Lola." Even over the Bluetooth, his sarcasm rang through.

"Okay, well, I'll have to check them. Sorry about this."

"Fine. But we're getting down to the wire."

"I'll call you when I've got the problem resolved."

"Make it snappy."

She tapped the button, but she was sure he'd already disconnected. Dammit. She wanted to pound her head against the steering wheel. Instead, she turned on her blinker, gunned the engine, and zipped around the slowpoke in her way.

It was gone, all that delicious bliss, even the phantom scent of Gray in her head. You just couldn't hold on to good things. She knew that; it was why she didn't like relationships. They never lasted.

*   *   *

UNLOCKING THE FRONT DOOR AND STEPPING INSIDE, LOLA could hear them. Their laughter didn't emanate from their room, which was first on her right, or the living room off to the left. It originated down the hall, and the only rooms down there were her bedroom and her office.

Lola began to seethe.

She was stealthy, tiptoeing so her sandals didn't slap on the front entry tile. Like a secret agent, she crept along the wall before her office door, then stuck her head around the jamb.

Harry was seated at the computer, *her* computer. William was on his knees, elbows on the desktop, watching as Harry typed.

They hadn't heard her unlock the front door. She whirled into the doorway, stood with her legs planted firmly apart, hands jammed on her hips. "What. Are you. Doing?" she snapped, three separate sentences booming across her office.

Harry jumped and hit William in the nose with his elbow, who in turn squealed and fell back on his butt.

"Aunt Lola." Harry stared, his eyes as wide as fried eggs.

"This is my office." She stabbed her chest. "And that is my computer." She jabbed a finger toward her desk. "Why are you using it without my permission?"

"I—I—" Harry didn't usually stammer.

"Step away from the keyboard. Now." She wasn't about to let them erase any evidence of what they'd been doing.

Harry stood, the chair flying out behind him and rolling into the wall. William scuttled away on his hands and knees, then slowly rose to his feet. They both held their hands in the air as if she were a cop with a gun on them.

She had a password for initial start-up but didn't employ a screen saver password. Obviously she should have shut everything down when she left this morning. And obviously she needed to deploy her office door lock as well.

She advanced on them. William rubbed his nose, but it wasn't swollen or bleeding. It wasn't even red. Though Harry's cheeks puffed in and out like a fish's gills, not another word came out.

"The files I sent to my boss were corrupted. What have you done to my computer?" She had no clue how they could possibly have screwed up her files.

Finally, Harry fired a brain cell that worked his mouth. "We were just doing our online driving instruction, Aunt Lola. Your screen is so much bigger."

Both her monitors were twenty-three inches as compared to their fifteen-inch laptop screens. And on the one they were using, she could indeed make out the driving school's logo. But maybe they'd had time to toggle from another window.

She narrowed her eyes. "Don't ever touch my stuff unless you have my permission." She couldn't remember what program she'd had open on her desktop when she left. She'd never considered it an issue. But she should have. "Have you used my computer before when I'm not home?"

God, they could have been sending spam emails from her account, surfing porn sites, infecting her computer with sneaky, dirty little viruses.

"We're sorry, Aunt Lola. We only used it today. Because it was already booted." Harry's gaze was an earnest, plaintive, puppy-dog brown.

But he was such a good actor. He could play Oliver Twist with that sweet, angelic face begging for another bowl of gruel, when inside beat the heart of the Artful Dodger.

"I am going to run scans and check registries and follow your history trail like bread crumbs"—of course they'd probably erased everything from previous uses—"and if I find anything . . . " She stared them down, left the threat hanging.

"You won't, honest, Aunt Lola. We were just running the driving program, I swear."

She moved aside, then pointed to the door. "Go. Do not bother me for the next hour." She glared a long moment. "Or there will be consequences."

They scuttled out.

And she asked herself what consequences? She felt for anyone who was a parent with a child who just would not listen. What could you really do? You couldn't beat them or starve them or lock them in a closet. So what made them behave if they simply didn't feel like it?

"I'm never having children," she muttered, then marched back out to the living room.

They were seated on the couch, laptops open, identical studious lines on their foreheads.

She held out both hands. "I want all cell phones, iPods, iPads, MP3s, video-game consoles." Was there anything else? She had no idea. "You can work on your driving instructions until we leave for the lesson. Then I want the computers, too. You are in total blackout until tomorrow morning."

When Harry opened his mouth to argue—if that's what he intended to do—she cut him off. "And we're having a chick flick marathon tonight on streaming."

They grimaced, and she had the insane urge to laugh. But they handed over everything. *Almost* everything. Harry clutched his phone. "What if we have an emergency call from Mom?"

"If she can't get hold of you, she'll call my phone."

He finally relinquished it, then swiped at his eye as if there might actually be a tear there. Lola wasn't moved.

With an armload of their gadgets, she gave them one last glare and a parting shot. "And when I'm done checking my files, we're going for a walk."

They gaped. "Walk?"

Teenagers never seemed to walk anywhere, except if you counted cruising the mall. "Yes, a walk. You need exercise after working on your computers."

"But we get *five hours* of exercise with Coach Barnett." William groaned.

Lola smiled. "That's tomorrow."

Turning her back on them, she marched down the hall. She stored their devices in her office closet. And from now on she would lock the freaking door when she wasn't sitting right there.

Forty-five minutes later, she'd found no ill effects on the computer. The twins had been in the online driving forum, so they hadn't lied about that. The history showed nothing, but she deleted her history every time she logged out, so that didn't mean anything. If they'd used her email program to send any funky emails, they'd deleted any evidence. The quick scan found no viruses, and she was running the full scan now. And there was absolutely nothing wrong with the FrameMaker files that she'd sent.

She dialed Paul Robinson and said she'd bring him a disk this afternoon after she'd dropped the boys off at the driving school.

"Look, we figured out the problem," Paul said without an ounce of apology in his tone.

"What was wrong?"

"George loaded some new software on his computer, and it screwed things up."

She stared at her computer screen without seeing it. "*George* messed up the files?"

"The files are fine. The software just wouldn't recognize them. But it's fixed now, so you don't have to bring the disk down."

George. Was this about the date she'd turned down? Had he

done it on purpose to make her look bad? It couldn't be. Because it made him look even worse than it did her.

She didn't want to think about George. Or the twins. She didn't want to think about the Fletcher project or Paul Robinson. She wanted to think about Gray and that glorious hour in his office. She wanted back the bliss she'd lost. She *needed* it back. So she called him. When he didn't answer, she left a message in the softest, sexiest of voices, so soft he might not even be able to hear.

"God. You cannot possibly know how good that was."

She was hooked. Completely. Now all she could do was hope the smackdown, when it came, wouldn't cripple her forever.

18

OH YES, HE KNEW EXACTLY HOW GOOD IT WAS. GRAY FIGURED
that his experience both before and after his marriage qualified
as far more vast than Lola's. So he knew their sexual connection
was unique, their chemistry rare.

Which was why, in the middle of a product-review meeting
when he should have been paying attention to his VP of development, Gray sent Lola a text reply to the voicemail she'd left earlier.

Very good, my naughty little slut. U performed well.

Seated at the head of the table, he kept the phone down on his
lap, the sound on vibrate so there were no tones as he typed.

Jones, on the high side of fifty, his hair thinning, his paunch
growing, was repetitive. Another time, Gray might have told him
to skip the corporate history lesson and move on to the meat of
the discussion, but for now he was content with the analysis.

The blinds were closed against the blast of August sun, and

consequently the room was stuffy with male sweat and conflicting aftershaves. The coffee had started to stew on its warmer. He didn't usually allow himself to become distracted, but the scent of her clung to his clothes, her taste lingered on his tongue, and the sound of her cries superseded Jones's sonorous tones.

The phone vibrated in Gray's hand. His heart actually began to beat faster in anticipation. There was definitely an added thrill with illicit sex. He could understand why employees succumbed to office affairs. Without dropping his gaze, he pushed the Menu button on the phone to open her reply.

Three seconds later, he glanced down to read.

I'm not the slut. U demanded I come there. U made me pull up my skirt. It was all U U U.

Returning to his view of Jones's weathered visage, he smiled inwardly. Yes, it was all him. He'd commanded, she had obeyed. She'd allowed him every liberty. When she'd climaxed, she'd contracted so tightly around him, she'd dragged him down with her. What a way to go.

And she was right. It was so far from punishment for her nephews' crimes. He no longer needed an excuse, not for her, not for himself.

Jones moved into the new-product release schedule, which was actually the point of the review. It was not simply an engineering or development matter. It was also about the reserves that were needed to adequately cover potential returns and allowances, which were higher in a product's infancy. The question was how much and when to increase accruals. Overestimating requirements affected the bottom line in the current period. Underestimation, however, could mean a big lump-sum hit at quarter-end or year-end. Bannerman, his CFO, was conservative—as an accountant should be—compared with Gray's more aggressive tendencies. Generally, they tempered each other.

He listened to the discussion as he typed on the phone's small sliding keyboard.

Dirty bitch, don't deny U loved it. U need more. U R obsessed with sex.

The brief sexual byplay via text made him feel alive. His skin seemed to hum like an electrical current buzzing just beneath the surface. He was semi-hard, ready. If she walked in the door, he'd take her on the conference table in front of his staff.

He decided to type exactly that.

She was back in a flash.

Naughty Coach. Look who's obsessed.

Oh, yeah. He was. And to use her words, she couldn't possibly know how good that felt.

U R my filthy little whore.

He loved the dirty talk, especially because of the place in which he sat, at the head of the table, chief executive officer in the middle of a meeting.

Jones and Bannerman were looking at him, waiting for his input. Gray slid his phone into his pocket.

"Ten percent is far too high," he told them. "What's the failure rate in QC, Reynolds?"

Reynolds was his head of manufacturing. Quality control was his bailiwick. Tall, dark-skinned, with classical features like a black Apollo, he was the youngest of Gray's staff. But he knew his stuff. Gray had been impressed during the interview and had never had an occasion to revise that first opinion downward.

"We're seeing two percent." Which was pretty damn good. "There's always a slight bump in the field, but ten percent failure rate isn't supported by any of my data."

They settled on three percent for August and the fourth quarter and moved on to other issues. When Gray had an occasion to check his texts later, he found another from Lola.

If I'm your whore, then where's my payment?

Oh, she would have payment, most definitely. He started planning her remuneration right then.

And he was still considering his plans far into the evening. As he ate dinner. While he reviewed a couple of spreadsheets on his laptop. Exactly how much did she deserve? And would she like his payment, since it wouldn't exactly fit under the heading of traditional?

He was returning from the master bathroom at the far end of the house. A noise in the kitchen pricked his ears, and while he wasn't an alarmist, he padded lightly down the hall to investigate.

Rafe leaned both elbows on the breakfast bar, his hands supporting his chin. Gray's keys, wallet, and cell phone lay on the tile counter in front of him.

"What are you doing?" he asked sharply.

Rafe jumped, slamming his hand down on the counter. It landed on the phone. Gray discerned a slight movement of a pinkie finger as if he might be hitting a button or two.

Then his son stammered, "I—I—well . . . " He slapped his lips shut, opened them again. "I was just waiting for you. I heard you back in the bathroom."

The only way Rafe could have heard the water running as Gray washed his hands was if he'd walked all the way back to the open master bedroom door. Just as Gray hadn't heard him enter, Rafe wouldn't have been able to hear him if all he'd done was come in and enter the kitchen. Why hadn't he called out to say he was here?

"Were you looking at my phone?" He hadn't erased the string of texts to Lola. He hadn't mentioned her name, and it should show only her cell number.

"Of course I wasn't," Rafe said too quickly. "I was just thinking."

He was lying. He'd probably been trying to figure out who had been here that night last week when he'd dropped by unexpectedly. Rafe was checking up on him.

Gray entered the room, stepped to the opposite side of the counter. The screen was once again blank. He didn't have an extended time on the lighted screen.

He could call Rafe a liar, but it was counterproductive at this point. It would only create another argument between them, which he was loath to do after the good weekend they'd had. Saturday evening they'd enjoyed pizza and a movie. Sunday they'd gone for a hike in Edgewood Park. Rafe had shown no signs of his usual sullenness.

He was probably waiting until the new car was insured and the registration sticker on the license plates, then he'd revert to his usual attitude.

"Did your mom mention anything about the insurance?"

Rafe ran his thumbnail along a line of tile grout. "Yes. That's all done."

"Good."

Finally Rafe looked up. "The guys really like the car. You were right, Dad. It's pretty cool."

Something warm and tender wrapped itself around Gray's insides. He'd been stupid to fight getting the car. The aftereffect of the purchase was this truce between them. Maybe it wouldn't last, but he wasn't going to question it now.

"You want to stay for a movie? I got the new Jason Statham." Rafe liked the high-action actor.

He was still fingering the grout. "I kinda told Mom I wouldn't be that long."

"All right, I can save it. Thanks for stopping by and letting me know about the guys." It didn't matter which guys. It only mattered that Rafe had actually admitted his father was right about something.

These days, that was a huge step between them.

THE EMAIL WAS TIME-STAMPED WITH 9:45 AM PST. TUESDAY. THE subject line read *YOU*, and the address was a generic gmail account. She would normally have discounted it as spam. Except that the letter had arrived in this morning's mail. Lola's sixth sense was telling her the letter and the email were connected.

"Okay," she said softly, "bite the bullet."

She double-clicked the mouse, and the email filled one of her twenty-three-inch screens.

BITCH WHORE SLUT. Over and over on the page. All caps, in different sizes and different colors. It was actually quite creative.

But it wasn't funny. And she couldn't dismiss it. Not after the letter had come in this morning's ten o'clock mail.

That was still lying on the desk beside her. Mailed in Menlo Park on Monday, it had taken one day to arrive. The address had been typed rather than handwritten. The return label was phony, no name, just a street address. And she was pretty damn sure there was no road named Ho Lane in Menlo Park. *Ho* as in *whore*. At least that was her interpretation based on the contents of the letter. It was also typed, no signature. Short and to the point, she'd read the missive enough times to memorize it.

I know who you are, Bitch, and I know what you're doing.

That sounded like a melodramatic old movie.

You can't treat people like this. You'll be sorry for what you've done. You will pay. And you'll never hurt anyone like this again. I promise you.

And on the monitor, each epithet in the email seemed to pulsate, especially those in red.

Who takes that kind of time to color and size each word separately?

It wasn't at all like George. He'd never said a bad word in front of her, never acted like a drama queen, certainly never to the extent of the letter. *That* was total drama queen. She'd always thought of George as . . . a nerd. How mean was that? Maybe he'd sensed the thoughts she'd had about him, and when she'd rebuffed him, he'd gone off the deep end. Maybe he'd even sabotaged the files she'd sent and only confessed when Frank, or even Paul, figured out George was responsible.

She could sit here ruminating in front of the computer all she wanted, but it didn't solve anything.

Get off your butt and go see him.

She wasn't the type to complain to his boss before she'd given him a chance to defend himself. And she certainly wasn't going to mention it to Frank in the off chance he had a clue. No, it was big-girl time. She might dislike confrontation, but she had to ask George.

Forty-five minutes later she turned into Fletcher's parking lot. She'd chosen jeans and a loose T-shirt sporting the figure of a tabby cat doing aerobics. On the back, it was paws up. She wasn't quite sure whether it was supposed to be exhausted or dead.

Her card key allowed her access through any door, so she

chose one in the back, closest to engineering and the factory. Hopefully, she could avoid Paul that way.

She wended her way through the racks of equipment being assembled, smiling at a technician, a stock guy delivering parts to the floor. The ceilings were high, sound echoing above her in a dull roar.

She checked the lab. It was empty. Engineering consisted of rows of cubicles made of blue cloth partitions. She came at George's cube the long way around, avoiding Frank.

George was seated at his computer monitor, his back to the cubicle opening. His hair was cut so short, she could see white skin through the black strands. Music played softly. Elevator music. He was actually listening to elevator music. Only old people of the Lawrence Welk contingent enjoyed that kind of music.

Although she had to admit the song was kind of pretty.

She was stalling. If she didn't get on with it, someone else would see her standing here and she wouldn't get the chance to speak privately. But God, she did *not* want to do this. She clenched her fists and stepped inside the blue fabric walls, which were adorned with the periodic table and posters of the planets and constellations.

"Hey, George."

He whirled in his chair and looked up at her, taking a moment to focus behind his horn-rimmed glasses. "Lola."

"Yeah. Hey. Can we talk for a minute?"

He blinked. There was only a light spot of ink on his shirt pocket today, red that had faded to pink. "Ah, okay, sure."

She hooked a thumb over her shoulder. "How about coffee in the break room? I haven't had my morning cup yet." She sounded so lame she could have rolled her eyes at herself.

"Yeah, okay." He used both hands to shove himself out of the chair and followed her.

Past midmorning but not quite lunch yet, the break room was

empty. The coffeemaker sat on a counter along one wall, with three carafes next to it, then a bin holding little pots of creamers, sugar packets, stir sticks, cups, and beside that, a microwave. The refrigerator hummed, and the scent of coffee still hung in the air.

"I thought you wanted a cup," George said when she sat down at one of the four tables without pouring.

"Changed my mind." She held out a hand, indicating the chair next to hers. She was afraid if he sat across, she'd have to speak too loudly.

He blinked again, then finally sat. "You're uncomfortable because I asked you out."

Thank God he started it for her, but how did an adult tackle the issue? Really, did being older and an adult make it easier to say *Hey, I've been getting weird messages and I wondered if you've been harassing me*?

No, it didn't get easier, so Lola stepped into the void in the conversation. "Yes, I'm a bit uncomfortable with that. It feels like it might have changed our working relationship."

Staring at the table, George gave a wry smile. "I'm used to women turning me down. It doesn't alter how I do my work."

She heated with embarrassment, yet something tightened in her chest. It felt like putting out food for your own cat and shooing away the hungry stray kitten sitting on the edge of the porch. "I'm sorry, George."

He shrugged. "Don't worry. I came out of the blue at you. You weren't expecting it."

She wondered if anyone ever said yes to him. Which made it all the harder to say, "Can I ask you a question without hurting your feelings?" A dumb thing to ask. Of course, it would hurt his feelings.

"Sure." A polite reply. He was still staring at the table.

"I got some flowers the other day. And a letter today. I was wondering if you sent them."

He glanced up from the table. Behind his lenses, his eyes were wide. Or maybe the thickness of the glass just made them seem that way. "I didn't send you anything." Then he added, "To your home, you mean?"

"Yes."

"I would have had to look your address up on your contract."

"Yes," she agreed, "you would have to do that." Since it wasn't on her invoices.

"Or followed you home."

Lola didn't say anything.

He pressed his lips together. She could read his thoughts. The tone of her voice indicated she wasn't asking because the flowers were expensive roses or the letter full of pretty, glowing prose.

She felt a bit sick. It sounded so bad, even mean, as if she assumed the weird guy at work had to be the guilty one. She wanted to explain that there were no other suspects—if she discounted her nephews. Yeah, it sounded bad. Unless he really had looked up her address or followed her home.

"No, I didn't," he said finally. "Is it the kind of thing you should call the police about?"

Okay, she really felt like crap now. She didn't want to say the flowers were dead or that the letter was vaguely threatening. And honestly, she wouldn't go to the police for something like that. What were they going to do, stake out her house? Not.

"No," she said, "nothing like that." She met his gaze earnestly. "It's not about you," she said. "It was just the timing, that's all. I got the flowers the day after."

He laughed. It was a nice sound, and somehow it completely transformed him. "Of course it was about me, Lola. I don't have any illusions." The statement reminded her of Harry when he'd said that people needed their illusions. Maybe George wasn't like everyone. "You wouldn't have thought it was Frank if you'd turned him down," he went on. "But then you probably wouldn't have turned him down."

She gaped. "Good Lord, of course I would have turned Frank down. And I would have asked him about the flowers, too." She didn't add that Frank was even lower than George on her dating protocol. "But you're both so much younger than me." She paused, felt the words before she actually said them. "And I'm seeing someone."

"How old is he?"

"Forty-five."

"Hmm." George rolled it round in his mind. "Maybe he sent the flowers."

"They were dead," she had to admit. And Gray wasn't the flower type at all.

"Well, you never can tell." George leaned back in his chair, not reacting to the *dead* part. "I'm glad I asked you out. It's good for me, you know, putting myself out there and all."

"I'm sure it is."

He narrowed his eyes behind his glasses. "And don't tell me I should get contact lenses or change how I dress because I am who I am."

"I wouldn't dream of changing you." She pointed at his shirt. "I was just trying to help you save on dry cleaning bills."

He looked down at his pocket. "The hair spray worked." He grimaced. "Sort of."

"You need the pocket protector. I saw one at Fry's with SpongeBob on it."

He laughed again. And she really did like his laugh. Maybe everyone didn't need illusions. Maybe they just needed to accept exactly who they were and like it.

He wiped the corner of his eye behind the horn rims. "So SpongeBob is my style?"

"They had Spider-Man, too. And Wolverine and Iron Man."

"No, I'm definitely more a SpongeBob guy."

He was. And proud of it. She put a finger to her lips, considering. "You never know, you might get it for Christmas."

"I don't think I can wait that long. I've ruined a lot of shirts."

"You should try clicking the pen closed before you put it in your pocket."

"I could do that. But then no one would have anything to laugh at around here."

"They'll love SpongeBob then." She gave him a wry smile. "George," she said, "you're actually a cool guy. I'm glad we had this talk."

She could no longer imagine him sending her dead flowers, nasty email messages, and threatening letters.

But she still had a problem. Someone knew her email address, her cell phone number, and where she lived. Whoever was doing this knew her. And didn't like her.

That, of course, made her think of the twins. She ran a couple of errands, then headed across town to pick them up at the high school. She'd been parked at the curb a couple of minutes when the players exited the gates in a herd, stampeding toward the waiting vehicles. Harry let William have the front seat this time.

"Hey, Aunt Lola, are you okay?" William leaned in, almost breathing down her neck.

"I can't reach the gear shift when you're that close."

William backed off, but Harry leaned over the seat. "Wow, you do look a little pale, Aunt Lola. Is something bothering you?"

She narrowed her eyes and started the engine. "I'm absolutely fine."

Harry pointed at her brow. "You've got lines on your forehead like you're anxious about something."

She looked at him in the rearview mirror, hard. "I'm fine. Now sit back and put your seat belt on."

They were extremely weird children. And she was back to thinking it was the twins who'd been sending her those messages. Maybe that's why they'd been on her computer, they were looking for her email address.

19

OVER THE NEXT THREE DAYS, LOLA RECEIVED ALL THE RED-LINES, worked late into the night, made the corrections, and sent off several more completed chapters. She needed another training session with George and Frank to write the section on troubleshooting. It was close to one on Friday, and since the twins had their driving lesson, she could have fit the engineers in this afternoon, but the best she could get out of them both was three o'clock on Monday. That would have to do. She would still be on track for sending the completed package to everyone the following Friday for a final round of red-lines, all eyes required. After that, it would only be a matter of getting all the guides formatted and up on the website. She might very well be ahead of the ship date despite having the twins around.

In the same three-day period, there had been no more letters, emails, or phone messages, and no dead flowers. Funny everything should stop right after she talked to George. Coincidence?

Proof of the twins' innocence? Whatever, it was over, and she could stop thinking about it.

What she couldn't stop thinking about was that in those same three days, there had been no texts from Gray. No phone calls. No voicemails. Nothing.

Why did he do that? He ran hot, then suddenly he was cold, ignoring her. The problem was obsession. She was obsessed, he wasn't. This was why relationships were bad. You got dependent. The man got distant.

Arriving at the high school, she had the notion of parking in the lot and walking down to the field. For a glimpse of him. God, she needed to get a grip. If he wanted her, he'd text or call.

Please, please, please, call this weekend.

She shut down the pathetic, needy voice in her head and turned the car into the pickup loop to idle. She was *not* running onto the field to catch the coach's eye.

Stinky Stu ambled out of the gate and climbed into his mother's minivan. Had he lost a bit of weight or was that her imagination? She inched forward when the van left. More boys tumbled out of the gate, more cars left.

Where were the twins? Maybe she'd have to park and go in to find them.

Yes, yes, yes, the needy voice clamored.

"No," she said aloud.

At last they bounded through the gates, gym bags slung over their shoulders, grabbed the door handles, then flung themselves into the car, Harry in front, William in back.

Her pathetic little heart dropped because she wasn't forced to go inside looking for them.

"Good day?" she asked.

"Coach is a slave driver," Harry said. It was what he always said, yet he didn't seem particularly moody or unhappy.

"I think I pulled a hamstring," William complained. He always pulled something, until they were free for the afternoon and suddenly everything had healed.

"I guess that means you won't be able to drive today," she said with a smile.

"Oh no, I'm fine for that. It's the other leg."

Of course, he was. Her phone rang as she pulled out of the loop. Her heart leaped. Maybe it was the coach. Then it dropped. No way. He knew she was with the twins.

"Hello?"

"Lola Cook?" The voice filled the car, raspy, one she didn't recognize, an older man.

"This is Wilson Blanchard, your nephews' driving instructor. I'm afraid I've been in an accident. I won't be able to take them this afternoon."

Beside her and behind her, the boys groaned.

An accident? That wouldn't look good on a driving instructor's record. "I hope you're all right."

"I'm fine. We should be able to continue on Monday. Why don't you have them do some online work for today instead?"

Lola glanced at Harry and gave him a look, did the same with William in the rearview mirror. "All right. Thanks for letting me know."

Damn. She was stuck with them for the afternoon.

IN THE LOCKER ROOM AFTER HIS PLAYERS HAD LEFT, GRAY SHOWERED and changed into his suit for work. Rafe was now driving himself to and from practice.

Gray hadn't texted Lola since Monday—when he'd let himself get carried away in the meeting—so he'd almost given in to the urge to walk out with Harry and William to tell her he needed to speak with her.

That always put the fear of God in the twins. *I'm going to talk to your aunt.*

They hadn't done much today that required punishment. William tripped over Tom's feet and claimed he'd pulled a hamstring. Gray checked him over and found no evidence of an injury, but he'd had him sit out the last forty-five minutes.

Hmm, faking an injury could be punishable. Perhaps he would give Lola five swats on the ass for William's infraction.

The strength of his need for her was a tad alarming. Not because it existed but because he actually liked it. Over the past three nights, he'd enjoyed working himself up, needing to call her, wanting it so badly he ached to hear her voice. Then denying himself. By the time he had her in his clutches again, he would be absolutely wild for her. And he couldn't wait.

In the parking lot, he tossed his sports bag in the trunk, then climbed in to start the car. He sat for a moment, the engine idling. He was hard again. Just like that. A few moments of fantasy about her—spanking her, taking her in his office, dragging her into the locker room and having her against the tiled shower wall—and his body had gotten rip-roaring ready. He closed his eyes and imagined sinking into her depths, sliding out, feeling her shiver and shake . . .

Christ. He was torturing himself. And it was so damn good. Maybe he wasn't the dom at all. Maybe he needed to let her dominate him.

He rolled out of the parking lot and turned right.

Harry and William had their driving lesson this afternoon. He wondered what she'd do with the alone time. He could call her and find out. He could order her to touch herself for him. Her moans would fill the car as he drove.

His cock pulsed like a metronome. A dull ache throbbed in his balls. He wanted her bad. Right now.

He made another turn, then stopped for the light a block down.

Closing his eyes, he felt her breath on his cock, then her hand wrapping around him, her mouth sliding down, engulfing him.

The SUV on his tail honked.

The freeway was ahead, but his car turned right, then right again. Maybe he should have called her deep in the night, come with her, taken the edge off. But it was too late for maybes. He was no longer in control. The primeval part of his brain was. And it wanted her. Now. Right now. Screw work. Screw everything and take her.

He knew the area in which she lived. He'd often used it as a shortcut up to Highway 280. Entering three driveways in her condo complex until he found her number, he parked in a guest spot.

Before climbing out, he texted her.

Need to be buried deep inside U. Need to hear U scream.

She would read the text and by the time he got to her door, she'd be wet and ready. He'd take her right there in the front hall. Then he'd have her in her bed.

He found her unit, rang her bell. His blood raced through his veins pounding out an incessant beat of *do her do her do her*.

Noise inside, running feet, and the door burst inward.

Harry stared at him, William one pace behind. They both wore swim trunks and had towels slung over their shoulders.

Fuck. They weren't supposed to be here. She was supposed to be alone.

Something angry and testosterone-infused raced through him. "Get your aunt. I want to talk to her."

Harry gaped a moment, his mouth worked, then words and a breath wheezed out. "But we didn't do anything."

"Get. Her." Two separate and distinct words.

He wasn't in control. His need was too great. And he didn't give a damn if they were home or not.

HIS TEXT HAD HER GOING BEFORE SHE EVEN FINISHED READING the first sentence. She'd closed her bathroom door in the back of the condo and indulged herself with his dirty words, his need.

The boys were in the living room, presumably doing some of their online work before they went down to the pool. That was the compromise they'd agreed on for the afternoon's activities. She should have checked to make sure, but honestly, if they didn't do it, they only hurt themselves.

She started typing.

Call me. Now. Make me come.

She didn't care if the twins were home. She could come very, very quietly.

"Aunt Lola!" Harry. Shouting her name. With something like terror in his voice.

She pushed Send and snapped the keyboard on her phone shut. Flinging open first the door of the bathroom, then her bedroom door, she scurried into the hall. She saw a flurry of white as Ghost darted under the bed.

Gray stood in the front entry, his fists bunched at his sides, a glower on his face. The twins flanked him, their eyes wide.

"We—we didn't do—do anything, Aunt Lola." William actually stammered.

"We need to talk." Gray's jaw was as clenched as his fists. The lines of his face were strained. And something Neanderthal glittered in his eyes.

She almost couldn't speak. He stole her breath, even her power to move her mouth. All she could do was point to her office, and back up the couple of steps to get there before he was on her.

"Inside," he ordered.

Her knees felt like jelly and her calf muscles almost failed.

Need to be buried deep inside U. Need to hear U scream.

Oh God. Oh yes.

Gray stormed past her. She shot the boys a look. "Are you ready for the pool?" she asked, a bit amazed she could say anything at all.

They nodded in unison, their eyes still saucer-wide.

"Then I'll take care of whatever's bothering Coach Barnett." They remained rooted to the spot, so Lola pointed toward the open front door. "Go."

They jumped, ran out, the door shaking in its frame behind them, the pounding of their feet on the outer stairs shuddering through the whole condo. As if the sound was his cue, Gray yanked her inside the office, shoved the door closed, and pushed the lock. Then he was on her. Grabbing her waist, he hauled her up. Lola wrapped her legs around his hips, and he stepped back, then turned. At the desk, he kicked aside the chair and plopped her down on top of papers and folders, a pen jabbing her backside. Lola didn't care.

Gray reached past her and flipped the blinds closed. Cupping her cheeks in his big hands, he held her head, his mouth descending. But before he actually kissed her, he growled, "I am so going to fuck you."

There were a million questions, not the least of which was *So if you want me so bad, why haven't you called me or texted me for three days?*

Then his lips were on hers, his tongue invading, his relentless kiss pushing her head back. He devoured her. She had never been so consumed by a man, so powerless beneath his need. His desire fueled her own. Her hands on his arms, she sank her nails into the material of his suit jacket. Tightening her legs around him, she dragged him closer, until his body met the juncture of her thighs, caressed her, turned her liquid, then set her on fire.

She was dizzy by the time he pulled back.

"You want me to fuck you, Lola?"

"Yes," she whispered, her voice raspy, unlike herself at all.

"Then pull up your skirt."

She wriggled, shoving aside the folders and knocking papers to the floor, and yanked the skirt up over her hips until she was bare-assed on the desk. The thong she wore didn't count for much, and he tugged it aside. The fragile fabric tore. He didn't apologize, simply jerked harder until the whole thing tore away. Thank goodness, it wasn't the ruffled Macy's panty.

He sucked in a breath, shot it back out. His eyes glazed as he looked down at her. "You're so fucking wet for me. I knew you would be the minute I sent you that text."

"You made me want to touch myself," she admitted.

"Do it now." He looked up, captured her gaze, compelled her.

She pushed the keyboard over, nudged a monitor out of the way, then leaned back on one hand and spread her legs wider. The skirt rode higher.

"Jesus, I need to see." Impatient, he tugged her hand down.

Then she was touching herself, slipping in all her wetness. "You do it. It's better when you do."

He covered her fingers, his big hand over hers, and together they massaged her. Then he slid down, penetrated her with two fingers. Lola gasped. Her body contracted.

He put his head back, let out a long exhale. "Christ, I love it when you do that on my cock."

Then he shoved a hand in his suit pocket and produced a condom. "Open it."

"Do you always carry those?"

He laughed softly. "Since I met you, yes. I protect what's mine."

The possessiveness in the words edged her higher. She bit her lip as a wave of pleasure rushed over her. Not an orgasm, but a precursor.

He played the button of her clitoris as she took the condom packet and tore it open. "I don't know how I'm supposed to concentrate when you're doing that." Her chest heaved as she started to pant.

"You're a smart multitasker," he said. "Undo my pants."

Her hands shook as she unzipped him, leaving his belt buckled, just as they had on Monday. His desk, now her desk. His cock was huge in her hand when she pulled him from his briefs. Unable to resist temptation, she curled her fist around him, stroked lightly, swirling her finger in the drop of pre-come on his tip.

He loosed a long sigh. "Damn you." But he didn't halt her exploration.

Damn him for driving her mad with his fingers. She pushed him away—"Stop it"—then slowly rolled the condom down his length. Holding him at the base, her hand clamped around the bottom of the condom, she worked the crown of his cock, trapping him in the circle of her thumb and finger.

"Dirty bitch," he whispered with feeling.

"You love that I am."

"Yes, I do." He cupped her face in his palm. "I love what you do to me." He leaned his forehead against hers. "Now quit playing and put me inside you before I go stark raving mad."

She wanted him stark raving mad. Everything he said, everything he did made her feel special, ratcheted her tension higher. She *needed* to hear it.

"Whatever you want, Coach." She reeled him in with her legs around his waist, locking her ankles at his back.

Holding her breath, she closed her eyes as he slid slowly inside. His breath fanned her cheek, and his words drifted through her mind.

"Oh God, yeah, baby, so good."

She liked all his dirty words, but *baby* was better than *slut*. *Slut* was dirty, crazy desire, but *baby* slipped into wild need for her alone.

"Fuck, fuck, fuck," he murmured. "You're so tight. So perfect."

He filled every inch of her, all the way to her throat, her heart. And he was right, it was better than good, it was perfect.

He dropped his chin to her shoulder, buried his face in her hair, and clutched her butt in his hands. Then he hauled her closer and began a slow grind against her, inside her. Her nerve endings fired. A fast pump was good for the end, but this slow riding of her G-spot melted her, made her quiver, turned her into mere flesh and need.

"Lean back," he demanded. "I need to see."

She went back on both hands. He was fully dressed, his cock the only naked thing about him. Her legs were spread; her body filled with thick, hard flesh. The decadent sight was enough to steal her breath all over again.

She rolled her lips between her teeth, bit down, the pain intensifying the pleasure.

"This is beautiful." He leaned back for better exposure.

She squeezed her muscles.

He let his head fall back. "Oh fuck. What you do to me, baby." His breath sighed out.

She tightened her legs in a fast move, yanking him deeper, a spear of pleasure shooting through her. "Stop playing," she demanded, ready, needy. "Faster."

Her words, maybe the command in them, suddenly made him wild. He pounded into her. The desk was sturdy but the monitors swayed beside her. The wood groaned beneath her.

Then she didn't care about anything, only this, his cock in her, his hands on her, his mouth taking hers as he dragged her down with him.

20

FUCK. WHAT HAD HE DONE?

As ill-advised as it had been, it was also too damn good to disparage. She was tight in his arms, her face pressed to his chest. He was still inside her, still pulsing, his body still electric like a live wire. Papers were scattered on the floor at their feet. Her ruined panties were a scrap of blue against the beige carpet, the torn condom packet a yellow splotch.

"You okay?"

"Mmm," she mumbled against his chest.

Palms to her cheeks, thumbs under her chin, he tipped her head back. Lashes fanned against her skin, her eyes were closed. "You okay?" he repeated.

"Fuck yes," she said on a breath.

He laughed softly. It was his word, not hers, but it said it all.

"Did I scream?" she asked.

"Hell if I know. I'm not sure about myself either."

"You're bad." She still hadn't opened her eyes.

"Hell, yes." He flexed his cock inside her for good measure. She moaned.

"Do you think they came back?" he asked.

"Who?"

"Heckle and Jeckle." She'd mentioned the names somewhere along the way.

"Who are they?"

"Your nephews."

"Do I have nephews?"

He laughed. "How easily we forget."

She smiled and finally opened her eyes. "What you just did to me blew a few brain cells."

"It fried some of mine." But it was so damn good, he couldn't pull out. "I'm supposed to be working."

"So am I." She closed her eyes and hummed a little pleasure sound. "But who cares."

"The monsters weren't supposed to be here."

She shook her head. "I didn't know I kept you so well apprised of their schedule."

"I make it my business to check."

"Their instructor had to cancel. And to answer your question, no, they won't come back. Not until you're long gone. You terrified them."

He stroked her hair, smoothed it for her. "A little terror keeps them in line."

He kept talking because he didn't want to pull away. She was so goddamn warm and slick around him.

But his phone vibrated in his pocket. Work. Things to accomplish. Obligations. There was nothing to do but ease out of her. Grabbing a tissue from a box on the desk, he removed the condom, tossed it in her trash, then zipped up.

When he turned, she was pulling her skirt down. She reached

between the monitors to open the blinds again, then straightened her papers and folders, picked up the ones that had fallen to the carpet.

Gray swooped down to grab the discarded condom package and scooped up her panties at the same time. He handed them to her.

She looked at the torn material a long moment.

"Sorry I ripped them."

When she glanced up, her lips curved in a sultry smile. "I liked it. Very sexy." She put her hand to her hair. "Do I look okay?"

Not that it mattered since the boys were gone, but she was more than okay in his eyes. Her cheeks glowed with a light blush of color, her lips were just-kissed plump and red, her hair as smooth as silk. She looked good enough to spend the afternoon in bed with, then the night. And the next day, too. But he went for understatement. "You look perfect."

She patted his hair, straightened his collar, adjusted his tie. "You're good, too. All set for work." Then she skirted him, heading to the door.

"You know that wasn't punishment," he said. "We've gone way beyond that."

Hand on the doorknob, ready to unlock it, she said, "I know. But I still have to give the twins an excuse."

"Does it matter? They think I'm a slave driver anyway."

She smiled, then snorted a soft laugh. "And I totally agree with them on that, since you've made me your sex slave."

He took the three strides to her, wrapped his hand around her nape, and hauled her up against his chest. The kiss was hard and fast, but her taste consumed him.

She had it wrong. The one enslaved was him.

*　*　*

"YOU KNOW, YOU'VE BEEN EXTREMELY STINGY WITH DETAILS." Charlotte nursed her skinny soy vanilla latte.

The boys were getting their daily exercise courtesy of their slave driver coach at football camp, and being that it was a gorgeous Saturday morning, Lola had craved a white chocolate mocha. Of course, one couldn't truly enjoy a calorie-filled coffee drink and whipped cream topping without company, so she'd invited Charlotte. And not because she wanted to talk about that stupendous episode in her office, of course.

The coffee bar was packed, the order line seven deep, some of those being couples or families, and another five or six hovering by the pickup counter. The corduroy couch and its two armchairs were taken, the four chair groupings full, and the five tables in the back occupied. Charlotte and Lola had swooped in on a departing couple and snagged two comfy leather chairs with a small table between them. The air was redolent with coffee concoctions and baked goods heated in the oven. The house specialty was a gooey cinnamon roll dripping with frosting. Lola had not ordered the cinnamon roll, just the mocha.

"Details embarrass me," she said. Plus, they were in a packed coffee house where anyone could overhear them. Sure, the noise was close to deafening, but that just meant they had to speak louder to be heard.

Charlotte leaned on the arm of her chair, her legs curled beneath her, her upper body extending over the table between them. "You cannot possibly be embarrassed around me. Not only am I your friend, but honestly, honey, I've heard it all."

Lola rubbed her napkin over a smudge on the table. Yesterday in her office had been extraordinary, thrusting her a step higher on the terrifying heights of the can-I-live-without-him ladder. First it had been *Sure, I can live without this, but it's a lot of fun.* After Monday in his office, it was *God, this is so good that I could actually tolerate it all the time.* Which wasn't the same as saying *I can't live without him.* Today was *I can't stop thinking about him, wanting him, needing him.* Still not quite *I can't live without him*, but horrifyingly close.

"Charlotte, I think I'm in over my head."

Charlotte gasped and put a hand to her chest. "Do tell."

"It started out as just sex." Lola mouthed the last word. "And it's still just sex"—she mouthed the word again. "But I think I'm pretty hooked on him. And when our six weeks of football camp and punishment are over"—and they were halfway through their six weeks—"I don't think I can bear it when he dumps me."

Charlotte dropped the eager-for-dirty-details attitude and gave Lola's problem real consideration. "First, it's not *when*, but *if* or *maybe*. And you told me he said it wasn't punishment any longer. That doesn't sound like he's thinking about dumping you at the end of the six weeks either."

"And then there's his kid," Lola heaped on. "I get the sense they don't have a great relationship and that he would totally resent his dad dating anyone."

"So what you're saying is that you're a cliché, damned if you do and damned if you don't."

"Exactly." She'd be crushed if he walked away. But she couldn't handle a teenage kid either, especially a resentful one. The darling princelings were a perfect example. Really, what kind of woman would make up all sorts of not-so-nice names for her nephews? A woman who really couldn't get along with kids in general.

"So you want him but not his son."

Excuses popped into her mind. No, of course she didn't mean

that. It was just stepping into a difficult situation. What if she made their relationship worse? But that's what they were, excuses. So she admitted the truth. "Yeah, I'm not ready to handle a guy with . . ."

"Baggage," Charlotte supplied.

"God, that makes me a terrible person, doesn't it?"

"It makes you honest. But let me throw out something you might not have considered." Ah, there was the psychologist in Charlotte. "Maybe he doesn't want to introduce you to his son either. There's no requirement that you need to have a relationship with his son to have a relationship with him. You could date, you could have sex, you could go on holidays together, and do all the things that normal couples do."

"Just not on the weekends he sees his son." Though she still wasn't exactly sure what his custody arrangements were.

"Precisely." Charlotte gave her a smug, self-satisfied smile.

Lola eyed her. "Is that what you would recommend to one of your clients in the same situation?"

Charlotte pursed her lips. "Not precisely."

"Because it wouldn't really work."

"No. Because most of them come to me when the kids are already a problem. I'm offering you a suggestion so that he doesn't become a problem. Limit your contact with the kid now."

"What if Gray doesn't go for that?"

"You won't know until you ask him."

"But I don't really want a relationship like normal people have relationships. I'm just not ready for him to walk away."

"So tell him exactly what you do want."

"Umm . . ." She didn't know what she wanted.

"Chicken," Charlotte goaded.

Yes. Totally. She didn't want to define it only to have him say no. But she didn't want him to say yes, then change his mind later. God, she was crazy. "How old do you have to be before you stop being chicken?"

"Depends on the chicken. But even chickens can change their spots if they want to."

"You're mixing metaphors. I think that's a leopard."

"Whatever." Charlotte flapped her hand, barely missing her coffee cup. "Most people don't say what they really want. They wait for the other person to figure it out. And the other person is waiting for them. And nobody says anything and nobody gets what they want." She huffed out a breath, then smiled and put a hand to her chest. "And then they come to me."

Lola laughed. "Has anyone told you that you're actually pretty amusing?"

"No, they use the word *amazing*."

"That, too."

"And you don't even have to pay big bucks for all this advice." Then she leaned in very close and said softly, "I suggest first you figure out exactly what you want. And, Lola, make sure you don't use his kid as an excuse to get out of a really good thing just because you're afraid of getting rejected later on."

Brilliant. Lola's phone chirped once, softly, signaling a text message. And saving her from answering.

"Oh my God." Charlotte grabbed for the phone. "Is it him?"

Lola beat her to it. "Don't you dare touch that." She glanced at her watch. He was texting her from the football field.

"Hah, it is." Charlotte's smile was wide enough to show her gleaming teeth. "This is a paranormal event. We're talking about him, and miles away, he senses it."

"Don't be silly."

"What does he say?"

Lola hit the button and read. Her heart began to thump. "You're not going to believe it."

Charlotte gave her a wind-up motion.

"He wants to have dinner."

"Wow." A sparkle grew in Charlotte's eyes. "It really is paranormal. Telepathy. He heard what we were saying."

Lola ignored the absurdity. "Dinner. I don't know."

Charlotte threw her hands up and huffed out a breath. "Are you crazy? You said you wanted more from him."

"I said I don't *know* what I want. And then we started talking about his son. And I'm really not ready for all that."

Charlotte stared at her deadpan. "If you do not say yes, I am going to have to send you round to his house for a really big spanking."

"But what am I supposed to do with the boys?"

"Tell them you have a date. They're old enough to stay home alone for a few hours."

"But—"

Charlotte shook a finger. "Do not *but* me. Tell him yes."

She typed Yes because she really wanted to. She'd think about his son and relationships and getting hurt later.

He came back with: Tonight.

She was suddenly terrified, why, she had no idea. They had sex. She'd gone to his house, his office, he'd come to her place . . . "He wants dinner *tonight*."

"So say yes." Charlotte made everything sound easy.

Lola typed another Yes. Again, because she really wanted to.

After several back-and-forths, they agreed to meet at six on the downtown's main street, which had several good restaurants.

"Why don't you let him pick you up like a normal date?"

"Because I don't want to have to explain anything to Heckle and Jeckle." She stopped Charlotte with a look. "You're the one who said we don't have to tell his son. Same goes for my nephews. It's my business, not theirs."

Charlotte put up her hands in surrender. "You've got me there. What are you going to wear?"

"Something sexy."

"Let me help pick it out."

"I can choose my own clothing, thank you very much."

"But that's no fun." Charlotte pouted.

Lola's phone buzzed with another text, and she immediately hit the button. And there, all over the little screen, was BITCH WHORE SLUT. In capital letters.

"What's wrong?" Charlotte touched her arm.

Before she could stop her, Charlotte turned the phone to read. "He is a dirty one, isn't he. From asking for a date to calling you filthy names."

She should just let Charlotte think that. Then she wouldn't have to explain. Wouldn't have to analyze. Instead, what came out of her mouth was "It's not him."

"Who is it?"

Lola checked, but she already knew. "It's from a blocked number."

Charlotte gave her a narrow-eyed glare. "You don't seem surprised."

"I've had some calls and emails."

"And the dead flowers." Charlotte wasn't stupid. "For some strange reason, I get the feeling you know who's doing it."

Lola chewed the inside of her cheek. After her talk with George, she didn't believe it was him. She still didn't despite this new message. "I think it's the twins."

Charlotte gaped. "No way. They're bad, but *that* bad?"

"I got an email on Tuesday morning"—she didn't load it on by saying she'd had a letter, too—"and when I picked them up from football, they were so concerned that I appeared to be nervous and anxious. They asked if I was okay. Was something bothering me? And they did the same thing about the dead flowers. Remember they bought me another bouquet?"

"Yes, at the mall."

"That's not like them. And now, only a few minutes after Gray sends me a text, I get *this* text"—she pointed at the phone—"not a call, but a text. As if they *can't* call, but they can send a surreptitious message." Which meant Gray hadn't confiscated their iPhones today.

"Why would they do that?"

"Because it's fun." It made perfect sense to Lola. And the coincidence of this latest text message coming only minutes after Gray's was confirmation. They'd probably been watching him and assumed—correctly—that he was texting her.

"It could be something worse. They could be serial killers in the making." Charlotte leaned in. "Have you seen small dead animals around the condo complex?"

Lola rolled her eyes. "They're yanking my chain. That's why they're being so good. Because they're playing this game." It was dirty and underhanded. And just like them.

"Then you should call the police. That would scare the crap out of them."

Lola pressed her lips together and narrowed her eyes. "I think I'll just observe and evaluate, gather evidence. Then I'll think of how I'll make them pay." This wasn't a matter for the police. It was a game. And she had to outsmart the twins.

21

"SO, YOU'VE GOT A DATE, AUNT LOLA." WILLIAM SMIRKED.

"Someone from work?" Of the two, Harry was the better actor. He didn't overdo with more than passing interest, barely looking up from his video-game console. He'd attached this one to the TV, and, from what Lola could see, the game was excessively violent with buildings blowing up, tankers exploding, gunfire erupting, but, thankfully, very little blood and guts. "Does your mother approve of these games?"

"They're just games," Harry said, his fingers and thumbs flying over the controls.

"All right, fine. I'm not sure what time I'll be home. The lasagna in the oven will be done in thirty minutes." She'd felt honorbound to produce a meal. "Don't have anyone over and don't burn anything down."

"Have a wonderful time, Aunt Lola," they said in unison. Harry added, "And thanks for the lasagna. You really make the best." Okay, *now* he was laying it on thick.

"You look really nice, Aunt Lola," William added. Yeah, *way* too thick.

"Thanks, boys. Be good." If they weren't, she probably wouldn't figure it out anyway.

She'd chosen a stretchy white top with a square neck that made her breasts look more tempting than they actually were. She'd never bemoaned her chest size enough to do anything about it, but the top and the push-up bra at least gave her a hint of cleavage. On a normal date, she would have paired it with tight jeans, but this was Gray. And after dinner, well, who knew what was in store. So she wore a skirt. Panties or no panties didn't matter; if he wanted her, he'd tear them off. It had given her a delicious thrill yesterday in her office when he'd ripped the delicate material.

By the time she'd parked in the downtown lot behind the grocery store, locked her car, put her phone on vibrate in her purse, and headed out to the sidewalk by the bank, a tiny thread of anxiety had her nerve endings thrumming. Dinner. Conversation. What would they talk about? What topics were off-limits? The only things she knew about him were that he was a divorced CEO with a teenage son who didn't seem terribly fond of him. And he liked football. Which just about described every man. Oh wait, she also knew he'd had an exciting sexual summer in his sixteenth year. Which is when he learned to enjoy spanking and various other forms of bondage, dominance, and submission. The safest topics would be sex and work, forget his divorce and fatherhood.

A warm evening breeze fluttered in her hair like the light touch of fingers. Diners thronged the sidewalks, heading to outdoor seating along the street. A couple with a well-behaved poodle were drinking champagne cocktails and consuming a plate of sliders at one eatery. The dog didn't even beg. For a small San

Francisco suburb, the town had more than its fair share of restaurants, from Italian to Chinese to steak and seafood, upscale, middle of the road—but no fast food, at least not on the quaint main street.

Where was Gray? She glanced at her watch. Okay, she was early. But she felt conspicuous standing alone at the corner of the bank. A couple of men looked at her, looked away. What did that mean?

Then something brushed her backside. A palm cupped her, squeezed. She turned her head slightly and said, "Please don't squeeze the Charmin."

He laughed softly, his breath minty against her hair. "May I squeeze something else?"

"Not in public."

He stepped around to face her, dressed in a black button-down shirt and jeans. God, yes, she'd let him squeeze anything he wanted.

"So what do you want to eat?"

Lola glanced up and down the packed avenue. "You didn't make a reservation?"

He shook his head, shrugged his shoulders. "I didn't think it would be so crowded at six o'clock."

"Then let's eat at the first place that has a table available right now."

"You're easy."

Yes, she was.

He took her hand in his. It was the oddest feeling, holding hands with him, in public, where someone he knew might see them. Like it was a real date. He didn't scan the sidewalk for familiar faces, in case he needed to duck into a doorway quickly. He didn't hurry her along. He was just there, with her. A big, handsome man, turning female heads. But with *her*.

"Their salmon is great here." He pulled her through a doorway. There was a fifteen-minute wait for an outside table, but they could be seated right away inside.

Once they were in the booth, Lola understood why. "God, it's loud."

The ceilings were high, and the bar was in the middle of the restaurant, surrounded by people waiting for one of the outdoor tables. The grill and the brick oven were separated from the diners only by a wall along which the chef set out the completed dinners for the waitstaff to swoop by and pick up. The tap of high heels and men's dress shoes echoed off the terra-cotta tile floor. With so much open space, the mix of voices became a cacophony.

Gray slid around the booth until his thigh rested against hers. "The noise just means we have to sit close." He leaned an elbow on the table, propping his chin on his hand to look at her. "That top you're wearing is hot."

Miss Manners would have shaken her finger at the elbow on the table, but Lola loved his rapt attention, as if she were the only woman in the room. She could melt under that gaze. Yeah, she *was* hooked. "And you're hot in black."

He didn't acknowledge the compliment. "I was watching you for a few minutes out there." He quirked an eyebrow. "And I thought I might have to bash a few heads in."

"Why?" She wasn't quite sure where he was going with it.

He tugged on the top's neckline, pulling it up slightly, his knuckles brushing the swell of her breast in the push-up bra. A flush of heat raced across her skin.

"Too much drooling," he said. "There were a couple of guys about to turn around and accost you. I had to step in."

She didn't believe him. He was teasing. And she liked it. "But I thought you wanted to do me in front of an audience. So why would you care if some guys were checking me out?"

He clucked his tongue. "There's a huge difference. One thing is all about *us*"—he waved two fingers back and forth between them—"the other thing is about *other* men."

"So it's okay for men to watch me as long as I'm doing naughty things with you." She liked the idea. It was proprietary, even if it was kinky.

"Now you're getting it." He trailed a finger down her nose, which was another intimate gesture. "And I asked you to dinner because I wanted to take you somewhere I couldn't touch you. Where I could only feast my eyes on you and imagine what I'd do to you later."

"That's why you asked me out?" So it *was* about sex.

He trailed a finger down her arm. For someone who couldn't do any touching, he was doing a lot of it. The tug on her neckline had been very intimate.

"After yesterday, I need to tease myself."

"What does that mean?" She wasn't sure it was good. Maybe she was too easy for him.

His eyes darkened. "I like how crazy you make me. Dinner in public, no chance to jump you, it'll make everything hotter"—he gave an eloquent pause—"later. Tell me what you do."

"What I do? I—" She did whatever he wanted. When he wanted it.

"For your work."

"Oh." She hadn't even realized they'd never discussed it. Of course, it brought home the fact that they were all about sex and nothing else. Why was that starting to sound bad? "I'm a technical writer. Cell phone transmission equipment."

"Very interesting."

"It's not."

"You underestimate yourself."

They talked quietly, intimately close, so they could be heard over the dinner traffic. She could see darker specks of brown around his irises, the shadow of whiskers along his chin. She wanted to touch him.

"Can I get you something to drink?"

Totally engrossed in Gray, she hadn't seen the waiter approach or heard him slide the breadbasket onto the table.

Gray deferred to her.

"I'd like a glass of Riesling," she said.

Gray ordered a German beer. When the waiter was gone, Gray went back to the intimate position on the table and asked, "So tell me about all your lovers."

She choked back a startled laugh. "My lovers?"

"Yes. I told you about my projectionist. Tell me about your most formative experience." He grinned. "In exquisite detail."

That was the problem with getting down and dirty with a man on the first date—or whatever you called the first time she'd gone to his house. They could skip all the preliminary stuff about where they were born and how many siblings they had and jump straight to the subject of lovers. "I . . . ah . . ."

Saved by the waiter bringing their drinks. She could have kissed him.

"Are you ready to order?" He withdrew a pad from the pocket of his dark blue apron and held his pencil poised.

Lola hadn't looked at anything besides Gray. But he'd already decided. "I'll have the salmon." He dragged a menu close, opened it, then handed it to Lola.

"I'll have the salmon, too." She couldn't be bothered to look.

They spent another couple of minutes with choices and sides—they both passed on salads—then the man left and Gray tucked his beer mug close as he leaned on the table once more. He slid the glass of wine to her. "Drink. It'll make it easier to bare your soul."

Who was this man? He wasn't the coach on the football field. He wasn't the man who made her bend over a chair so he could spank her. He wasn't even the man telling her about his sexual experience in the projectionist's booth. He was almost . . . playful. And that was a word she would never have applied to him.

But Lola drank as ordered.

Then he issued another order. "Now talk."

"I . . . um . . . my ex-husband."

"Your husband was your first lover?" He didn't seem surprised that she had an ex-husband. Maybe she'd told him, but she couldn't remember.

"He wasn't my first"—he was the second—"but you asked about formative. And he was." Mike had done a lot of forming.

Gray put a hand on her knee beneath the table. "As formative as the projectionist?"

Oh yeah, but in a far different way than he meant. "Probably, but not as good."

He raised one eyebrow. "An asshole?" Then he snorted. "Of course he was an asshole or you wouldn't have divorced him."

"He divorced me." She felt a twinge in her stomach having to admit it.

"Then he was an asshole *and* an idiot." The hand on her knee started to move, caressing her, warming her. Or maybe that was just the sentiment in his words. "Did he cheat?"

"No." She rolled the stem of her wineglass between her fingers. "Do we have to talk about this? I don't want to be a pathetic whiner."

Gray laughed. Her heart flipped over. He was absolutely gorgeous.

"You're the furthest thing from a whiner." And that hand rose tantalizingly higher on her thigh. Heat spread through her body. "I'll bet," he said, "that he was the whiner."

Well, yeah, Mike could be described that way, but to be diplomatic—and not to come off as the typical divorced woman who couldn't stop complaining about her ex-husband—she said, "I didn't measure up to his standards, that's all."

"What were his standards?" Something about him had changed, a slight tension in his jaw, an infinitesimal flare of his nostrils.

"He just wanted me to dress better, do my hair differently, change my makeup, do a better job with the housework. And the cooking." And at her job. And . . . well, the list went on and on. She wasn't nice enough to his mother. She'd forgotten to send a thank-you note to his aunt. Everything about her had been disappointing.

"Why did he marry you?"

The callousness of the question shocked her until she looked right into his eyes. And saw something soft there, empathy. "I don't know why he married me."

"I know exactly why." The harshness of his tone belied the softening she'd seen in his gaze. "Because it made him feel like a big man to put you down. It made him feel better than you. He was the type that needs to put down someone else in order to feel superior."

"Charlotte said the same thing."

"Charlotte?"

"My friend."

"The one who took the photo of the panties?"

She gave a small laugh. "Yes."

"Well, she's right. And I'm right, too. He was an asshole. There's nothing wrong with you." He twirled a lock of her hair around his finger. "You're perfect."

She swallowed, didn't say anything, didn't admit how much she loved that word on his lips.

"What I've learned about marriage is that people often end up despising the things they loved you for in the beginning."

"And he loved me because he could put me down?"

"Maybe."

"And he left when it didn't make him feel like a big man anymore."

"He probably needed fresh meat to grind."

He couldn't know how true that was. Another small laugh hiccuped out of her, then she bit her lip.

She'd known all that, figured it out for herself in the aftermath, but it was the way Gray put it that amazed her. That's exactly what Mike had done. He ground her down. And when she was just a pile of meat at the bottom of the bowl, he had to find new meat to grind, starting all over again. She'd heard he'd been married and divorced two more times. He was probably looking for a fourth piece of meat to grind right now.

"I've never heard it put quite like that, but you're right." She tipped her head to examine him. "Is that what happened to you?"

He shook his head and didn't hesitate answering. "Not the meat grinder. My wife loved me for my ambition. Then she hated me for becoming a workaholic."

"I thought it was all your women that bothered her." If she had to bare her soul, Gray did, too.

"Are you referring to what my son said?" There was a distinct tightening of his facial muscles.

She nodded.

"I'm not even sure if that's what he was implying."

She pursed her lips and huffed out a breath.

He heard what she was saying. "All right, he was implying it." He cocked his head. "Do you believe it's true?"

She saw the waiter arriving with their plates before he did.

"Our food," she said as the waiter flipped open a folding table and slid the tray onto it.

Gray didn't move, concentrating on her. "Do you think I did?"

"Your salmon, ma'am?" The waiter's voice rose in question when Gray didn't move.

Lola ignored him, her gaze on Gray. "No, I know you wouldn't."

22

RELIEF COURSED THROUGH HIM. HE DIDN'T CARE WHAT PEOPLE thought of him. He knew who and what he was. He had flaws. If they needed fixing, he fixed them. Of course, there were the flaws only in other people's minds, and then there were those he chose to live with. But he couldn't let her think he was capable of betraying his marriage vows. It was her hesitation that had gotten to him. Even after she answered, he wasn't sure.

But he hadn't intended to get so serious, or to remind her about her asshole ex-husband.

Straightening in the booth, he let the waiter place their plates, inquire about additional drinks, et cetera, then stride away to another table.

"This looks like a great choice," Lola said. She closed her eyes, breathed in. "Smells yummy, too." She was discreetly changing the subject.

He wasn't going to let her. Breaking off flaky pieces of salmon with his fork, he kept his other hand on her thigh. "You still haven't answered me about all the naughty things you've done with your lovers." Which wasn't exactly how he'd phrased it, but he wanted to discount the ex. The man deserved a thrashing.

She muffled a laugh around the fork in her mouth. After swallowing—and moaning over the taste and texture and deliciousness—she said, "I haven't done a lot. And I haven't had a lot of lovers."

"How many?"

She tipped her head, obviously counting in her mind. "Five."

"And you were divorced when?" It was hard to believe she hadn't had throngs of men at her feet.

"Ten years ago." She swirled her fork in the mashed potatoes. Most places complemented fish with rice, but here, they served the most excellent whipped potatoes with just about every dish unless you specifically asked for something else.

She obviously loved sex, so that wasn't the issue. And she would have had any number of offers. Perhaps she was gun-shy after her divorce.

She answered in the midst of his contemplations. "Contrary to popular belief, most men, after you've been with them any length of time, and this is presuming that there was mutual enjoyment, of course"—she punctuated with a swirl of her utensil—"most men want a relationship."

"And you don't?"

She hesitated, poked at the salmon, ate a bite, then finally said, rather quickly, the words rushing out, "No, I didn't. I just wanted the sex. Women can be like that, you know, just wanting sex. I didn't want a man around telling me—" She stopped.

He knew exactly what she hadn't said. She didn't want a man telling her she wasn't good enough, wanting to change her, then never being satisfied with the changes she made. Been there, done that. She was definitely gun-shy. Since he knew the answer, he skipped to the other part of the question. "But before they got around to wanting a relationship?"

She pursed her lips and widened her eyes dramatically at him. "I was a very missionary kind of girl until I met you."

He laughed loud enough to turn a couple of heads despite the noise level. "I don't believe you."

"My favorite flavor was vanilla."

"Was?"

She raised an eyebrow saucily. "I'm starting to think there are other flavors out there which might be much better."

"Like chocolate and strawberry?"

She flapped a hand at him. "No. Like cake batter. Or blueberry cheesecake."

"Or a spanking?" He held her gaze.

"Definitely." She dropped her voice and leaned in, the fruity scent of her shampoo mesmerizing him, and murmured, "Or up against a tree in the middle of the woods. Or blindfolded and handcuffed."

"There are so many more choices." It was the perfect time to mention his plan for tonight. But that might come so much better as a surprise.

"I'm sure there are some flavors I've never even dreamed of." Then she pulled back. "And now it's time for *you* to tell all."

He'd had varied experience before and after his marriage. In the five years since the divorce, he'd indulged himself—and fully admitted it—in reliving his youth, stepping up the kinkiness. Maybe that was due to twelve years of sexless marriage. "You've had a taste of what I enjoy." This time he leaned in. "I want you tied to my bed for an entire weekend where I do anything and everything I want." He smiled wolfishly. "You can get up to eat, drink, and use the bathroom, that's all."

"Have you ever done that to a woman?"

"I've been saving it for you." He'd been saving it for the right woman, and Lola was it.

She worked at the vegetables on her plate, which was only half-empty. He was closer to being done. "How many women have you spanked?"

He listened to what she didn't ask. *How many women had come before her?* "Maybe ten since I've been divorced. I wouldn't call what I did with any of them unforgettable." He wanted her to be well aware of that. "I'm not sure how many before I was married." He winced. "I have to admit I was a horndog when I was in college."

"Aren't all young men?"

"Remember when you said that after being with a woman for any length of time, most men wanted a relationship? That wasn't me. I was perfectly happy with just sex and nothing else." If he took Rafe out of the equation, he might actually have been better off remaining a horndog. But despite the current issues with his son, Gray felt that Rafe was worth everything.

"I should have met you then." She gave him a sexy smile. "We could have been—"

"Fuck buddies," he supplied.

"Yeah."

But he was fifteen years past being a horndog. By forty-five, he'd learned it took more than just the physical to make sex cataclysmic. It took chemistry. It took connection. It took two people with equal desire. And it took more than what fuck buddies had. It took what Lola had given him. A freshness, her willingness. Her acceptance. And the intensity of emotion, the like of which he hadn't known since his very first time. But she was wary of relationships and a man getting in her business.

"The perfect fuck-buddy relationship"—he used the word purposely—"is between two partners"—he used that one purposely, too—"who are willing to experiment." He gave her a long look. "Are you willing?"

"Haven't I proven that already?"

He studied her. There was a bloom in her cheeks brighter than before. Beneath that quite delectable top, her breasts rose and fell faster. A pulse beat visibly at her throat, and a scent rose off her, sweet, partly shampoo, but something earthier, the scent of woman, the perfume of arousal. Oh yes, she'd proven her willingness. She gave further proof of it now with her body's reaction.

"If I touched you, would you be wet?"

She nodded, swallowed. "If I touched you, would you be hard?"

"Give me your hand." He seduced her with the softness of his voice.

She didn't question. She didn't gasp at the public nature of what he wanted. She simply laid her hand in his. He brought it to his lap, molded it around his cock under cover of the table. No one would see, or if they did, they would guess that her hand was on his thigh or simply clasped with his.

"Does that answer your question?"

Instead of pulling away, she squeezed, then stroked him, keeping her eyes locked with his. "It most certainly does."

"Then finish your dinner. Because I have a surprise for you tonight."

They were going to indulge in a very kinky experiment.

HE DROVE THEM INTO THE HILLS AGAIN, BUT THIS TIME IT WAS a real road that ended in a real driveway, not a bumpy, winding track that led to a weed-choked clearing. The evening was still light.

Lola was sated with dinner and satisfied with their talk. It had been both sexy and tormenting. They'd dug at each other's wounds, then applied a seductive salve to smooth them away again. They had both failed at marriage, for different reasons and with different results, but they were still failures. They came out of their divorces battle-scarred and wary. She'd told him the truth about avoiding relationships and wanting only sex. Charlotte would have said it was the opportune moment to discuss what she wanted out of her relationship with *him*. She'd chickened out. Or maybe it was more fair to say that she still didn't know, so she'd opted for her usual answer.

As for him, she wasn't sure whether he meant he'd spanked ten women or that he'd dated—fucked—ten since he'd been divorced. She hadn't asked. It didn't matter. It wasn't a huge number. Right now, everything he did and everything he said made her feel special, made her feel like he was crazy for her and obsessed and willing to do anything. Maybe *that's* what she was looking for, all the giddiness of a new relationship, but none of the pick-pick-pick. God, it was just like Harry said. Illusion. She didn't want reality. She wanted the illusion of hot sex and a hot relationship without all the messy stuff. And she wanted to pretend it wouldn't end on the last day of football camp.

In profile, he was absolutely divine. She'd turned in her seat to watch him, the play of muscles as he turned the wheel, the strong, shadowed jaw.

"What?" He glanced at her, then turned back to the winding driveway.

She thought of an old saying her mother used. Cannot a cat look at a king? In this case, it was more like: Cannot a mere mortal look at a god?

"Nothing," she said with a naughty little smile. It had been sexy and wicked squeezing him in the restaurant, all those people around them. He wanted experimentation. He wanted to tie her to his bed for an entire weekend. It wasn't punishment. It wasn't torture. It was a fantasy come true.

"Where are we going?" She asked but didn't care. She'd go wherever he led.

He shook his head. "It's a surprise."

The driveway was smooth and long, flanked by trees, bushes, and scrubby grass, the acreage natural, not manicured. Side roads with mailboxes occasionally led off into the distance.

Then they turned a corner into a circular drive rimmed by parked cars, not a single clunker among them. The stucco house wasn't a mansion but still large enough to support a three-car garage, with wide stone steps leading to a double door. Through the floor-to-ceiling windows along the front, people were clearly visible, milling about, talking, drinking.

Gray parked behind the last car. "It's a house party."

For a moment, she thought he'd brought her to some sort of work function, cocktails and business. Then he said, "Take off your panties."

So, not a work function. Her pulse kick-started. His fantasy. He'd said he wanted to have her in front of a crowd of people. There were more than enough cars to make this a crowd.

"Do it," he demanded. He was back to being the coach. And she was his slave. A rush of heat flashed across her skin.

Lola lifted her skirt, slid the panties down her legs, and handed them to him.

He held them a moment. "Damp. I could smell how wet you were in the restaurant."

Most people did dinner and a movie. They were doing dinner and a sex party. Her heart thrummed in her chest, and she was very, very wet.

"Here are the rules. You don't say anything unless I give you permission. You do whatever I tell you to do. You don't touch anyone. And you don't let anyone touch you."

"Starting now?"

His eyes seemed to glow as the sun began its descent behind the mountains. "Starting now." He grabbed her chin, held her. "You are my submissive, and you will not shame me in this place by questioning my orders. Nod if I make myself clear."

Lola nodded. She wasn't sure she was ready, and yet anticipation sizzled through her veins. Her breaths were fast, her heart panting, and inside her push-up bra, her nipples were diamond-hard.

This was excitement. To be thrust from a normal dinner date into . . . a sex party. Her nerves jangled in horror, her stomach turned over with fright, but she was hot, wet and breathless with need. She'd do whatever he wanted.

Her high heels tilted on the dirt shoulder of the driveway as she climbed out. Gray rounded the hood of the car and held his hand out.

She took it, loving the big, warm feel of him. "Are you allowed to hold a submissive's hand?" She had visions of having to walk three paces behind him, her head bowed.

Leading her up the drive, he shook his head. "Didn't I just tell you rule number one was silence?"

She hadn't forgotten. She just liked a bit of disobedience when no one was listening.

"You'll have to be punished for that. But to answer your question, your hand in mine is a stamp of ownership."

"Are they all doms and submissives here?"

He glowered.

She made a face. "You should have told me over dinner and let me ask all my questions then," she groused.

"I will tell you once only, then no more questions. I have no idea whether they're doms and subs. It's a private swingers party I discovered on the Internet. There'll be sex. The rules I just gave you are not house rules, they're my rules. Now you will follow them and shut up."

He finished by silencing her with a hot, probing kiss that melted her nerves.

They climbed the wide steps, but the front door opened before they reached the top. The man who answered was tall, silver-haired, and trim-figured in black slacks and a blue shirt. He had his arm around a woman of similar age, late forties to early fifties, with upswept blond hair. Her green cocktail dress plunged in a vee that was deep enough to expose the upper edges of her nipples, and the slit up her right thigh reached almost to her pubic hair. She was admirably well-kept for her age. A very good surgeon. Or Botox.

"Oh, goody," the woman said, grabbing Gray's arm. "Just what I've been dying for. Fresh meat."

And Lola realized that with all his rules for *her*, Gray had never said that *he* couldn't touch and be touched.

23

WITH THE DOOR CLOSED BEHIND THEM, GRAY EXTRICATED
himself from the woman's grip.

"I'm Jackie." She put a hand flat to her chest, a move designed
to bring attention to the rather impressive size of her breasts, or
to the fact that her nipples were damn near popping out of her
dress. "And this is Charles. We're your hosts for the evening."

"Nice to meet you. Gray." He held up Lola's hand. "Lola."

Charles flourished a hand. "Come on in. Have a drink. Eat a
little. Mingle." Looking at Lola, he licked his lips. "Then we can
all get down and dirty."

There was something about the lascivious swipe of his tongue
along his fleshy mouth that raised Gray's hackles. The look burning in the man's light blue eyes was . . . crass. And beneath Lola.
Yet that's exactly what they were here for, to see and be seen, to
have Lola admired and desired. He had to expect a certain
amount of prurience.

What the host lacked, his home made up for. The oversize

living room was nicely appointed with tasteful furniture, hardwood floors, expensive rugs, and a monstrous fireplace. The dining room lay through an archway, the table laden with an elaborate spread of appetizers and an open bar. And it should have been elaborate for the amount Gray had paid. The party was free, but one contributed toward the food and drink. They certainly hadn't skimped.

"Everyone." Jackie clapped her hands and called out, "We've got newbies. Gray and Lola. After they've gotten themselves a drink, come on over and introduce yourselves." Then she turned back to him, lowering her voice. "The rules are simple and few. Anything goes, but only with permission from both husband and wife. No poaching. Don't touch unless invited. And don't be a nuisance. No means no. But we're all exhibitionists here, so look as much as you like. Everything clear?" She puckered her red lips at him.

"Perfectly clear." The rules were posted on their website.

Lola's fingers tightened around his, and he read nervousness in her eyes. He wouldn't let anything bad happen to her, but a big part of the kick was anticipation. A little nerves would add to it for her. So he gave her an imperious *dom* nod, then led her through the assemblage of brightly plumed women and their escorts. That's one thing that had attracted him when he was looking online: This was a couples-only gathering.

He had a vague plan in his mind. First a little voyeurism, giving Lola an eyeful of rampant sexual activity. Then, if the mood was right, he'd cultivate any exhibitionist tendencies she might have. Mostly he was just willing to see where the evening led them, and, if this crowd was the right crowd, to let Lola's inner slut loose.

The crowd came in all varieties, from thin to paunchy, blondes, brunettes, redheads, bald men, a few wearing obvious toupees. They weren't an overtly good-looking bunch, as if everyone had stepped out of the pages of *Vogue* or *GQ*. They were average, some more appealing than others. For the most part, they weren't young. In fact, the majority were middle-aged, and, if he judged correctly, a few even in their sixties.

Conversation rose around them again, echoing slightly in the open-beamed ceilings, as he led Lola to the dining room.

"What would you like to drink?" he asked, surveying the array of liquor bottles.

"Champagne, please." She sighed. "So am I not allowed to say anything if one of them introduces themselves?"

"I will speak for you."

She glowered. It made him hot. He filled a glass, keeping the foam to a minimum, and handed it to her. "And that's the last word I want to hear out of you. Unless you want me to punish you in front of everyone." The idea had some appeal, and he enjoyed giving her orders. Dropping the dom thing on her in the car had been a last-minute decision, mostly with the intent of heightening her anticipation. It had the added benefit of heightening his own.

She muttered something under her breath and sipped, then she smiled. The champagne was not the cheap stuff.

He wended his way through the company, glad-handing like he was attending a business meeting, except that no one asked about his work.

"Oh, honey, I love that—she's not allowed to speak." This from a midforties balding man who obviously worked out regularly.

His wife, a bit on the stout side, slapped his arm. "Don't even think about it, Kenneth. I am not shutting up for you or any man."

Kenneth laughed, then palmed his wife's ample ass. "Don't worry, honey, I'll shut up for you instead." And he zipped his lips.

Lola held fast to Gray's hand as he maneuvered through the gathering, which he estimated at twenty or so couples. She smiled when he introduced her, and threw him looks with daggers in them when no one was watching. At one point, he chucked her under the chin and whispered, "Do you know how hard it makes me when you look at me like that?"

She shot him a multiple-dagger glare just as another couple moved in on them.

"We've been swinging for five years now," the redhead told them after introductions and a bit of small talk. Wearing a miniskirt that was meant for someone ten years younger—Lola would have looked magnificent in it—the woman wrapped herself around her husband's arm, clinging like a vine. "I can't tell you how much better our marriage is because of it."

The husband in question—florid-faced with a body that threatened a heart attack in the not too distant future—eyed Lola with undisguised desire. He was practically drooling.

The redhead leaned in, lowering her voice conspiratorially. "My husband would love to have a go at your sub. And I'd love to watch." She cupped her husband's package, squeezing, molding, manipulating. "See how hard he is."

Lola's eyes went wide, unable to take her gaze off the growing—and fairly impressive—package the woman held in her grip. Gray wondered if she always pimped for her husband.

"Thank you for the offer," he said politely. "Let me take it under consideration later in the evening." Lola made a choking sound and tightened her hold on his hand almost to the point of pain.

Finally Gray led them closer to the fireplace, pulling away from the main crowd to lean against the mantel, tucking Lola beneath his arm. "Shall I give you to him?"

She shook her head violently. He had no intention, but he

enjoyed her reaction. He liked it when she got feisty. Then some activity caught his eye. "Look at that, baby," he whispered into her hair. "It's starting."

On a leather corner group, a woman lay back between her partner's spread legs as another man pushed her skirt to her waist and buried his face at the apex of her thighs. The sight was almost ignored by many in the company, only a few heads turning. But Lola was suddenly flush up against him, her arm around his waist.

"You've never seen a live sex show."

She shook her head, the movement disturbing the air around them. Her scent rose. Arousal, sweet, hot, and thick.

The woman on the couch began to moan and thrash. Her husband held her arms, whispered dirty things in her ear. They were attracting attention now, and the activity caused a ripple effect, a hand down a dress here, beneath a skirt there, slacks unzippered over there, stroking, kissing, touching, watching.

"Do you want to be the center of attention like that?"

Against him, Lola didn't move, her gaze intent, but her tension vibrating along his side. It was part nerves and part sexual, he was sure.

"Roll her over and fuck her doggy, Bert," a male voice called.

"Make her suck cock at the same time." That was a woman, the redhead. Gray recognized her smoky tones.

Bert reared back and in conjunction with her partner, they rolled her to her knees. She immediately unzipped the pants right in front of her and starting sucking while Bert donned a condom and impaled her. For long moments, there was only the slap of flesh and the slurp of her mouth. They had their audience's rapt attention. Lola's fingers clutched at his back.

"You want that, baby?" His lips were close enough to taste the sweetness of her skin as he spoke. She didn't answer, she didn't move. She barely breathed. He enjoyed the show, but mostly for her reaction, for how tightly she held him.

The tableau on the couch became a three-way simultaneous orgasm, a lot of shouting, groaning, moaning, much of which Gray believed was exaggerated. Then they collapsed in a heap on the leather. A round of applause followed, and from amid the audience, a woman strode to the couch, lifted Bert's head by his hair and said, "My turn, sweetheart. But I want her to do the licking." The applause was followed by a burst of laughter and a lot of whispering.

Jackie was on them almost immediately after the show's conclusion. "Oh, you two can't hide out over here all by yourselves." She began a slow massage of his arm. "Why don't you give me an idea of what you're looking for specifically." She pointed a long-nailed finger. "We're always happy to accommodate such a lovely"—she put her hand on his chest, discovering his nipple and squeezing—"couple."

There was no *couple* about it. Jackie was only interested in him. He could smell the arousal rising from her, the scent slightly off-putting, nothing like Lola's sweetness.

He glanced down at her, then at her hand, a hint of disdain curling his lip, and finally at Lola. Just in time to see the glass in her hand tip slowly to the side, pouring champagne all over Jackie's spike-heeled shoes.

LOLA WAS QUIVERING WITH JEALOUSY, DESIRE, AND FEAR.

That horrible Jackie was staring at her shoes, her mouth open. And Lola felt utterly satisfied.

Gray had dropped his hold on Lola and fixed her with a look that made her bottom tingle in anticipation and terror. With a deep breath, she stared him down. Oh, she wanted to push him, goad him. All she had to do was speak.

He spoke first. "What did you just do?" His eyes were dark, unreadable.

She was allowed to answer his questions. So it wasn't breaking a rule. Too bad. She felt like breaking a *lot* of rules. She arched an eyebrow and added a sly little smile for him. "It was an accident."

One minute she'd been mesmerized by raw sex right before her very eyes, the next that woman had put her hands on him. She didn't like any of these people, the way they looked her up and down as if she were horseflesh for sale. But mostly she hated seeing that woman's harpy-red nails against Gray's shirt, hated the pinch on his nipple. She was sure he'd liked it. That was the worst part. And she'd simply lost control. So it was an accident. Sort of.

"Are you lying, Lola?" His voice was low, menacing.

Lola swallowed, her mouth suddenly dry. Nerves. Anticipation. It was a good feeling. She nodded her head.

"Then tell me why you did it?"

"She didn't ask for permission. And the rule is that you have to ask for permission from the partner."

Jackie snorted. "Permission for sex, not for simply putting my hand on his chest."

Lola narrowed her eyes on the bitch. "You pinched his nipple. That's sexual."

"Oh, please." Jackie pursed her lips. "She's your submissive, Gray. You need to control her. She ruined my shoes."

Gray stood back, arms folded over his chest. "Lola's right. You didn't ask for permission. And she deserves the courtesy even if she is my submissive." He looked at Lola, dark and forbidding. "But she does need to be controlled. Bring me a chair." Then he added, "Now," when Jackie didn't jump at his command.

"A chair?" The woman's voice came out in a squeak.

Lola's heart started to pound, and she suddenly realized the implications of what she'd started. *Please, please, please don't make me get naked in front of these people.* She sent him the message with her eyes. The idea had been exciting and frightening when they first walked up those steps, now it was simply terrifying. She didn't like them. She didn't want them. The live sex show had been exciting, gotten her wet, but she realized she didn't want to be one of the performers. Not with these people. They were too . . . lascivious.

Gray didn't read her silent message. Or he ignored it. Grabbing her arm, he hauled her across the living room, parting all those horrible people, dragging her through them like a naughty child who'd just thrown a tantrum in the middle of a crowded department store. Then he stood her behind a dining room chair and said, "Assume the position."

He would lift her skirt. She was naked underneath. They would all see. Lola's face burned at the thought of being exposed before them all. Yet she was wet for him. Wet for his hand on her, smacking her, caressing her. Two opposing sets of emotions. Her whole body quivered, wanting, needing, and hating it all at the same time.

"Assume. The. Position." He snapped out each word separately.

She could have walked away from him. She could simply have said no. She could have begged and cried. There were any number of things she could have done to make him stop. But Gray was looking at her, commanding her. And Lola wanted his hand on her despite their audience.

She wrapped her fingers around the chairback, bent slightly, legs spread to balance herself, and presented her bottom for Coach to take advantage of.

The first swat was muted through her skirt, not full flesh on flesh. But it stung. And she got wetter. He slapped her again, his hand lingering. Then again and again, slap, caress, slap, caress. He'd made her love the pain as much as the pleasure, the punishment as much as the reward. She wanted more. She needed it. She no longer cared about Jackie. She didn't care about the avid, greedy crowd watching her, devouring her, demanding satisfaction. She cared only about his touch. Only about him.

She closed her eyes, absorbed the blows, the sweet torturing touches. Panting, her fingers tight and painful along the top rail of the chair, she eased back, giving better access. If he'd lifted her skirt and taken her right then, in front of everyone, she wouldn't have fought. She'd have come. So close. God. Almost there. *Please.*

Then he stopped. Lola could have cried.

"I apologize. My submissive was obviously not ready for this excursion. My fault. A master is responsible for what his submissive does." He shackled her with a hand around her wrist. She felt him bow courteously. "If you'll excuse us."

Lola kept her eyes closed, allowing him to lead her, trusting him.

The house had felt hot and stuffy, too many bodies, all that perfume. But the night air caressed her skin. Her body was still quivering, needy. She almost tripped on the steps. Gray held her up. She opened her eyes, skipping to keep up with him as he marched to the car at the bottom of the drive.

The same imp that had gotten hold of her when she let the champagne glass slip sideways in her hand suddenly took over again. She pushed him up against the driver's side door, fisting his shirt in her hands. "I am not letting some witch like Jackie have you, do you hear me?"

He wrapped his hands around hers. "I had no idea you were such a jealous little wench."

"I'm not." She raised her nose in the air. "I just didn't like her."

"There were plenty of others," he said mildly, but against her stomach, he was hard.

"I didn't like *any* of them."

He moved suddenly, turned with her, pressed her against the car, lifted her, and plopped her down on the hood. Her bottom stung pleasantly, the metal still warm from the afternoon heat and the drive. She spread her legs to accommodate him, then locked her ankles at his back, trapping him to her.

"But you liked watching the sex. You were wet." He insinuated a hand between their bodies, palmed her. "And you are so fucking wet right now."

She couldn't deny what he could feel for himself. "I am not taking my clothes off in front of them. I am not exposing myself." But watching had indeed been sexy and tantalizing. And his hand between her legs was pushing her back up on the same cliff he'd taken her to with his spanking.

"So you'll watch, but you won't do."

"I don't want any of them to have a piece of me. Not even to watch me." And hell if she'd let them have a piece of Gray.

Then she couldn't resist her own needs. Hands on his face, she pulled him close. "Stop talking." She kissed him, opened her mouth, invaded his, tasted, took. Like she was the mistress and he was her slave.

He growled deep in his throat, melting her bones with his returning kiss. Her skirt was suddenly up around her hips, his hands all over her, his fingers filling her. Lola had to break the kiss, throwing her head back, gasping. "Oh God."

"Oh Gray," he said for her.

Then he was freeing himself, his flesh spilling into her hand. She stroked the rock-hard length. "I love how you feel in my hand." She loved the look of him, the thick, hard flesh. She found a bead of pre-come on the tip and swirled it around his crown. Then she looked up.

His eyes glittered in the moonlight. "Tell me you need it. Beg me to fuck you right now."

"God, please, yes, Gray. I need you inside me." He'd tossed her up on the ledge with his spanking. Now she needed him to push her off into bliss.

He made fast work of the condom he had in his pocket. Then he stopped at her entrance. "Put me inside you."

Lola curled her fingers around his cock, stroked herself with him, up, down, circling, made him wet with her natural lubricant.

"Stop playing." His voice was strangled.

"I like playing," she whispered. "I like you right *here*." She demonstrated, using him to stroke her clitoris, a soft moan slipping past her lips.

"Fuck, you make me crazy." He took her mouth, kissing her hard, deep, forcing her head back. His hand wrapped around hers, directed, and with one hand on her hip, he plunged.

Then he was pounding. Lola lost count after the fourth thrust. She was gone pretty soon after, high-diving off the cliff edge, and dragging him right along with her.

24

"FUCK," HE WHISPERED AGAINST HER FRAGRANT HAIR. LOLA mumbled an agreeing sentiment.

She made him lose his mind. It took long minutes for him to find it again. His cock was still throbbing, and he savored the feel of her around him.

How the hell did she do that to him? He'd planned . . . God, what? To get her excited to the point of letting him do her in front of that crowd. It had sounded like a good idea. But she'd poured that glass of champagne over Jackie's shoes, turned his plans upside down, and given him something so much better.

The spanking had been spectacular, their audience more enraptured than they'd been watching a three-way fuck.

Then Lola had taken him. Owned him.

He shuddered with orgasmic aftershock. She wrapped her arms tighter around him, her face buried against his chest. "Are you all right?" he asked softly.

She mumbled into his shirt. He figured it was a yes.

He loved her jealousy. Maybe in the back of his mind, he'd set out to incite it. Whatever, it had given the night a twist that knocked him sideways. Somehow, he found himself unable to expose her. Like she was his and his only. They could have a bare minimum taste, but the rest was all his.

"We can't stay like this all night." But he wanted to. Her hair stuck to his lips. He pulled it away. "Baby."

She leaned back in his arms. Blinked lazily. "Why not?" Then she seemed to focus on something past his shoulder. "Oh my God."

Gray turned, following her gaze. The party guests lined the windows, dark shapes with the light behind them.

"They were watching." She bit her lip.

"Yeah." He smiled. It was actually quite perfect. The aftershock. He flexed inside her.

Lola's lips curved. "It's kind of hot. Like having sex out in the woods, not realizing anyone is watching, then not stopping when you catch a glimpse of movement."

"So it's okay out here, but not in there?"

She put a hand to his cheek. "They can't see everything up close and personal. It takes the raunchy out of it and makes it simply sexy."

The woman had some crazy limits. Being an exhibitionist was okay, but only at a distance. He could remember that. In fact, he was already planning a hike in the woods.

She'd taken his fantasy and made it ten times better than anything he'd imagined. That ability was another reason she was special. She always managed to give him more than he expected. She always surprised him. She always enhanced his wildest dreams.

* * *

LOLA WAS STILL SEEING STARS LONG AFTER GRAY DROPPED HER off at her car. Hard to believe, but it wasn't even ten o'clock. She'd thought about begging him to let her go home with him for a while, but honestly that was way too needy. She'd already given enough away by letting him know she was jealous. That, however, could be written off as part of the sex-party fantasy, like she was *supposed* to be that way, an act.

So she'd let him kiss her sweetly in the front seat of his car, then climbed into her own. He'd waited until she'd turned on her lights, started the engine, and waggled her fingers at him. She'd checked her phone for messages from the twins. None, thank goodness, just as there'd been none when she'd looked right before getting into Gray's car after dinner and heading out to the house in the hills.

She couldn't categorize her emotions about that row of onlookers. It had been sexy. First that initial *Oh my God,* then the sweet little lick of heat through her body saying *Wow.* It was like sneaking a furtive sexual interlude in your office very late at night. Then realizing the trash can you'd left just outside the open door was now empty. Then you had to wonder how long the janitor had stood there watching.

Yes, that was hot. She could do it again. Plan a naughty assignation in an out-of-the-way place and hope someone stumbled across their hiding place. Or make sure they did. Who knew how, who cared? Gray would figure out how to make it work.

God, she was changing. He wasn't forcing the changes; she was simply adapting to his will. It was terrifying. She was too needy. He could cut her off at any time. He might very well be planning for it to end the day football camp was over for the summer. The thought shot a spasm of fear through her belly. Yet she loved how he made her feel. She enjoyed every new test he gave her, even if she had to twist it slightly, like she had tonight. She had to stop worrying about tomorrow and enjoy everything he gave her today. Or she'd go crazy. As if she wasn't already. It was Harry's illusion analysis. She wanted this *now*. She wanted her illusion. And that meant not thinking about the end of football camp.

Her Bluetooth chirped just as she was pulling into her carport. Her phone was still in her purse so she immediately punched the answer button on the dash before shutting the engine off. Her heart beat faster, harder, and she was suddenly breathless. It was him, he needed more of her. Just the way she needed more of him.

"Hello?" Excitement threaded through her voice.

"Bitch. Whore. Slut." Words flooded the car in a gravelly, indistinct voice.

It seemed so loud, coming at her from everywhere.

"Bitch. Whore," shouted out at her in an eerie, subhuman drone.

Lola found her voice and her anger. "Who the hell is this?" The call had destroyed her high.

"Bitch" was the only answer.

"I'm not afraid of you. I've called the police. They have equipment that can trace calls even from blocked numbers."

"Whore."

"So now you're screwed."

"Slut."

"Yeah, come on, stay on the line, give them all the time they need to find you."

"Cunt."

Ooh. That was a bad one. Then there was the dead air of a disconnected call. She grabbed her phone, checked the received list, but it was a private number. She'd lied to her anonymous caller, of course. She hadn't phoned the police. She didn't know if they could trace private calls. She got all her information from movies.

She was beeping the remote lock when a car sped by, far too fast for the relatively narrow lanes of the condo complex's parking area. By the time she stepped from beneath the carport, there was nothing but distant taillights.

She'd barely put her key in the front door's lock when she remembered she wasn't wearing panties. She'd left them with Gray. Darn.

"Hello, I'm home," she called out.

There was a scrambling in the living room, laptops slammed shut, then Harry dashed into the hall. His feet were bare. "Aunt Lola. You're home early. Didn't everything go well with your date?"

"My date was just fine."

William was close behind at Harry's shoulder. "But you look a little worried. Are you sure the date was okay?"

She eyed them both. Why were they so anxious about her date? "It was fine. But I didn't plan on being very late." Andrea would have had a fit. During the usual morning call, the boys would be sure to tell her that Lola had been out until all hours of the night. "What did you guys do?" *Make any nasty phone calls, boys?*

"Watched movies," Harry was quick to say.

"Played video games," William added before Harry completely got the words out.

She glanced at her watch. "It's not terribly late. If you want, I can get out of these shoes and watch a movie with you." Then she could watch them for any telltale signs of their *real* evening's activities.

She still couldn't be sure they'd made the call. It was just conjecture. A sixth sense.

"Okay, Aunt Lola. We'd really like that. And if you want to talk about your date or anything else that's bothering, we'd be happy to listen."

She stared at Harry. "You guys are totally weird. I told you I'm fine." Oh yeah, her sixth sense was working overtime.

Then she backed down the bedroom hallway as if their heads might suddenly split open and some alien creature with a long, spiky tongue would shoot out to get her. Did she believe in the movies? Nah.

After closing the door, she sat on the bed, toed off her shoes, and kicked them at the closet. Ghost didn't come out from under the bed to join her. She slipped into fresh underwear, then hung up the skirt, threw her top in the hamper, and pulled on a pair of capri pants and a T-shirt.

Ghost still hadn't come out. "It's just me out here," she called softly.

No Ghost. On her hands and knees, she pulled up the bed skirt. No little eyes blinked at her. She checked the usual hiding places, then opened her bedroom door and checked the office, too. When Lola wasn't home, Ghost limited herself to those two rooms. Then again, maybe the cat was starting to make friends with the interlopers.

"Have you guys seen Ghost?" she asked, standing at the edge of the living room.

They were slouched on opposite ends of the couch, laptops open again.

"No, we haven't," Harry said for both of them. "She's always in your room, and we'd never go in there."

Fifteen minutes later she'd checked every nook and cranny. Ghost wasn't in any of the usual places. She wasn't in any unusual ones. She wasn't anywhere.

*   *   *

"WHAT DO YOU MEAN, YOU MIGHT HAVE ACCIDENTALLY LEFT THE screen door open?" Lola's entire body vibrated with anger. The finger she was pointing at the offending porch screen was actually shaking.

"It was hot, and we went out on the deck for a little while," Harry said rather plaintively. Cowering in his corner of the couch, William let his brother do all the talking.

"Why didn't you close the door?"

He didn't answer that, made excuses instead. "But the cat never comes out of the bedroom. And we would have seen her anyway, if she wandered out on the deck."

Lola closed the screen door behind her as she stepped out to stare into the darkness of the woods below, the muscles of her face tense. The deck hung out over the steeply sloping hill. At the far end it was four feet off the ground, but right next to the condo wall, the drop wasn't more than a foot. A cat could easily slide out the door and jump off the edge.

"Gho-ost," she called. "Here, kitty-kitty." She held her breath, listening for a rustle or a soft mew. Nothing.

She turned back to the door, the boys' faces oddly dissected with the closed screen between them. "Do you know what's out there?" Her voice was shaky. "Coyotes and foxes and bobcats and—" She shuddered. "She doesn't have any claws. She can't fight back if something attacks her. How could you do that to a defenseless animal?" The same way they could pick on defenseless boys like Stinky Stu. The same way they could make nasty phone calls to her.

Harry came to the screen. "Are you sure she's gone?"

"You saw me check everywhere. Were you making a lot of noise? Did you scare her?" If they'd gone back to her office or her bedroom, Ghost might have automatically run the other way, out to the living room.

"We were just"—Harry glanced back at William—"playing video games and stuff."

She threw the door open so hard it banged loudly on the end of its track. Harry jumped back. She found the flashlights in a kitchen drawer. Marching back into the living room, she handed one each to Harry and William. "We are going outside and we are going to find her, do you hear me?"

They scrambled to follow her, right on her heels. She'd terrified them. And they damn well better be terrified. Because if— she couldn't even let herself think it.

"William, you check the carports and along the front of the condos." She pointed up the steps, and William took them two at a time to do her bidding. "Harry, you come with me."

She led him around the wall of the condo, which was an end unit on her building, shining the flashlight and softly calling for Ghost. They came out from between the buildings right by the side of the deck. "You go that way"—she pointed to the right—"and I'll go this way."

"She's gonna be okay, Aunt Lola." His words were sure, but Harry's voice actually shook as if he was truly worried.

"If you see her, call for me," she told him. "Don't try to get her yourself. You'll only scare her off."

Harry headed into the darkness, tracking slightly down the hill, then along the row of decks that would eventually lead him out to the street. In a few moments, all she could see was the beam of his flashlight weaving back and forth across the dense shrubbery.

Lola headed in the opposite direction. "Gho-ost." Her flash-light showed nothing but bushes, shrubs, and greenery so thick, the light couldn't truly penetrate it. The hill sloped all the way down to a ravine shrouded by oaks and pines. A coyote howled in the distance. Another answered, closer. Lola started to sweat. At least they weren't chasing anything yet. You could always tell when they'd found something, the sound of their furious barking and yipping filling a quiet night with terror for small animals.

They searched for more than an hour. Her head throbbed and her eyes ached.

"I'm sure she's inside, Aunt Lola," Harry offered. "Cats always find new places you'd never think of."

The anger was gone, nothing but a sense of helplessness was left. "She'll be fine. She'll be back in the morning when she's hungry," she said. But she didn't believe it. Ghost didn't have claws. She'd never been outside the condo. She was lost. She wouldn't find her way back.

"We're sorry. We didn't mean to let her out." Harry gazed at her, his eyes swimming. She could almost believe he was upset. No, he *was* upset; he wasn't faking.

"We'll find her in the morning," William added, his gaze as stricken as Harry's. "She'll be all right, we promise."

There was no movie. There were no computer games. Lola sent them to bed because she knew they couldn't possibly keep that promise, and she couldn't stand to talk about it a moment longer.

She didn't sleep. She couldn't even think about the sexy evening with Gray. She could only think about poor little Ghost lost in the woods.

Much later the coyotes started up with a frantic, ballistic cacophony of yips and barks somewhere down in the ravine. Lola covered her head with the pillow.

25

"AUNT LOLA." A TINY WHISPER SEEPED UNDER THE BEDROOM DOOR.

Lola opened her eyes, blinked. Sunlight streamed through the window, reflecting in the bureau mirror. It would last fifteen minutes, then the sun would move into the shadow of the building next door. Which meant it was eight. The last time she'd looked at the clock it had been five in the morning.

"Aunt Lola," the whisper hissed beneath the door.

She tossed aside the sheet and climbed out of the bed. Passing the mirror, her reflection scared her, wild-eyed, mascara-streaked, party-haired.

She threw open the door. Harry and William were down on their hands and knees, cheeks resting on the carpet. "What," she snapped, "are you doing?"

Harry jerked up. William followed.

"She's out on the deck, but when we open the door, she scampers away again."

"Ghost?"

Their heads bobbed in tandem.

Lola jumped over them, ran down the hall, flew around the corner, and burst into the living room, then skidded to a stop. Ghost flashed across to the far edge of the deck and disappeared.

Seeing the cat, Lola simply wanted to cry, but she waved a hand behind her, warning the boys. They stopped. Silently she crept across the living room carpet, slid both the screen door and the glass door open, then backed up slowly to the edge of the living room again.

They waited. The wall clock ticktocked in the small dining area. She counted thirty ticks and tocks before Ghost appeared again. The cat closed in on the open door with stealthy steps, her whiskers twitching, then suddenly, she was a flurry of white fur across the blue carpet, dodging the three humans in her way like cones on a driving course, and disappearing down the hall.

Lola closed the screen and the sliding glass door and turned to glare at the boys. Inside, her heart was hammering, her eyes stinging with relief.

"Aunt Lola, before you say anything, let us explain."

She narrowed her eyes and pursed her lips. Her only signal that Harry could speak was the fact that she didn't start screaming at him.

But William started. "It wasn't our fault. We didn't do it."

Lola ground her teeth.

Harry took over before she could jump on William and throttle him. "Arby stopped by."

"Oh," she snapped, "so you're blaming your friend instead of taking responsibility yourselves. And I told you *not* to have anyone over."

"Well . . . um . . ." Harry did some hemming and hawing, and just when Lola was about to yell, he blurted out, "He sent the flowers."

She stopped, her finger up and ready to make a pointed stab at the air in front of his face. "The *dead* flowers?"

Harry nodded vigorously.

"We thought it was just a game," William rushed on.

She forced herself to breathe evenly. "What else did he do?"

Harry shrugged, stared at the floor, very un-Harry-like. "A couple of text messages. Some voicemails."

"And a phone call last night?" Her teeth clamped so hard she thought they'd chip.

"Yes. But you answered. So he left in a rush."

The car speeding down the lane. Lola narrowed her eyes. "So you must have given him my email address and my cell phone number."

Harry rolled his lips between his teeth and bit till the flesh turned white around his mouth. "We thought it was just some harmless fun to pass the time."

"Harmless fun." She did *not* screech. "Stalking and harassment is harmless fun?" This was why they'd been so good to her face. Because they were stabbing her in the back. She'd suspected it, but now she *knew* it, and she was livid.

William fluttered his hands helplessly. "We thought it was fun until last night when he let Ghost out."

"You *saw* him let Ghost out?" In a moment she'd be out of control. And they might need a trip to the hospital.

"No, no, no," Harry jumped in. William was only making things worse. "We didn't *see* him. We wouldn't have *let* him do that, Aunt Lola, I swear it. But, well, we were in the kitchen making sandwiches, and he was out on the deck and the door was open and"—he shrugged again—"we didn't know she was gone until you got home."

Her fists clenched and unclenched, almost as if they had their very own brains controlling them.

"That's when we decided Arby had gone too far," William added. He probably thought that explanation was helping.

"So nasty messages and letters aren't considered going too far?"

"Letters?" they echoed together.

She didn't bother to say it was only one letter. "Yes. *Threatening* letters."

"He didn't say anything about letters, Aunt Lola, we swear." Harry gazed at her earnestly. As if he was actually sorry for the whole thing.

It didn't make a damn bit of difference whether it was a letter or a text or a phone call. "What did my sister teach you? Do you do this kind of thing to kids at school?"

"No, no, it was just that Arby was so upset."

None of it made sense. She shook her head slowly. "What have I ever done to Arby? I don't even know him." Andrea was right. She should have insisted on meeting the kid.

And really, had she treated the twins so badly that they'd participate just for *fun*?

Harry gave her a look, one that was close to having his usual spunk. "Because of his dad, of course."

"His dad? What does his dad have to do with this?" She didn't know any dads. She only knew people from work. She only knew . . .

Oh. Oh no.

"His dad is Coach Barnett."

GRAY PUT HER PANTIES IN HIS BUREAU. HE COULD STILL SMELL her on him, a faintly flowery scent spiked with the essence of her arousal, and he wanted her sexy aroma to permeate his clothes, his mind, his soul.

He was officially obsessed. So obsessed, in fact, that he'd been carrying them around in his pocket since last night. They would be there now if Rafe hadn't called and said he wanted to come round.

It amazed him. Since the car purchase, Gray had suddenly become a cool old man. Who said you couldn't buy love? Of course, he wasn't an idiot and Rafe was only seventeen; he'd change his mind again tomorrow or the next day, or the next time he wanted something and Gray didn't immediately give it to him. But for now, he had an opportunity to do a little bonding, maybe fix one or two of the many threads that had come loose between them, and he wasn't going to blow it.

Tonight, he'd get back to Lola. Maybe a little phone sex. Maybe he'd order her to drop everything and come over.

The possibilities were endless.

"THE *COACH*?" LOLA WHISPERED, HORROR SEIZING HER HEART.

They nodded like bobblehead dolls. The sight made her woozy.

"He saw your car at his dad's house, and well, he kinda saw it there a few times."

"Arby is Coach Barnett's son?" She was repeating, but she couldn't wrap her foggy brain around it. Then she tipped her head like a dog that can't figure out where a sound came from. "So, let me get this straight. You've been meeting Arby—" God, it wasn't Arby, it was *RB*, which stood for Rafe Barnett. She could have smacked herself in the head for being so stupid. "So you've been meeting Rafe Barnett at the mall and the movies, and"—she spread her hands—"you guys *followed* me?"

"We only drove by his dad's house a couple of times," Harry said reasonably, as if that *wasn't* spying and following.

"You drove by his dad's house?" She was utterly horrified. Then an even worse thought occurred. "Did you follow me last night?"

Harry waved both hands frantically. "No. Of course not. You had a date."

What difference did a date make?

"Do you swear?" She narrowed her eyes to near painful slits. "If you lie to me, I'll call your father."

They quaked. "We didn't, Aunt Lola. We swear it." Harry poked William in the ribs, who nodded vigorously.

Okay, she had to believe them. Anything else would make her crazy. And if they had seen anything going on at that house, she didn't think they'd be quaking right now. Instead, they'd be blackmailing her.

She pointed at the couch. "Sit. Both of you. And I want to know *every* detail."

THE DETAILS MATCHED CONSISTENTLY WITH HER OWN MEMORY of the last few days. Gray's son and the twins had sent her voice-mails, texts, and messages—and the dead flowers—then the twins had reported on her reactions. They'd looked on her computer to find out her email address, just as she'd suspected. Of course, they could have just asked their mother, but subterfuge was more fun. They'd driven by Gray's house when she said she was going to work, and they'd seen her car there. They hadn't actually followed her, thank God, so they didn't know about last night. And she believed them about that. They'd planned and plotted against her almost from that first day at football, when Rafe had caught his dad checking her out. After the night she'd been hiding in Gray's bathroom, Rafe Barnett hadn't confronted his father. It was much more fun to harass her. The darling, devious, malicious little princelings claimed that for them it was a game to while away the endless hours of boredom. Until Ghost got out and they suddenly realized they might have gone too far.

Lola needed a walk, fresh air, and sunshine to decide what had to be done. The midmorning heat warmed the top of her head and leached down into her bones. Her quick stride stretched her muscles, and her elevated heart rate oxygenated them. She reached that blissful, near-trancelike state where your feet did all the walking and your mind did all the thinking.

Okay, the calls and messages hadn't hurt anyone, and Ghost was fine. The fact that the cat had gotten out was an accident. Probably. And there was that old saying about boys being boys. Running to Gray with some horror story about his son stalking and harassing her would come off as completely over-the-top.

And yet . . .

If you allowed them to get away with a pattern of misbehavior, they would begin to think it was acceptable. No matter how she looked at it, the intent was nothing nice, nothing innocent. And therefore unacceptable regardless of the severity.

So she had to deal with it. The question was whether to approach Gray first. Or his son. In a way it was like George; she'd gone right to the source. She hadn't complained to his boss. She'd asked him. If the issue had needed escalating, she'd have done it, but she owed him the benefit of the doubt.

Her foot hit a rock, skittering it across the sidewalk. A car passed. She realized she'd walked several blocks downhill. Now she'd have to climb back up. Fine. More thinking time.

The fact was she didn't owe Rafe Barnett the benefit of the doubt. She owed everything to Gray. That's what twisted her stomach. She was going to have to come between him and his son. There was no way around it. Rephrase, she'd already come between them—hence the messages and phone calls—and now she was going to make that even worse. Because she knew the only right thing to do was tell Gray. And once she told him . . .

Despite the heat of the day and the climb back up the hill, her chest was suddenly tight with cold. She'd always known this thing with Gray would end. It was inevitable. It was just sex, after all. They were having fun. But that's when it was all a secret.

It wasn't secret anymore. His son knew. His son was pissed. And everything had changed. Now Gray's family relationships were compromised. It was messy. Gray would have to make choices. His son. Or her.

It wasn't fair to force him to make that choice. It wasn't fair to come between them. She should have cut it off the night Rafe had almost discovered her in his father's house. As her mom always used to say, *Better late than never.*

Except that it was a little too late for Lola. Because letting Gray go now was going to hurt like hell. She should never have allowed herself to get attached. She hadn't allowed it to happen since the divorce. Yet somehow, in a few short weeks, she'd thrown away years of resistance. Still, it was better to rip your own heart out right now rather than let someone else tear it to shreds later. And it wasn't what Charlotte accused her of. She wasn't rejecting Gray before he rejected her; she was simply making it easy for him.

She knew what she had to do, what was right, what was best.

At least she did until her car was rolling slowly down Gray's street. He was in the driveway.

And so was his son.

THEY WERE OUTSIDE WASHING THEIR CARS TOGETHER BECAUSE it was a guy thing to do. Gray basked in the warmth of camaraderie. Rafe had squirted him. Gray had run him down, wrestled the hose away, and sprayed him back. It was a good day. He wouldn't question why his son had offered it to him.

Now they scrubbed their individual cars in companionable silence, and the only sound breaking the quiet was the gush of hose water rinsing off the soap.

Until a car rolled up curbside and stopped.

Lola climbed out.

His heart contracted with need. Her white shorts and tank top bared enough tanned skin to make his mouth water.

Beside him, Rafe growled. It was the only word he could use to describe the rumble in his son's throat. "What's *she* doing here?" The tone was so derisive, Gray's hackles rose.

But Lola didn't approach him. She walked straight to his son and stuck out her hand. "Hi, I'm Lola Cook. We haven't been officially introduced."

Rafe looked at her hand like it was a snake. Then he looked at her face, some indecipherable emotion swirling in his eyes. "I know who you are."

She smiled pleasantly. "I really want to thank you for taking care of the twins these last few weeks. It's been a great help. They were so lonely with nothing to do around my house."

Gray studied Lola. She hadn't even looked at him yet. And he studied his son. Rafe was jumpy, his hands shoved in his cargo shorts for an appearance of nonchalance, or maybe to check that the car key was in his pocket. His eyes darted from Lola to the Subaru's driver's side door, then to Gray.

"You took them to the mall," Lola went on, "the movies, squired them all over the place. And even coming over to the condo when I had to be at work"—she paused—"or elsewhere. That was above and beyond. Oh, and don't worry, the cat came back after you accidentally let her out last night."

"The cat?" Rafe couldn't seem to help opening his mouth at that point.

But Lola waved him off. "No, don't say anything. She's fine. It wasn't your fault that the door was open. I've just never known a sweeter boy. I mean, you're seventeen and they're only fifteen and a half, no friends in the area. And your ages are miles apart in teenage years. But you took them under your wing with no ulterior motive."

What the hell was she talking about? Rafe had ignored the twins.

"Oh, and the flowers." She closed her eyes briefly in an expression of absolute bliss. "That was so sweet of you."

"I didn't give you the flowers," Rafe said, but his voice was weak, his gaze on the concrete. He removed his hand from his pocket, his fingers working the keys.

"Don't be so modest. You can tell your dad. He'd be so proud of you." She finally looked at Gray. "They were all dried and ready to be pressed. Absolutely perfect." What was she trying to tell him? He didn't have a clue.

Rafe swallowed, looked at him, then just as quickly his gaze darted to the car. His feet even shifted a step closer to the driver's side.

"And all those lovely messages and texts you sent me. I can't begin to tell you how good they made me feel. If I'd known they were from you, I would have immediately thanked you." She winked at Rafe. "But you sly devil, you blocked the number and sent the emails from a generic account. You just didn't want to take credit for being so nice, did you?"

Rafe remained speechless, a flush staining his cheeks red. Embarrassment? Gray was beginning to realize it might actually be shame.

"But the sweetest thing was that letter." Lola put a hand to her chest. "It truly touched me."

Rafe cocked his head. "I didn't send a letter."

She waved a hand at him. "I know you don't want to take credit for such heartfelt words." She smiled sweetly. "So eloquent."

"But I didn't send a letter," Rafe insisted.

She fluttered her eyelashes at him. "Well, never you mind. I'll leave you two alone, and I'm sure your dad will want to hear every detail of your benevolence."

"But—" Rafe's hand shot out as if he wanted to grab her. But he stopped dead instead.

Reaching into the purse dangling from her arm, Lola pulled out a folded piece of paper which she handed to Rafe. "And just in case you forgot all those wonderfully eloquent words you wrote"—she wrinkled her nose at his son—"I thought you'd like a copy for a keepsake."

For a moment, the paper hung in the air between them. Then Lola opened her thumb and forefinger, the folded sheet falling, and Rafe reached out to snatch it before it landed in the puddles on the drive.

Stupefied by her performance, Gray realized he hadn't said a word. It was time to take charge. "You should stay and tell me more about it yourself." Because he sure as hell didn't know what was going on, except that there was a subliminal message threaded through everything she'd said. And Rafe knew exactly what she was referring to.

But Lola was stepping back from him, too. He not only saw it, he felt it, the sudden distance that was more than just the few feet between them.

"No," she said. "I think it's time for me exit stage left. Rafe can tell you everything. You don't need me in the middle. In fact, I shouldn't be between you at all. It really was a bad idea."

He could read between the lines. *Don't call me. And I won't call you.*

What had she said last night? That contrary to what most people believed, men were the ones who ended up wanting a relationship. And that's when Lola exited stage left. She didn't want a relationship. And certainly not with a man who had parenting issues. She was walking out, cutting her losses.

He felt the ache in his gut, and she hadn't even left yet. When she turned, her sandals slapping on the concrete, the ache became a tear across his midsection. Then she was gone.

26

LOLA DROVE AWAY, HER FINGERS NUMB ON THE STEERING WHEEL.

Gray had let her go. He hadn't tried to stop her. He hadn't even asked what the hell she was talking about. He'd just looked at her with resignation. Like he knew that letting her walk away was inevitable.

When she'd thought it up in the split second between seeing Gray with his son and pulling up to the curb, the method had seemed perfect. She'd tell Gray without telling Gray. She'd lay it on so thick that the boy would be rolling on the ground with remorse. Okay, it was the same thing Julie Andrews had done in *The Sound of Music* when the children put a frog in her pocket and a pinecone on her chair.

Except that where the children had started crying, Rafe had done nothing at all. And Gray let her walk away.

It was over. Just like that. She was alone again, the way she liked it. She was free to come and go as she pleased—at least as soon as the twins left. No attachments, no one to pick-pick-pick until she couldn't stand it a moment longer. No one trying to mold her into something else. No man she was dependent on to make her feel good about herself. In charge of herself, her life, and powering through the next project. Yep, the way she liked it. Alone.

The way she *used* to like it. Before Gray.

IT TOOK GRAY SEVERAL MOMENTS TO COLLECT HIMSELF. HE couldn't act like Lola had walked away with a big piece of him in the palm of her hand.

"Are you going to tell me what that was all about?" His voice came out husky, laced with an edge of emotion.

Rafe didn't answer. He was reading the letter Lola had given him, and with each second that ticked by, his face grew more pallid. Then he swallowed.

"I didn't send this letter," he said. "The rest of it was just a little fun. But I didn't send this." He shook the paper emphatically. "I wouldn't send this, Dad, I swear."

What the hell? Gray held out his hand. Rafe passed it over, his fingers shaking. And Gray read the *wonderfully eloquent* words.

I know who you are, Bitch, and I know what you're doing. You can't treat people like this. You'll be sorry for what you've done. You will pay. And you'll never hurt anyone like this again. I promise you.

His belly crimped. He looked at his son. "You better tell me the rest of it. Now."

Rafe told him. About the flowers—which were all dried and ready for her to press rather than *dead*—the texts, the voicemails, the emails, all with words like *bitch*, *slut*, and *whore*. About plotting with the twins, how they were to gauge her reaction. How he'd noticed Gray watching her that first day of camp. He'd seen Lola looking back, too. His son wasn't stupid. He'd read all the signals. He'd seen her car at Gray's house.

"It was just a game, Dad. Harry and William said she was on their case all the time, taking their phones and their video games when they"—he finger-quoted—"misbehaved."

Gray stared at him. "Did I actually raise you? Because if I did, I failed miserably to teach you *anything*." The words came out like they were from someone else's mouth.

For the first time, Rafe's face turned sullen, his lip curling slightly. "*You* called her those names, too. I saw your text to her."

He remembered that night in the kitchen, the phone on the counter, Rafe's obviously furtive and guilty expression. "If I were you, I wouldn't choose this moment to admit you invaded my privacy."

A lawnmower started up next door, but he didn't raise his voice. Rafe could hear every word. "Words have appropriate uses and inappropriate ones. Sending a woman anonymous messages calling her a bitch and a slut is one of those inappropriate uses." He threw his hands in the air. "Don't you realize that's harassment? How could you do that?"

"It was just a game."

"Don't use that excuse again. It wasn't a game. You were pissed because I was dating her, and you punished her instead of being a man and talking to me about it."

"I tried to talk to you about it that night. But you said you were busy." Rafe's voice rose. "You've always been busy. You were too busy for Mom. All the times she used to cry when you didn't answer your phone while you were traveling. You always have time for everyone else. Even the kids on the football team."

He ignored the stuff about Bettina. It was a battle he couldn't win. But he needed Rafe to understand about football. "I started the camp for you. To spend time with you."

Rafe shot the explanation down. "You don't spend time with *me*. You're busy with drills and game plans and exercises and wiping Stinky Stu's nose or Pete's butt." He stabbed a finger at his chest. "I even had to beg you to buy me a car so Mom didn't have to drive me around all the time. I just wanted to make it easier on her."

It always came back to Bettina, but she was beside the point now. "You think I'm too busy so you harassed a woman?"

But Rafe wasn't listening anymore. His fingers clutched around the keys, he turned on his heel, ran to the car, backing out of the driveway while Gray watched.

He wasn't angry. He was defeated. After all the years of trying to make things right, he finally accepted that they never would be. He had lost his son. And he had lost Lola.

HE WAS DEFEATED, BUT IT WASN'T IN GRAY TO GIVE UP ON HIS SON. He climbed in his car, started up the engine, and followed. Of course, Rafe was nowhere in sight, so Gray chose option one on the list of places he would have gone: home.

He had to admire the way Lola had gotten her point across. She hadn't gotten angry; she'd praised Rafe. She hadn't shouted; she'd simply sounded amazed and appreciative. The result was shaming his son in a way she could never have accomplished with anger. And Rafe deserved shaming without a doubt. He could only hope his son learned something from her method.

The Subaru was in Bettina's driveway, the hood still warm as he passed his hand across it on the way to the front path.

He knocked. Bettina opened the door. "What on earth did you do to him this time?" Frown lines slashed her forehead.

"I'd like to talk to him," he said politely. He didn't want a boxing match with her as well as Rafe.

"Well, he's up in his room and he doesn't want to see you." She barred his way, arms folded, defensive. Her hair was perfect, her blouse ironed, everything about her crisp, even her walking shorts.

He closed his eyes for one second and breathed deeply. "Bettina, I still pay the mortgage on this house, and I don't need permission to speak with my son."

Wrong thing to say. She drew her mouth into an ugly purse, lines marring her upper lip. "You don't have any rights here. You gave them up when you abandoned us."

He wanted to laugh; she was so good at rewriting history. But he was interested in Rafe, not Bettina's never-ending grievances. "We have an issue with our son, so I would appreciate coming inside to discuss it."

Bettina hated it when he got reasonable. "What issue?" she snapped, not opening the door even an inch wider.

"Bettina," he said calmly, "you don't want to air our dirty laundry out on the porch, do you?"

She hated his equanimity, but she hated publicly airing her quarrels with her ex-husband even more. She stepped back and let him in, but no farther than the high-ceilinged front entry.

It was a two-story house, living room on the right, dining room on the left, a hall leading back to the kitchen and family room, and the stairs to the second level straight ahead. Rafe's room was directly across the landing, his door open. Anything said down in the hall could certainly be overheard.

Gray stated things flatly without embellishment or emotion. "Rafe has admitted sending harassing messages to the aunt of two of the boys on our football team."

She scowled. "He wouldn't do anything like that."

"I just told you," he said evenly, rationally, maintaining composure. "He *admitted* it."

"Well, he must have had a good reason."

Gray put steel into his voice. "There's never a good reason for harassing anyone. There's always a better solution for addressing any problem."

"Well." She tossed her hair, gave a slight shrug of her shoulders. "I want to hear his side."

"Fine. By all means"—he thrust a hand out in the direction of the upstairs landing—"call him down."

Bettina didn't. "Who was she?"

He'd already told her. "She's the aunt of two of the boys on my team."

"So this is the little floozy you've been screwing?"

Gray didn't say anything because if he let one word out, all the rest would come. And getting angry with her wouldn't help Rafe.

Bettina went on as if he'd spoken. "Rafe told me all about her. All those heated looks"—she rolled her eyes—"you and this woman have been giving each other out on the football field whenever she picks up her brats."

He glanced to the head of the stairs and Rafe's open door. Were those his words? Or Bettina's?

"I'm appalled at the way you've exposed our son to your rampant sexual activity."

This was her usual modus operandi, put him on the defensive, make him start explaining. And the original point was dead, buried, and forgotten.

Not this time. "My private life isn't the topic of discussion. We need to come to some resolution on Rafe's behavior."

Two steps closer, Bettina stuck her finger in the center of his chest. "*Your* private life is exactly why he did what he did. You leave your cell phone around where he can see whatever filthy texts you're sending to your paramours."

"He had to push several keys on my cell phone to get to any messages I might have sent." Dammit, she was making him explain, diverting him.

"He told me about them. All your filthy language, your degradation of women. I won't have him exposed to that." She stabbed his chest for emphasis, and it was all he could do not to shove her.

He had never understood her anger. She didn't want sex, but she sure as hell didn't want him to have it with anyone else either.

"Bettina." He struggled for that equanimity she hated, and his hesitation allowed her another volley.

"I don't blame him for sending a few nasty texts and emails to the little harlot. I'm sure she must have deserved everything he said in that letter."

It was still in his pocket. The letter had been the worst, seeing Rafe's threatening words in black and white.

"I'm not going to punish him for something that's *your* fault," Bettina said. "She should have to pay for putting my son through this. You should both pay." Another stab for emphasis.

But Gray didn't feel the hard jab. He was listening to her, hearing her, absorbing her words. "I didn't mention a letter."

She dropped her hand down to her side. Opened her mouth, closed it, then finally said, "Of course, you did. You said he was sending this slut of yours messages and letters."

"I only mentioned messages."

She shook her head and huffed out an exaggerated breath. "Whatever. You said messages, I thought letter. Who cares?"

"And I never said what was in the messages."

She pursed her lips, but she was no longer meeting his eyes. "Isn't it obvious? I just made an assumption." She backed up a step.

Gray reclaimed the step. "I have the letter in my pocket. And Rafe says he didn't send it."

"What does *that* matter?" she snapped, her voice rising. "What *matters* is that you have reduced your son to harassing your little whores and sluts because he's dying for your attention. And all you've ever done is ignore him. I find that to be a perfectly reasonable explanation, and I won't punish him for standing up for me."

"For *you*?" he asked very softly.

"For *himself*," she stressed.

"Mom." Rafe stood at the top of the stairs.

They both glanced up, then Bettina dashed to the bottom of the stairs. "I'm not mad at you, sweetie. I understand completely."

"I didn't send that letter."

"It doesn't matter," she said, hanging on to the banister.

"Yes, it does." Rafe covered three stairs and stopped. "Dad's right. What I did was wrong. I shouldn't have told you about Lola Cook or looked at Dad's cell phone."

Gray watched the exchange, then he asked, "Did your mother ask you to check out my phone?"

Rafe didn't answer. He wouldn't take that final step and desert his mother for his father. He wouldn't blame her. He'd stood by her, loved her, and protected her for five years, all the things he believed she needed. But Gray knew it was true in the way Bettina bit her lip waiting for Rafe's next word. And in the way Rafe looked at her, a sadness in his eyes that was far too deep for a boy his age.

"I know I didn't send that letter, Mom," he said gently, just a slight change in the wording but such a big shift in the meaning.

Bettina couldn't seem to open her mouth, her knuckles white with her grip on the banister.

Gray answered for her. "I know you didn't, Rafe. And your mother knows it, too. Do you think you and I can go somewhere and talk about this, son? Clear the air. Decide between us where we go from here?"

Rafe swallowed, his gaze on Bettina. Then his son gave Gray the words he'd been waiting more than five years to hear. "Yeah, Dad. Let's go somewhere and talk."

Out on the porch, he put his arm around Rafe's shoulder for a brief moment before they headed down the path, leaving Bettina standing in the open door.

She hadn't admitted a thing. She would never admit she'd sent that letter. She would never own up to manipulating Rafe. It was a fine line to walk now. Gray had to resolve his relationship with his son, try to undo the damage Bettina had done, give him guidance, divert his path from the one his mother had started him down. Gray couldn't do all that by bashing her in front of him. But there was one more thing that needed to be said, without their son listening.

"Why don't you get in the car, Rafe? I'll be back in a minute."

"Dad—" Rafe started.

"Don't worry. I won't be long."

Rafe nodded, accepting, and jogged the last few steps to the driveway.

Gray returned to the front porch and his ex-wife.

"Don't you start in on me," Bettina said.

He didn't give her a chance to say more. "Don't butt into my life again, Bettina. And don't use Rafe to get to me."

"Is that a threat?" She glared at him, but he detected a tremor in her hands that she tried to cover by crossing her arms beneath her breasts.

"All I'm telling you is that he's figured out you manipulated him, and if you keep it up, you'll lose him."

"And I'm sure that's exactly what you want," she snapped. "For him to hate me."

"That's where you're wrong. I want what's best for our son. He loves you. I don't want to see him have to choose. But if that's what you want, just keep on doing exactly what you've been doing."

That was all he'd come back to say. Maybe it was a threat. Maybe it was just a warning. He didn't know if Bettina would listen. He only cared for Rafe's sake, because the boy still loved his mom. Having said his piece, Gray ended the discussion by turning away from her, his stride eating up the walkway back to his car.

Now it was time to fix his own issues with Rafe. In a very big way, it was Lola who had given him this chance. He wasn't going to blow it.

27

GRAY HADN'T CALLED. HE HADN'T TEXTED. LOLA REALIZED HE wasn't going to. She'd told him this morning that she shouldn't be in the middle, essentially that she didn't want to be. He'd taken her at her word.

The computer screen was a blur, the words swimming in front of her eyes. She'd been sitting here all afternoon, and honestly, she couldn't remember changing a single word. She was close to being done, almost there. The only thing left was the trouble-shooting section, which she'd take care of on Monday. The goal was within her reach, but somehow she just didn't care.

An instant message popped up on the screen. George. Working on a Sunday. A dedicated guy. What had he said to her in the cafeteria? That he didn't care what other people thought, he was happy with who he was.

She liked her career, she was proud of her work, but somehow she couldn't say those same words. She didn't want to have to change to make a man happy, but she wasn't so sure she wanted to be alone anymore either. Gray *had* changed her.

Configuration, section B, George wrote. Big boo-boo, Lola.

A week ago, even yesterday, her stomach would have dropped as low as it could go. Now, *the big boo-boo* was just another thing to deal with. She scanned the cited section and couldn't find the error. About to type back a more specific question, she suddenly saw it. She'd typed *do* instead of *don't*, but the eye saw what it expected to see and she'd glossed over the mistake. One little word was a big error in the scheme of things, but just a tap-tap on the keyboard, and it was fixed.

She thanked George for saving her butt. Then she stared at the computer screen. For a long time. Until the monitor went dark. Her reflected face stared back at her. The lips moved.

Do you really want to be alone, Lola? Are you sure you want to let this one walk away?

Of course it was her imagination.

You reject men before they can reject you. Charlotte's words of wisdom.

But this time it wasn't her choice, not really. She'd had to do what was right.

Aren't you just protecting yourself like you always have?

She was really starting to hate that reflection.

He's not like Mike. He's not trying to make you into someone acceptable to his code. He thinks you're perfect the way you are.

Thank God, she was saved from answering her reflected self as the walls began to shake and the monitor wobbled with a magnitude seven on the Richter scale, which could only mean two teenage boys were headed her way. Ghost shot down behind the desk to hide. A moment later, Harry and William crashed through her office door, fighting for who would be first.

Harry won. "Aunt Lola, can we go to the mall?"

It was four o'clock in the afternoon. She generally prepared dinner between five-thirty and six. That wasn't much time at the mall. "Fine," she said. "Whatever."

"Will you drive us?" William asked.

"And we'll have dinner in the food court so you don't have to fix anything," Harry sweetened the pot.

"It's a win-win," William declared.

"You can have the whole evening to do whatever you want without us bugging you." Harry beamed at her.

They'd been good all afternoon, taken a walk *to get some much-needed fresh air and exercise*. They'd powered through their online driving lessons. They'd even made *her* a sandwich for lunch. And cleaned up afterward. They were really trying to make it up to her. Maybe she could give them this one little thing.

"All right," she said, slapping her hands on her knees.

They hooted and did little dances around the room.

She narrowed her eyes on them. They were laying it on too thick again, a dead giveaway. "What have you two got planned?"

"Nothing," Harry said with singular innocence.

William nodded agreement. "We were just bored."

"We'll probably see a movie," Harry explained.

She could be suspicious until they were old and gray and had gone home to their mother. Or she could take them at their word when they said their devious ways were over.

Lola gave them the benefit of the doubt, and fifteen minutes later they were tumbling out of her car at the mall. "What time is the movie?" she called.

They raced to the ticket window, jostling each other to read the schedule, then dashed back. "It's a seven-thirty showing and lets out about nine-thirty."

"Then I'll be right here at nine-thirty."

"We could call you."

"No, I'll be here." She wanted a time limit so she didn't have to hang out all night.

"Okay," Harry agreed, and a broad smile darn near split his face in half. "Have a good time, Aunt Lola." Then they were off again, this time heading to the mall entrance, playing with their phones, texting or something. Kids always had fingers to the phones. In a few years, everyone would start complaining about carpal tunnel thumbs.

She turned down a parking aisle, intending to circle back around and out to the traffic light. The cell phone chirped with a text message. Her heart skipped a beat and her skin was suddenly warm.

Pulling into a vacant spot, she grabbed the phone. Gray's number flashed like a neon sign. She hit the button to view his message.

U need punishment. U walked out without explanation. B here in 5 mins or U won't sit down 4 a week instead of a day.

She couldn't breathe. They weren't done yet. *He* wasn't done. She'd have more time with him. Enough time to find the courage to tell him that she didn't want to be alone anymore.

She drove very slowly and made sure she was at least fifteen minutes instead of the five he'd dictated. She would definitely deserve a nice long punishment for that.

LOLA RANG HIS DOORBELL, HER NERVES JITTERING. WHAT HAD happened with his son after she left? Did they talk, work it all out? Or were they still at odds, even further apart than when she'd first opened her mouth?

The door opened with a jerk, and her heart did a somersault

in her chest. He looked good enough to make a girl cry, the shadow of beard on his jaw, compelling deep brown eyes mesmerizing her, black jeans and black shirt hugging all that perfect masculinity. Or maybe she was just biased.

Nah. He *was* perfect in every way.

But she knew from that dark look in his eyes that she wasn't getting any of her questions answered.

"You're already ten minutes late. Are you going to make it worse by standing out there on the doorstep?" His voice was low and mildly harsh.

"No, Coach. I'm coming in." Yes, please, she wanted in. She didn't want to be alone.

The door closed behind her with a loud click. And he was glaring.

Through the living room archway she saw her naughty chair in her very naughty corner. And Lola got wet. "Where do you want me, Coach?" He could have her anywhere.

"When do you have to pick the boys up?"

How did he know she'd taken them somewhere? Best not to question him in his present mood. "Nine-thirty at the mall theater."

He looked pointedly at the chair. Then down the hall. And finally back at her. "That gives us five hours."

Yes, it most certainly did. She was wet, *and* her blood was rushing through her veins, her skin jumping. Her mouth watered for a taste of him. "Five hours for what?" she ventured.

"For what I have planned." He pointed down the hall. "That way." Then he smacked her bottom when she didn't move fast enough.

Lola squealed and skipped ahead, stopping at the end of the hall.

"My bedroom."

She'd only peeked but had never been invited into his inner sanctum. It was a master suite, with opaque glass double doors, hardwood floor, manly mahogany furniture, and that massive king-size bed.

It was the bed that stopped her breath right in her chest. The wine-red comforter had been pulled back to the foot. Four scarves were secured to the bedposts and draped across the cream-colored sheets.

"Strip," he ordered.

Lola gulped. What was that fantasy of his? To tie her to his bed for an entire weekend and have his wicked way with her. It wasn't a whole weekend, but he had five hours.

Lola pulled her tank top over her head, then held it a moment, unsure what to do.

"Give me your clothes."

She handed the tank over. He folded it and laid it on the bureau behind him. Then he flicked a finger. "The shorts."

She stepped out of her sandals, then her shorts, and gave him those, too. He scooted the shoes aside and folded the shorts on top of her tank top.

"I like the thong." He moved in close enough to take a deep breath. "You smell good." He looked down. "Hot and wet." Then he backed off. "The rest of it."

Lola reached behind, unsnapped her bra, then slid her panties down her legs and gave both scraps of lingerie to him.

Being totally naked while he was fully dressed made her vulnerable, but the way his gaze traced her curves—what there was of them—heated her insides and turned her legs to jelly.

"Lola, Lola, Lola, the things you do to a man." He raised his eyes to lock with hers. "You give me fantasies, Lola."

"What fantasies?" she whispered. *Dream of me, next year, the year after.* Dare she say she'd changed her mind about relationships, about a man in her life? Could she actually say that Charlotte was right, and her whole relationship phobia was really just a way of rejecting him before he rejected her? She had so many excuses to keep men at bay. But the fact was, Gray Barnett was perfect. And he thought she was, too. It was the only thing she'd ever needed, a man who wanted her just the way she was.

"Don't look at me like that," he said, his voice gruff.

"Like what?"

"Like—" He didn't finish the thought. "Facedown on the bed."

She didn't want to be facedown. She wanted to see everything. She wanted to see his face. *Ask for what you want, Lola.* "Face up," she said softly.

"Then I can't spank you."

"So spank me," she paused meaningfully, "before or after."

He held her gaze, his eyes dark and unreadable. "Turn around."

Lola did.

"Hands on the bed, ass in the air."

She did that, too.

He smacked her hard, following up with a delicious caress between her legs. Lola bit her lip to trap the moan inside.

"Wet," he whispered. "So damn sweet and wet.

Her whole body quivered. "Do it again," she told him.

"Dirty, needy little bitch." There was a crack in his voice.

Then his hand came down, again and again, until she was panting and on the very edge of climax, ready to tip over. "Take me now," she ordered him. And honestly, there was so much more in that than just the words. She wanted more than six weeks. She wanted him to take everything she had to give, as terrifying as that was.

His fingers filled her. She'd wanted *him*, inside her, a part of her, but she couldn't stop the tumble down into mindless orgasm. He touched her, moved her, pushed her, prodded her. When she surfaced, she was flat on the bed, spread-eagled, and tied down with scarves at her wrist and ankles. At his mercy. But at least she could see him.

"Now let me tell you how it's going to work," he said, soft menace lacing his words. He tugged off his shirt, revealing all that bare flesh with a dusting of dark hair across his pectorals.

"You're beautiful," she whispered, her mouth moving before she could think.

Gray was on her almost immediately, his hand between her legs, cupping her sex, then trailing moisture across her abdomen. "This," he said, "is perfection. I'm going to fuck the hell out of you for the next five hours." He grinned roguishly. "And when we've got more time, it's going to last a whole weekend."

She was hot from his touch, his words, the burning look in his eyes. She'd never had sex for five long hours in her life. She'd never had sex for a whole weekend. She'd never done it twice in one night. Until Gray.

Hands on his belt, he toed off his shoes, then he stripped down, pants, briefs, everything, until he was gloriously naked. And hard.

He'd used his mouth on her, his fingers, he'd been inside her, but she'd never seen him completely naked. He stole her breath.

She wanted this man. Everything about him, from his dirty, kinky mind to his beautiful body, his intelligence, his humor, his spankings. Every damn thing. She did not want to give him up because she was too afraid to have a relationship. He wasn't the kind of man that would ever pick-pick-pick her to death.

Hands on his hips, he stood at the side of the bed, his cock jutting proudly. "Here are the rules." He pinched her nipple. Lola arched off the bed, the pleasure greater than the pain, or maybe greater because of it.

"I will always want to do naughty things to you in the privacy of our bedroom."

Our bedroom? Always?

"I will spank you." He swatted her flank lightly. "I will tie you up." He fit two fingers beneath the scarf binding her wrist. "I will blindfold you." He covered her eyes with his hand. "And I will gag you." He put his palm to her lips. Then he bent close, his breath on her cheek, the musky scent of pheromones tingeing the air. "And you will love it all, won't you, Lola?"

It was a question. He required an answer. "God, yes."

He backed off. "We will be wild and kinky"—he raised one brow—"when it's appropriate." Trailing a hand between her breasts, down her belly, to her mound, he stroked between her legs.

"Other times, we will pretend we're vanilla like everyone else." An evil smile curled his lips. "Like on the occasions when you meet my son."

Lola gulped. "I've already met your son. I don't think it was an auspicious beginning."

He narrowed his eyes, his lashes dark. "You will meet him, and he will apologize for what he did to you."

"You can force someone to apologize, but you can't make them mean it."

He climbed on the bed, straddled her waist, the hair on his legs soft against her sides, his balls warm on her skin, his cock between her breasts. "Don't contradict me. He means it."

"But—"

He swooped down, planting his lips on hers. Lola immediately opened to him, taking his tongue. Her mind whirled, and she no longer wanted to argue about his son.

"Rafe has had a change of heart where you're concerned." His breath against her mouth was minty and sweet.

"He doesn't have to meet me. We can be secret again once the twins are back with my sister." He wanted secrecy. She wanted him.

Gray crawled down her body, between her spread legs. She was open to him, unable to move. He licked her, and Lola moaned. She was a slave to the things he did to her.

"These are the rules," he said, then dove on her again, licking, sucking, filling her with his fingers, taking her from zero to sixty in two seconds flat the way he always did. Then he backed off to ride her G-spot and murmured, "This particular rule is that we aren't secret anymore."

"Yes, Coach, God yes, please." She writhed on the bed beneath him.

"I'm Coach in the privacy of our bedroom, but outside it, I'm Gray."

"Yes, Gray." She loved the mastery in *Coach*. But she loved his name on her lips, too. *Gray. My Gray.*

He played her with thumb and forefinger. "We'll go out to dinner when we choose."

She panted. He took it for total agreement.

"We'll stay in and watch movies."

She groaned low in her throat. He seemed to take that for complete agreement as well. "We'll spend time with my son."

She nodded. With his fingers in her and his thumb circling her clitoris, she was in absolute accord with everything he wanted.

"You'll attend company functions with me."

"Yes, yes, yes," she cried out and came in a blinding, crashing wave of pleasure.

* * *

GRAY WAS INSIDE HER BEFORE SHE CAME DOWN OFF THE HIGH. Short-stroking gently, he kept her body on edge. The fit was excellent, tight, slick, hot.

He didn't think she got what he was telling her. It didn't matter. She was his. He had time to make sure she understood all the rules, that she was in his life and he was in hers.

He thrust deep. Lola's body clenched around him, her arms and legs tugging at the restraints. There was heat in having her tied beneath him. But he missed her legs gripping his waist, pulling him in, and her arms holding him tight. They'd do that later. And later, he'd roll her to her stomach and have her that way as well. Every way. Any way.

"The rule is that you're mine," he whispered, filling, withdrawing, plunging again.

Lola tossed her head on the pillow. She couldn't hear him.

"The rule is that we're together." He pumped faster, climbing closer to the edge himself. Beneath him Lola strained, then she arched up and sank her teeth into the skin between his shoulder and neck. A love bite, the way animals mated, the only way she could actually touch him, tied as she was. Not exactly pain, but far more than pleasure. He thrust deeper.

"The rule is"—he gasped—"I'm yours, too."

Then he couldn't think of another rule, he could only feel, taking her hard, relentlessly, pounding, roaring, exploding.

He lay on her, full weight, for five minutes. Her scent made him drunk, sexy and sweet and salty from the sweat of their workout. Her skin was soft and smooth and slippery.

Finally, after that fifth minute passed, he could form coherent thoughts again. Stretching, he pulled the scarves loose from her wrists, then her ankles. Rolling to his side, he took her with him, his cock still buried in her. Her pretty little clit beckoned. He circled and stroked, her body twitching.

Lola opened her eyes. The pupils were large, like she'd taken a drug, her irises nothing more than a lighter outer ring. He drew his finger up her belly to her breasts, circled one nipple, then the other. Until finally he licked his fingers clean.

"You taste so fucking good," he whispered.

She never took her eyes off him, tracking each movement.

"I'm not letting you walk away like you have with all your other men when they started thinking about a future."

Lola bit her lip.

"I'm not keeping our relationship secret so that my son won't freak out."

She blinked.

Gray cupped her cheek. "You need to work with me on this. Try. Don't be afraid."

Lola swallowed.

He gripped her chin and held her close to nuzzle the soft hair at her nape. "Don't walk away this time." And then he gave her the word that held his heart. "Please."

LOLA LOVED HIS WEIGHT ON HER. HIS TOUCH ON HER CHEEK, her chin. The light throb of him still inside her.

Please.

That word. His tone. As if he didn't intend to rid himself of her when the football camp ended. As if he wanted . . . more. Not just sex, not just a weekend, but everything.

"I don't want to walk away," Lola confessed.

His body relaxed against hers, and she realized how tense he'd been. "Good."

"But—"

"Shit," he whispered. "I don't like *buts*."

"Your son." She wondered if the boy was still just an excuse.

His breath sighed through the finer strands of her hair. "He's a good kid. We talked. What happened is a lot about protecting his mom, taking care of her, making sure she doesn't get hurt. But he understands what he did was wrong. He's sorry. And he's willing to try. That's why he sent the text to the twins to meet him at the mall. He wanted to give us time to talk things through. I'm not saying it's perfect. He and I have a long way to go, but—"

"Your son sent the twins a message?"

"Yeah. We spent the afternoon together. I told him you were here to stay—" He stopped abruptly. "If you want to."

"I thought it was one of the rules that I couldn't walk away."

"The Coach tells. Gray asks."

She reveled in his heat, the prickly hairs on his body, the softer ones, the hardness of his muscles.

Don't fight, Lola. She wanted this. She wasn't giving up anything to have it. Nothing except her fears. She hadn't put herself out there since Mike left her. She'd guarded her emotions, walked away when a man got too close, rejecting him before she was rejected. But Gray was worth taking a chance on. No doubt about it.

She'd been thinking so long that Gray stepped into the silence. "I'm a package deal, Lola. It hasn't been such a great package for you up to this point, but Rafe and I will work through this. None of that kind of crap will happen again."

He rolled suddenly, taking her up and over, then settling her on top of him, her knees bent along his sides. As Lola braced her arms on either side of his head, her hair fell down around them. In the slight darkness of the curtain of her hair, he held her face in his hands.

"I've never felt like this about another woman. Love me back,

Lola. That's all I ask. And we can make it work. I'll do whatever's necessary."

"You don't need to grovel," she said.

He grinned. "Whatever's necessary."

She went down flat on his chest, her lips almost on his. "I'll love you back, Gray."

"You will or you do?"

"I do." She had from the moment he'd stood in the locker-room office and told her she'd have to take the twins' punishment. Honestly, who wouldn't love a man as bold, brash, handsome, kinky, and delectable as Coach Barnett?

His eyes gleaming darkly, he asked, "What time is it?"

Lola glanced at the red numbers on the bedside table. "Five-thirty."

"Good. Four hours left." He rolled once more, pinning her to the bed this time. "First you get a good hard paddling for making me wait so long to hear you say it."

"Oh no, Coach." Her heart beat wildly in her chest.

"Then I'm going to lay you facedown on the bed and take you with your eyes blindfolded. And then—"

She grabbed him by the ears and pulled his head down, fastening her lips on his, thrusting her tongue deep, kissing him long and sweet. Until he was hard again inside her.

Ooh yeah, the spanking was going to be oh so excellent.

28

"WE'RE GOING DOWN TO THE POOL." HARRY STOOD IN HER OFFICE doorway, wearing baggy swim trunks, a towel slung over his shoulder.

She could hear William down the hall rattling things in the bathroom.

"Okay." That was good, they'd be out. She had some prep work for the troubleshooting session. She'd already spent too much time this morning lying in bed dreaming about last night with Gray. The fantasies were too good to give up. Her bottom was still deliciously sore, her muscles delectably achy. And then there was her heart.

"You wanna go with us?"

Lola stared a moment. The little scar by his eye gave him a crafty look. He was up to something. Then Lola realized that she always assumed Harry was up to something. Sometimes he was; he'd certainly proven that. But maybe kids lived up to *your* expectations. And she was *supposed* to be giving him the benefit of the doubt.

"You don't want some old lady at the pool with you," she told him. "It would cramp your style."

"You're not some old lady, Aunt Lola." His gaze on her was unwavering.

Lola swiveled in her chair to fully face him. She considered her next words and decided they needed asking. "Why did you scheme with the coach's son last night?"

"Scheme?" He raised a brow. The scar almost made it look like he was winking.

"Rafe texted you. Then you and William wanted to go out. All evening."

He stubbed the toe of his rubber deck shoe into the carpet. "We just wanted to help you. After the stunt we pulled. It was only fair. And we like the coach."

"You said he was a slave driver."

"He is. Doesn't mean we don't like him."

Last night had been more than she'd ever hoped for in the last ten years. The coach was more man than she could ever have dreamed up. "So going out was a gift, giving me time with the coach?"

"It was kind of like when Dad brings Mom chocolates after they've had a fight. Except that she throws them away when he's not looking because she doesn't want to get fat."

"I don't think I'm going to throw away the coach." But she almost had.

"So do you want to go to the pool?" He actually seemed eager.

Since the day they'd arrived, she'd been figuring out ways to get rid of them. Maybe, just maybe, you reap what you sow, to use another of her mother's old expressions. When she ignored them, they got bored. When she didn't like them, they didn't like her. Charlotte didn't have the same problem with the twins. They'd had a great time eating pizza and watching *Kick-Ass*. Maybe Lola was simply reaping her own feelings about them. She mistrusted them, so they'd proved untrustworthy. Not that it excused what they'd done.

It could also be true that Harry was a victim of his own philosophy about illusion. He wanted something new and different and exciting. He wanted to feel special, too. She'd denied him all of that almost since the day he was born. Maybe the twins weren't the only ones who needed to see things differently.

Lola tipped her head. "You know, I could use an hour at the pool." She couldn't remember the last time she'd relaxed by the pool. "But I've got a meeting this afternoon while you guys are having your driving lesson. Why don't you give me half an hour to get stuff ready for it, then I'll come down."

"Cool. We'll save you a chair." Then he dashed away, leaving the doorway empty. A moment later, there was a pounding like a herd of elephants, the front door slammed, the condo rocked as they raced down the outer stairs. Then everything fell silent.

Maybe the twins weren't *so* bad.

By Wednesday or Thursday, she'd have the manual done and off to the boys at Fletcher for final red-lines. Which meant there'd be no work for a few days. Maybe she should take the twins to the beach on Sunday. Try out the Giant Dipper at the Santa Cruz Beach Boardwalk. The coach and his son could come with them. Yeah, great idea. She'd love to see Gray in swim trunks, water sluicing down his chest as he came out of the waves. Oh yeah. Fabulous idea.

It actually felt good to be able to make plans. She hadn't made weekend plans with a man in ten years. It was new. It was exciting. It was special. And she didn't think that was an illusion.

She was digging in to her half hour of work when her little Skype window popped up. Damn. Hadn't the boys already talked to Andrea this morning? Since she hadn't hidden her address, she had no choice but to answer. Andrea *knew* she was there.

Her sister's face filled the screen. As usual, she was too close to the webcam. "Where are the boys?" Andrea yelled.

"They're down at the pool." Lola modulated her voice.

"Did you remember to tell them to put on their sunscreen?"

"They're old enough to figure that out for themselves."

"They're kids, Lola. They won't think about it until they've got skin cancer."

Andrea always called them kids or boys. Lola did the same thing. But they were almost adults. "Let's just assume they have good judgment about it." If you believed them capable of doing something right, they could actually become capable of it. A chicken could definitely change its spots.

"Speaking of judgment, Lola, I've got a bone to pick with you."

Andrea loved their mother's clichés, too. "Pick away," Lola said. She'd been picked at by the best of them, Mike. But Gray thought she was perfect. She might just start believing it.

"They said you let them eat out last night." Andrea's eyes went wide. "*Un*supervised." Ah, so she had talked to the twins already.

"As I recall," Lola said, "they're capable of feeding themselves. I certainly haven't had to hold a fork for them or cut their meat."

Andrea glared bug-eyed. "I *mean* they had *hamburgers* and *fries*. All that fat. They'll die of coronaries."

"They've been getting a lot of exercise every day at the football camp. I'm sure one burger didn't harden any arteries."

"You're creating bad habits."

Lola crossed her arms, sitting back from the monitor so her

sister could fully appreciate the position. "You know, Andrea, I think you should eat the chocolates instead of throwing them out."

Andrea's features wrinkled. "What?"

"The chocolates Ethan gives you after you've had an argument."

"How do you know about the chocolates?" Andrea sputtered.

Lola ignored the question. "I think you should eat them and savor them and share them with the whole family. Let Ethan know you appreciate his effort." She moved in, letting her face fill the little window and the big screen her sister could see. "Now *that* would teach the twins a really nice habit. Tolerance and forgiveness." She put her hand on the mouse. "Gotta go. I told them I'd be down at the pool in half an hour. See you soon. Enjoy yourself at the next party." She clicked the hang-up button and turned off Skype.

Half an hour later, she was ensconced on a chaise longue, sunglasses shading her eyes. The twins cavorted in the pool with three other teenagers, two girls and a guy. Marco Polo or some such thing. She'd had to borrow the twins' sunblock. See, they did know all about UV protection. She'd slathered it on because she certainly didn't want to ruin the skin Coach thought was so lovely.

Lola picked up her phone, punched Charlotte on speed dial.

"Hey, what's going on?" Charlotte sounded breathless.

"Did you know that people tend to live down to your expectations?" Lola mused.

"Well, they could live up to them. It depends on the expectation."

"I mean that if you think they're going to do everything wrong, they usually do. If you tell them they're failures, they usually are."

"Ah, yeah, that can actually happen."

"So I'm giving the twins the benefit of the doubt. No more assuming they're going to misbehave. I'm going to assume they'll be perfect."

"Hello? Is this my friend Lola Cook?"

Lola laughed. "Yes, it is. After all your hours and hours of counseling me, I finally figured out that if you expect that a man's going to reject you, so you make sure you reject him first, then obviously you'll never get hurt. But you'll never have a relationship either."

"Wow, that's profound."

She wasn't sure if Charlotte was being facetious. "I know."

"Does that mean you rejected Gray? Or he rejected you? Or . . ." Charlotte let the question hang.

Lola glanced to the left, to the right, straight ahead, and decided she was clear to speak. "It means that I let him tie me to his bed and do a lot of nasty things to me. And"—she paused dramatically—"I told him I wanted a relationship." Actually, he'd dictated that they'd have one. But she was in full agreement. And then he'd said he loved her. She was in full agreement on that, too.

Charlotte gasped. "So give me all the dirty details."

And Lola told her everything.

TUESDAY JUST BEFORE ELEVEN, GRAY HAD HIS GUYS LINED UP for a chase drill.

"Stu and Rafe, you first." Gray clapped his hands.

Rafe barreled down the field with the ball. It was neck and neck, so to speak. Stu was supposed to focus on the tackle first before attempting to cause a fumble. In the end, Rafe kept the ball, but Stu had given it a valiant effort. And so had Rafe. His son had really made the effort. "Good job, guys." He clapped his approval.

The sun beat down on his head. When they were done with this drill, he'd have them break for a drink and a power bar.

"Okay, Harry and William." Hands on his knees, he squatted slightly to watch their form. Not bad. Not as good as Stu and Rafe. But their hearts had never been in the game. Nevertheless, they executed passably and he gave them their kudos.

When they'd first arrived this morning, they'd apologized for their part in Lola's harassment. Gray had accepted without reservation.

Lola had been fifteen minutes late picking them up Sunday night. Monday at work he'd barely been able to focus, muscles aching, reminding him of each and every delightfully dirty erotic act they'd performed in their five perfect hours. Now he was dying to have her at his mercy for a whole weekend. Monday night Rafe had come over for dinner. After Sunday, Gray could definitely confirm Lola was here to stay. His son had actually said he was happy for him. He had no illusions that everything was resolved for good, that Bettina's jealousy wouldn't rear its head again, or that Rafe wouldn't side with his mother if it came down to another battle, but they had a working truce and a more open line of communication. It was a damn good start, the best he'd had in five long years.

"Excellent." Tom and Peter. Good boys. He had high hopes they'd make the high school team this year. He thought Stu had a damn good chance, too.

With the last drill executed, he clapped, then pointed. "To the tables and feast yourselves."

They ran in one big herd. Gray headed in the same direction at a slower pace. Then a glint of silver caught his eye at the far side of the field by the gate. A flash of white morphed into a figure. A tall woman, long brown legs, tanned bare shoulders, blue tank, denim skirt, silky black hair.

His heart settled into a faster beat. She was early. They had another hour of practice to get through.

But Lola came on, a sweet sway to her hips. His motor was purring, his mouth a little dry. At the table, he raised a bottle of water to his lips and drank thirstily, his eyes on her.

She didn't stop until she was at his side. The kids stared. She was a fine-looking woman, especially to an old man like him.

Harry and William said in unison, "Hi, Aunt Lola."

"Hey, guys." She wrapped her hand around Gray's arm. Then slowly went up on her toes and put her lips on his.

Jesus. What she did to him. His temperature hit one-oh-one and kept on climbing. And she hadn't even said a word to him. It was her sexy, sweet scent and the memory of what she'd done with that mouth just two nights ago.

Then she slipped back down to flat feet on the grass, and his world straightened.

"Hey, Coach, can I watch your players practice?"

He opened his mouth, and it took two seconds for his answer to come. "Sure." Wow. Very eloquent.

Then she flashed a look across to the huddle by the table. "That okay with you guys?"

"Sure, Aunt Lola." Harry or William, he didn't look.

The others sounded off in variations of *Sure, Why not,* and *Heck yes.*

Gray looked at Rafe. His son was smiling, not big, not snide, just . . . a smile. Which was an improvement. Then he said, "Sounds great, Lola."

Gray wanted to touch her. He wanted to lick her. But some things just weren't appropriate.

Then Rafe broke away from the group and loped over, the twins almost right on his heels. "Lola." He swallowed, looked back at Harry and William, then opened his mouth and started again. "I'm sorry for what I did. It was wrong."

Gray felt a loosening in his chest and an ache right behind his eyes. He hadn't coached Rafe on this, but his son was beginning to learn. He was even taking his lumps in front of the two younger boys.

"Thank you for the apology, Rafe. I accept." Lola stuck out her hand.

This time Rafe shook it. "And I didn't mean to let your cat out."

She nodded. "The twins told me it was an accident." Then she tipped her head. "I thought I'd take them over to the Boardwalk in Santa Cruz on Sunday. You think you and your dad would like to come?"

Gray looked at his son, waited, his heart damn near clogging his throat.

Then Rafe said, "That would be great." He turned to Gray. "Dad, can I drive?"

"We want to drive because we have to get in our practice hours," Harry argued. And the two started a good-natured back-and-forth.

Gray reached out, touched Lola's hand, then wrapped her fingers in his. She smiled.

Then he smiled, knowing exactly what she was thinking. If they kept arguing, he'd have a reason to send her to the naughty corner tonight.

Keep reading for an excerpt from
the next book by Jasmine Haynes

TEACH ME A LESSON

Available April 2014 from Heat Books

CHARLOTTE WORKED TUESDAYS AND THURSDAYS AS A GUIDANCE counselor at the same high school she'd graduated from twenty years ago. She had, in fact, planned her future in this very office, from the opposite side of the desk. Carpeting had been installed over the linoleum tiles, but the desk was the same, its veneer slightly more battered, as was the credenza beneath the window, though now it was filled with her files. She'd requisitioned a small conference table and four accompanying chairs, two of which sat in front of the desk, and her chair—which she'd bought herself—was ergonomic.

She spent money when it was necessary—like on the ergonomic chair—and she pinched her pennies on things that didn't matter—like brown-bagging it. Brown-bagging could be much healthier since you chose your own ingredients. Pinching the pennies was worth it.

Sometimes she ate her lunch outside, but today, seated at her small conference table, she gazed out the blinds at a sky that was heavy with dark clouds, rain threatening at any moment. Last week, Halloween had been gorgeous, in the seventies, warm enough for short sleeves, but come November, the temperature had dropped and the clouds rolled in. November in the San Francisco Bay Area was typically one of the rainier months, though not always. Sometimes the beginning of the month brought a deluge while on Thanksgiving Day you could practically eat outside. That's what she loved about the Bay Area, the variety.

Since she had a student meeting at one o'clock, Charlotte should have been studying the file open on the conference table in front of her. Instead she was thinking about spanking, not the discipline kind, but the fun kind. Lola loved her sex play with Gray Barnett, though even after three months, she was still scant on details. But these days, Lola damn near glowed. Charlotte didn't think it was *just* the kinky sex. It was Gray. For the first time in ten years, Lola had a real relationship. Charlotte was happy for her best friend.

But she kept thinking about spanking. And wild sex. And how long it had been since she'd had sex, wild or not. Besides, as a therapist, it was her duty to find out what this bondage thing was really like from an experiential perspective. Although she'd start with just the spanking. And damn if she didn't get hot and bothered thinking about that. She wanted to try it. Needed to. If she'd heard this kind of sentiment from a client, she'd have started using the word *obsession*, but Charlotte wasn't obsessed, just curious. Highly curious. Extremely. Okay, maybe slightly obsessed with sex itself and the lack of it in her life for the past six months.

All right, work, she needed to stop daydreaming. Flipping a page in the folder, she absently stabbed a fork into her salad. Somehow the plastic tub had moved—God only knew how or when—and her fork almost upended the container. She grabbed the fork clattering on the table, spraying balsamic dressing across another folder, but she managed a magnificent save before the entire salad was tossed to the beige carpet. The only casualty was her apple, which tumbled off the table and rolled under the desk. Hopefully the carpet saved it from bruising.

She went down on her hands and knees, stretching an arm beneath the desk, her face and chest practically smushed to the carpet before she could reach the errant apple. Ah, got it.

"Lose something, Miss Moore?"

Charlotte gave a tiny squeak and banged her shoulder on the underside of the desk. She snapped up straight, the apple in her lap, and smoothed her skirt down over her knees with one hand.

Principal Hutton lounged in her doorway, arms crossed over his white shirt and red tie, shoulder braced on the jamb.

Damn. Busted with her butt in the air.

"Are you all right?" he asked politely.

"I'm fine." Her shoulder only smarted a little. She held up the apple. "A delinquent. Tried to hide from me under the desk, but I found it out."

Principal Hutton raised a brow. "I trust you didn't bruise its fragile ego."

"Oh no, never." She waved the apple in the air. "Absolutely bruise free."

She was in a unique position, sitting back on her calves. Principal Hutton, at six-one or so, had always towered over her petite height of five-two-and-a-half—okay, maybe it was a quarter instead of a half—but from down here, he was a veritable giant, his chest broad, his shoulders wide, his thighs muscled from his daily runs. He was definitely attractive, she'd never questioned that, with salt-and-pepper hair, swarthy skin, and sharp, aristocratic features. And all those muscles. His female students were in awe of him. Not so Charlotte. At forty-eight, he was ten years older than her. And she liked her men younger. Once, a long time ago, she'd almost married a man who was more than ten years older. After a narrow escape, she'd realized that if she wanted autonomy in her life, in her career, and in her relationship, she'd be far better off with a younger man, one who would cede control to her. Only when it needed ceding, of course.

Yet, from down here on the floor, she was seeing Principal Lance Hutton in a whole new light. Or maybe it was the spanking thing infecting her thinking. Whatever the reason, he was suddenly more than merely attractive. He was big, he was strong, he was sexy.

She'd be willing to bet that receiving a spanking from Principal Hutton would be incredibly hot. And his age wouldn't matter at all. In fact, it would elevate the experience to mind-blowing.

Yes, yes, yes, Principal Hutton was the man she needed for this new adventure she intended to embark on.

ABOUT THE AUTHOR

With a bachelor's degree in accounting from Cal Poly, San Luis Obispo, Jasmine Haynes has worked in the high-tech Silicon Valley for the last twenty years and hasn't met a boring accountant yet! Okay, maybe a few. She and her husband live with numerous wild cats, one of whom has now moved into the house. Jasmine's pastimes, when not writing, are speed-walking in the Redwoods, watching classic movies, and hanging out with writer friends in coffee shops. She is the author of classy erotic romance and the popular Max Starr paranormal romance mystery series, and also writes quirky, laugh-out-loud romances as Jennifer Skully. Visit her at jasminehaynes.com and jasminehaynes.blogspot.com.